UNCANNY & UNEARTHLY TALES

A GRENDEL PRESS HORROR ANTHOLOGY

KASEY KUBICA

GRENDEL PRESS

ISBN: 978-1-960534-06-4 (Paperback)

Cover & Typesetting by Susan Russell
Story art by Dany Rivera & Daren Robertson
Edited by Kasey Kubica
Proofread by Rachael Swanson

Contributors:

"**Bound**" by Dan Peacock
"**The Mall Santas Ride at Moonrise**" by KT Wagner
"**The Soul Stone**" by Aly Faye
"**Good Intentions**" by Jessica Feather
"**A Chronological List of My First Hauntings by Jonathan Chen**" by Mei Davis
"**Rosebud**" by Amanda Cecelia Lang
"**Fortune of the Téméraire**" by DJ Cockburn
"**Helping Hands in the Acreage**" by Chris Kuriata
"**Rest Stop**" by John Haas
"**The Yakshi of Asthikaavu**" by Neethu Krishnan
"**To Catch a Bannik**" by Koji A. Dae
"**Hamlet's House**" by Anthony Engebretson
"**The Great Bath**" by T.S Vickers
"**The Greatest Show on Earth**" by Joel Reeves
"**A Final Offering**" by Akis Linardos

CONTENTS

1. Bound — 1

2. The Mall Santas Ride at Moonrise — 17

3. Good Intentions — 35

4. A Chronological List of My First Hauntings by Jonathan Chen — 59

5. The Soul Stone — 71

6. Rosebud — 83

7. Fortune of the Téméraire — 107

8. Helping Hands in the Acreage — 127

9. Rest Stop — 147

10. The Yakshi of Asthikaavu — 171

11. To Catch a Bannik — 187

12. Hamlet's House — 201

13. The Great Bath — 223

14. The Greatest Show on Earth — 245

15. A Final Offering — 263

About This Anthology

Uncanny & Unearthly Tales

We've long grappled with finding evidence of beings and places that transcend the laws of nature, never quite obtaining the answers we seek. But within these pages, one will not be able to ignore the truth when reality collides with the paranormal, leaving the question... are they myth or legend?

BOUND

BY DAN PEACOCK

I'd called ahead to tell the letting agent that I'd be a few minutes late for the viewing, but I'd neglected to mention my demon.

The agent was waiting for us by the front door, clipboard in hand, looking at something on her phone. Hearing our footsteps, she looked up, a well-rehearsed smile already spreading across her face—and then she saw us. I wasn't much to look at, and my clothes were unremarkable by design, but *he* was different. My demon sloped alongside me, a blackened gargoyle whose horns came level with my waistline. His barbed tail twitched and scraped along the floor, his charred wings folded tight against his back.

"Hi," I said, extending a hand. "I'm Rebecca. We spoke on the phone?"

"Hello," the woman said. She shook my hand, but her eyes hadn't left my demon. "Yes, you're the eleven o'clock, aren't you?"

I became acutely aware that it was past eleven. "Sorry. The buses."

"Well, shall we?" she said. I realised she hadn't introduced herself, and I tried to sneak a glance at the name tag pinned to her lapel. It was obscured by her hair, which fell past her shoulders in dark waves.

Inside the empty house, I found the familiar, generic aesthetic of every rental property I'd ever seen. Every wall was bare and covered indiscriminately with magnolia paint; the floors were a mishmash of pale laminate and off-cream carpets peppered with marks and stains.

"I should probably warn you upfront," the woman said, "that the landlord has an explicit policy against demon-bound tenants. Is it yourself you're looking for?"

I said that it was.

"Well, seeing as you're here... there's one bedroom upstairs, one bathroom. Feel free to have a look around, if you want."

"Oh, okay," I said. "Thanks." I glanced at the bare bones of the living room, at the faint impressions in the carpet that indicated where the furniture had been, and wandered through into the kitchen. It was tiny and dirty, the oven ancient, but much bigger than what we had. There didn't seem much point in going upstairs. My demon was still squatting by the front door, sinking his claws into the welcome mat repeatedly.

"I'm sorry," I said. "I didn't mean to mislead you, or waste your time." The letting agent's eyebrows raised slightly, as if suggesting both of those things were the case. "It's just that you're the last place we've tried. Nowhere else will even agree to see us. Nowhere else is taking tenants with demons."

She smiled, and it seemed a fraction more genuine. "I understand. It's not something we decide. The landlords just don't want the trouble."

"You don't have anyone that would accept us?"

"I'm sorry," the woman said. "We did have one landlord who accepted demon-bound tenants, depending on how they had, well, *acquired* their demon. But he had to evict the last one, and that was that. It was screaming and wailing at all hours of the night and the next-door neighbours were terrified. Their little girl had to go to therapy."

"Jesus," I said. My demon snarled at the name, and the letting agent flinched before realising he wasn't moving from his spot by the door.

"Look, give me your number," she said. "If I find anything, I'll let you know."

"Thank you." I scribbled my number on a business card that she offered, and gave it back to her. She handed me a fresh one to hold on to. Her name was printed on it—Angela.

"I really appreciate it." I shook her hand again, and went to leave. "Come on," I said to my demon, who was still kneading the welcome mat with his claws. "Leave that alone. We need to go."

He stared back at me, dark yellow eyes narrowing with hatred.

"Now," I said.

He growled, a deep, bass grinding that rattled in my chest, his lips drawing back to reveal rows of fine, sharp teeth. The lights overhead flickered, and the shadows in the corners of the room seemed to bulge and reach out, but then he relaxed his grip on the mat and everything returned to normal. He threw it to one side and slouched out of the open door. It slammed behind him, although he hadn't laid a hand on it, and there was no breeze. I offered my apologies to Angela, again, and followed him out.

It wasn't far to the bus stop back into town, and after I'd caught up to him, my demon kept close beside me. More people stared openly than those who pretended to look elsewhere. Demons were rare, especially in countries where the murder rate was low, but the implication meant that it was always a spectacle.

The other passengers gave us a wide berth as we waited for the bus, and when we got on, the seats around us remained vacant. He slumped in the window seat, horns down, occasionally craning his neck to look out at the buildings that we passed.

I felt the gaze of the other passengers on the back of my head, and in all honesty, I couldn't blame them. I remembered seeing my first demons when I was little. I'd been six or seven, and my parents had taken me out into town for a meal—I'd sulked when the only ice cream available for dessert was plain old vanilla—and we were on our way home. I'd raced ahead to the next crossing, jamming the button and waiting for the pedestrian light to turn green. Across the road, next to the entrance to the multistorey car park, a man was huddled against the wall, a cardboard sign beside him that read VETERAN COLD, TIRED, HUNGRY—PLEASE ANY HELP. His bottom half disappeared into a tattered sleeping bag, his top half wrapped in a blanket. His eyes were bloodshot and sunken into his face. Around him, three hideous creatures were snarling and tearing at each other, little bursts of flame flashing between their gnarled, charred bodies. They weren't much smaller than I was, and as I gawped, one of them had looked up at me. I cried, and then the others stopped and looked at me too, their eyes bright yellow and crackling with anger.

I snapped back to the present. My demon was shrieking and pounding on the bus window. Everyone was staring at us now. The bus jerked to a halt.

"Hey!" the driver shouted. "Get that thing under control!"

"*Stop it,*" I hissed at my demon. "I'm sorry," I blustered, trying to address the entire bus at once. "He must have seen a dog or..." I looked out the window. The bus had come to a stop beside the house we'd lived in together when he'd still been alive. The *For Sale* sign had long gone, of course, and a two-storey extension had sprouted on the side. He must not have noticed it on our way to the viewing.

He had definitely noticed it on our way back. He was still clawing at the window, growling, leaving deep lines in the reinforced glass.

"Right," said the driver. "Off." He heaved himself out of the driver's seat and stood with arms crossed by the open doors.

I hauled my demon off, feeling like I was carrying a writhing bomb. The bus left without us, the faces inside all but pressed to the windows to watch. My demon was still straining against me, and I could feel the fire that was baking inside him. My forehead was slick with sweat from both the heat and the effort of keeping him from breaking free. I'd tried to put a leash on him, once, but he'd grasped it in his hands and torn the chain apart as if it were liquorice. But he couldn't use his strength to hurt me any more than I could physically hurt him.

I half-carried, half-dragged him away from our old house. A few streets away, he stopped resisting, like he'd forgotten, or some spell had been lifted. I put him down, half-expecting him to bolt, but he didn't. He extended his wings and beat them a couple of times, stretching, and stepped back in line beside me, following me down the road.

Did he remember what had just happened? Had he already forgotten? I tried to stop thinking about it, but another thought arose. *What the hell are you going to do now?* Ashwell's had been the final letting agency that we hadn't already tried. We were out of options—we were going to be stuck in our tiny, damp, crappy room at the New Light Project forever. I could feel my breath quickening and my cheeks reddening. I stopped at the next bench and sat, head in my hands, doing my breathing exercises to get my heart rate back under control. The sick, tight feeling in my chest faded, and I looked up to see my demon staring at me.

"The fuck are you looking at?" I met his gaze and held it.

He looked back at me with the same familiar loathing, but suddenly, somewhere within the demon's dim, yellow eyes were the eyes of the man he had once been. Was there an *I'm sorry* flickering somewhere deep within them? It was probably wishful thinking.

My phone buzzed in my pocket. It was Julia.

Any luck?

No, I replied. *No luck. Game over.*

I'm sorry. Take your time—you're not due back online until after lunch. See you in the meeting!

Thanks, I typed. *See you soon.*

I got up from the bench and we set off for home.

From the outside, the New Light Project looked like a run-down, haunted chain hotel, which wasn't too far from the truth.

Glen was standing on the steps, leaning against the railing with a walking stick in one hand and a cigarette in the other. His demon was always strangely calm; it sat by his feet like an old dog, its horns thick and twisted with age. Glen stubbed the remains of his cigarette out on the stone wall beside the railing, and I expected him to toss the butt into the bushes, but it stayed between his fingers. I felt a longing to hold one myself again. Not to smoke—just to hold.

"Rebecca," he said, giving me a nod.

"Hey, Glen," I replied.

"Fine day today. How's your friend?"

I looked down at my demon, who glared back at me. "Peachy."

Glen smiled. "I'm glad to hear it."

"Thanks," I said. "I've got to get inside—got a meeting. I'll see you later."

He held up a hand in a lazy gesture of farewell. My demon snarled at him, tail swishing, as we passed them at the top of the steps. His demon didn't flinch, and it looked up to Glen for a moment, who smiled, as if some in-joke were passing between them. Then we were inside, past the big sign in the entrance hall that read *The New Light Project: sheltered accommodation for rehabilitated demon-bound residents c. 2015.*

I had my doubts that we were the ones being sheltered. No-one else ever came near the building, and delivery drivers dropped off any packages with near-superhuman speed.

The room we'd moved into after my release was tiny, with a single bed and a chest of drawers along one wall, and a half-baked attempt at a kitchen on the other—one cabinet with a little sink and one with a hot plate, a kettle and a microwave crowded together. A cramped bathroom sat off to one side, the edge of the sink preventing the shower door from fully closing.

It was easy to forget you were no longer on the inside. Sometimes I stirred in my sleep, hearing the other residents' demons howling and clawing at the doors from further down the corridors, and thought I was back there, with the other inmates' demons shrieking and throwing themselves against the walls.

Come to think of it, it was slightly larger than my prison cell had been, and the view out of the window was much nicer, looking out into the tree-lined car park rather than a gravelly inner courtyard. I'd relished the freedom at first, and found the size of the room comforting, almost uterine. I'd joked to Glen once that the kitchen/bedroom was en suite to the bathroom, and not the other way around. The joke seemed to go over his head, and his demon had stayed silent and placid as mine roughly sharpened his claws on the floor.

I had to face the facts. Every private landlord that I could find had raised their drawbridge, Mum and Dad still weren't talking to me and all my friends had made it clear during the trial that they blamed me for what happened. But I could make this work. And speaking of work—I looked at the clock. The meeting was going to start soon. I sat on the bed and pulled my laptop onto my lap, unplugging my bedside lamp so I could plug in the charger. It wasn't the best home-working setup, but working in the office wasn't exactly an option for people like me.

I opened my calendar and clicked on the meeting link, keeping my camera and mic switched off. I rubbed my eyes, hoping the dark bags under them wouldn't show when it was my turn to talk. My demon was flexing a half-closed fist over by the door, controlling the size of a little fireball that expanded and contracted within his grip. Little scorch marks on the wood showed the results of previous attempts.

"Hey." I clicked my fingers. "Cut that out. And be quiet. I'm going to be on camera soon." I put my headset on.

He held the fireball in his fist for a moment longer in a gesture of defiance before sidling across the room and settling on the windowsill, looking out. As I watched, he started to tap his claws on the wooden frame, at first randomly, then in something resembling a beat. *Tap-taptap-tap-tatatatap.* I frowned. He had always done things like that, when he was human. He'd always clicked his fingers, drummed with his hands on restaurant tabletops and hummed to himself. It had driven me crazy—even when I'd loved him.

The meeting was as unnecessary as it was inevitable. Each sub-team had to give a weekly update on their particular area—my team was just me. I mostly just set up the documents that the other teams used when they were out in the field with clients. It was easy work. A chimp with a rudimentary understanding of Google Docs could do it, and part of me suspected that Julia had given me the role out of pity. My application was brutally honest, telling them I was skilled and hard-working, but demon-bound, and that my job history had a gap of ten years due to my incarceration. When she'd hired me, she'd said she would keep those facts a secret from our other colleagues if I wanted her to. I'd accepted. I kept my camera and mic off whenever possible in meetings, and made sure he was well out of frame if I ever had to show my face. I had never been to the office in person. I couldn't.

"Rebecca," Julia said, snapping me out of my daydream. I turned on my camera and mic. "Would you be happy to update us on how things are going? You mentioned there were some issues with us moving to the new invoicing system."

"Hey, everyone," I said, giving a brief wave to the camera. "That's right—I think I've found a way around most of the issues, but..."

On the windowsill, my demon growled.

"Is that your dog?" someone said.

I shuddered and tried to laugh it off. "Yeah, sorry, guys. I think he saw a cat outside. Like I was saying, we..."

He growled again. The lights overhead dimmed to near-darkness for a moment, and the temperature in the room dropped so suddenly that I visibly shivered.

"Hey, Rebecca, think we lost you for a second there," Julia said. "Are you okay to carry on?"

"Yeah, of course," I said. With my arm out of camera-shot, I frantically waved to my demon to get his attention. He didn't notice me. Out of the window, I saw what was agitating him: a helicopter in the distance. He hated them, always snarling and straining upwards when he saw one, thinking he could catch them if he just reached a little harder. I never understood why, but I suspected they reminded him of prison. He had always screamed with fear and rage when one passed by outside, rotors thundering and the searchlight piercing its way into our room.

Agitated further by my memories of it, he started howling.

"Jesus, what's that?" someone else said.

"Sorry, guys, really sorry, just give me a minute," I said. I switched my camera off and yanked my headset away. My demon was still screeching at the distant helicopter.

I filled a big glass of water from the sink. "Will you shut the *fuck* up?" I said, and threw it directly onto him, the water splattering all around the window and onto the curtains. His cries stopped as if someone had cut the power to his vocal cords, and he spun around to stare at me, shocked.

"I hate you!" I shouted. "You ruined everything when you were alive and you're still ruining everything now that you're dead!"

He threw his arms and wings wide, filling the window, a fireball crackling within each hand. His foot-claws sank deep into the wood of the windowsill. His face was molten fury.

"You know what?" I yelled. "I'm fucking glad I killed you! At least now no-one else has to put up with your bullshit!"

He raised an arm, ready to throw the fireball into my face at point-blank range, and then he began to tremble. The fires in each hand sputtered out and his wings folded back down. He seemed to shrink and turned away, looking back outside, and he pulled the wet curtains closed behind him.

Taking a deep breath, I sat again and pulled the laptop back onto my lap. The screen had frozen, and my fingers automatically started to reach for Ctrl-Alt-Delete to kill the video-call program and start it up again. Then one of my colleagues moved their head, ever so slightly, and I realised it wasn't the program that was frozen. I'd deactivated my camera, but I'd forgotten to turn off my mic.

I slammed the laptop shut and pushed it away from me.

"Oh shit, fuck," I said. I grabbed my phone and typed out a private message to Julia, my hands shaking. *I am so sorry, he was making a scene and I didn't realise my mic was on! I really, really apologise.*

I saw the three dots appear to show she was typing back, then they disappeared. A few minutes later they reappeared, and vanished again. My demon had pulled a corner of the curtain back, and was watching me pace the tiny room.

My phone buzzed. *Take the rest of the day off. I will call you tomorrow to discuss.*

I picked up my pillow and screamed into it. I threw it to one side, grabbed my handbag and rifled through it—I'd given up smoking a long time ago, but maybe there was a forgotten pack somewhere in a side pocket? No such luck. An addict never forgets.

I opened the door and rushed down the hall, my demon barely making it out behind me before the door slammed shut. He had no choice, and neither did I. We couldn't stay too far apart.

Glen lived one floor down, close to the main entrance. I banged on his door and rang the bell simultaneously. It seemed like a full minute passed before the door creaked open.

"Rebecca?"

"I'm sorry to bother you. I really need a cigarette."

"Is everything okay?"

"Yeah. Well, no. Not really, no."

"Come in, please," he said, and pushed the door open. I didn't know this man, not really; I had spoken to him in passing outside the building, and helped him carry his shopping in once or twice. He always asked how my demon and I were, but I didn't know him. I needed a cigarette, though, so I went inside.

His room was the same as mine, but mirrored; the bed and kitchen were on the opposite walls and the bathroom was over to the left instead of the right. A little stone Buddha sat by the window, flanked by unlit tealights; otherwise the room was virtually bare. There was no TV, but a small radio sat on the kitchen counter, quietly playing classical music. His walking stick was propped up against his bedside table.

Glen opened the window wide and offered me a cigarette, lighting it for me. Not wanting to sit on his bed, where his old demon was already perching, I leaned against the sill, making sure not to knock into the Buddha. "Thank you," I said.

"Would you like a drink? I have water and tea."

"No, no thank you, just... just this." I took my first drag, feeling the heat working its way down into my lungs. I coughed, remembering how awful the taste was, and then sank into the familiar comfort of it. I took another drag and felt the warmth seep out into the rest of my body as I exhaled. I'd missed this. My demon's tail drooped slightly as it worked on him too.

Glen picked up a mug of tea he'd made earlier, and sat on the bed beside his demon. He reached out a hand and patted its shoulder. "Peter is worried about you," he said. It took me a second to realise he was referring to his demon by name. "As am I. Can you tell me what's happened?"

I shrugged. "*He* happened. Again." That sort of comment would normally have elicited a snarl from my demon, but he just sat at my feet, avoiding my gaze. His hands were curled into tight fists in his lap. I tensed for a moment at the sight, until I realised he was trying to stop himself from sinking his claws into things, like he usually did.

"If you don't mind me saying," Glen said, "you two do not seem happy together."

"No shit!" I said. "Sorry. But of course we're not happy together."

"Why not?"

I shrugged for the second time, and took another deep drag. "He ruined my life," I said, blowing the smoke out of the open window. "And I ended his. You can see why we're not on the best of terms."

Glen nodded and leaned back on the bed, positioned against the wall. He ran a hand through his thin, white hair. "Peter was my big brother," he said.

I had no idea what to say.

"I killed him when I was twenty-five and he was twenty-seven. A long, long time ago. I found him with my wife. Eleanor."

His demon had been gazing into the middle distance, but he looked over at Glen at the mention of her name.

"I was so angry," Glen said, "I think I would have killed her next. But then his demon appeared out of thin air, screaming at me, and I realised what I had done."

Peter was still looking at Glen, the demon's charred face calm as the old man spoke.

"We hated each other for a long time, just like you two. Even after we got out. The part of him that remembered who he was hated me for taking his life, and I hated him for taking mine. I never saw my wife again after that day, not even at the trial, and I don't blame her. But you need to make peace. You still have a long life ahead of you. Do you want to spend the rest of it shouting and screaming at each other?"

I glanced down at my demon who looked at me out of the corner of his eye. I didn't think he deserved forgiveness. And maybe, neither did I.

"What is his name?" Glen said.

"He's just my demon. He doesn't have a name."

Glen chose another question. "Who was he?"

I thought about deflecting again, then gave in. "He was my husband."

"Oh, I see," Glen said. "Do you think he really understands whatever it was that he did to you? When he was alive?"

"He knows who he is. He remembers."

"I'm not so sure," Glen said. "You will see little glimpses of him, here and there. These are just little stains, though, bleeding through from one life to another. You cannot find peace with your friend if you cannot let go of your hatred of who he was."

I finished my cigarette, and scanned the room for an ashtray. I thanked Glen before my demon and I returned to our room, both of us silent. The halogen lights in the corridors flickered as he passed under them. I closed the door behind us and he shuffled over to the window, jumping up to take his usual spot on the sill, looking out at the trees on the far side of the car park.

I poured myself a gin, forgoing the tonic, and sat to check my phone. I'd had no more messages from Julia, but I was probably fired. It was illegal to terminate someone purely on the grounds of being demon-bound, but after my outburst, I was sure they'd be able to find something to nail me on. I felt a sudden urge to throw my phone across the room, at my demon, but I looked at his slumped outline against the backdrop of the trees outside, and for the first time, I noticed how miserable he looked. Did I look the same to him?

His claws tapped nervously on the wood. *Tap-taptap-tap-tatatatap.*

I thought about the final minute of his life; how he had learned to be the one that was afraid.

"Richard," I said. It was the first time I'd called my demon by his name.

He looked back at me, and I saw that his eyes were blue.

About the Author

Dan Peacock is a sci-fi and fantasy writer from the UK. His short stories have been published or are forthcoming in F&SF, Kaleidotrope and Etherea. He is also a First Reader for Orion's Belt. You can find links to all his published stories at danpeacockwriter.com, and he tweets at @DanPeacock92. He lives with his long-suffering partner and daughter, along with a second-hand cat that hoots like an owl.

THE MALL SANTAS RIDE AT MOONRISE

BY KT WAGNER

December 21st, 1995, the eve of winter solstice, and Gwyn's world is twisting apart. Since childhood, Mall Santa season has been her favourite time of the year, but currently, it's proving challenging. Santa Eric phoned early this morning to deliver his resignation in a flat tone before hanging up. Gwyn called back and his line was disconnected. Like her former boss, Santa Eric has been with True North since the beginning. Absolutely everyone adores Eric and Oliver, and so does she, but now they're both mysteriously missing.

Her new cordless phone jangles—loud, shrill and not unexpected. With every ring, her kitchen table vibrates and the tiny poinsettia next to her computer shivers. She cringes and considers ignoring it.

There's no room in her postage-stamp apartment for a proper desk, and it's unfair to expect her to work from home. She's never heard of this kind of arrangement. It must contravene an employment standard, but she doesn't dare file a complaint. Complaints rarely end well for the employee.

Her hand hovers above the receiver. The new boss calls this time every day. She decides to not answer, though her mind tries to convince her otherwise: perhaps it's Oliver calling? He's been like a father to her, after all.

Oliver and the Mall Santas are the only ones who've ever accepted her for who she is; the only ones who feel like a real family. Her birth family act embarrassed of her. As an adult she rarely sees them, even though they all live in the same town.

Oliver promised to take her to see Bruce Willis's latest movie. She hadn't had the heart to tell him this one isn't set at Christmas. Perhaps his voice will rumble through the phone's speaker, telling her his disappearance was a badly conceived prank. That he didn't sell the rent-a-Santa business out from under her. That he didn't retire to sunnier climes without so much as a fare-thee-well. No matter what, she needs to know he's okay.

Brrrriinnggg. Brrrriinnggg.

She pulls her hand back, scrunches her eyes shut, holds her breath and covers her ears. One more ring and the machine will pick up. If her ghastly sounding boss can't get hold of her, he can't make any stupid demands for last-minute changes. She concentrates on her collection of Christmas Beanie Babies lovingly displayed on a shelf. Don't think about the phone—

Like it has a mind of its own, her hand snakes out and snatches the receiver from its cradle. "Hello?"

Hating how querulous her voice has become, she grits her teeth. Recently, it's like some outside force controls her reactions, but that's plain silly. It began just after Oliver disappeared, and the new owners of True North decided to change the focus of the business from Mall Santas to Private-Party Santas. It's simply stress affecting her.

The static at the other end of the line curdles her insides. Normally, she's a strong, confident person. She bites her lip to keep from whimpering.

After a long minute, the androgynous voice of her employer crackles through, "Gwyn, my dear. We have a lovely surprise for all three bookings this afternoon. Ensure your Santas are fully aware of the honour. Last night's engagement was… unfortunate."

There was only one engagement last night—Santa Eric's children's party—and, according to the clients, it was a resounding success. The message they left on her answering machine raved, "The best Santa experience ever" and "Please put us down for Santa Eric again next year".

Gwyn frowns. "What about Santa Eric's party? Do you know why he quit? Did he leave a new phone number?"

The static on the line increases in volume. Seconds tick by and a pit opens in her stomach. She bites her upper lip to keep from talking, but words slip from her mouth. "I'm so sorry for the behaviour of my Santas. I take full responsibility."

The voice shifts into sibilant tones. "The instructionsss are following in an email. As alwaysss, follow them to the letter."

Earlier in the day, yet another overdue-rent notice was pushed under her door.

Taking a deep breath, she tries to settle her nerves. "Of course, and—and, uhm, my cheque? Oliver always paid me at the end of each—"

Click. A dial tone pulses from the handset.

Gwyn shudders, burrowing deeper into her woolen shawl. She turned up the thermostat twice already today. Maybe it's broken. Crying might bring relief, but her eyes are dry. Besides, she's never been the weepy type.

Still in last year's dry-cleaning bag, her floor-length red dress and white apron hangs from the closet door. She loved working out of the now-closed True North Santa storefront office in the mall. Established in 1984, they'd been there since the mall opened just over a decade ago—the first indoor mall in town. She used to adore wearing her Mrs Claus costume to work, but True North's new owners cancelled the store-front lease. Now she works from one end of her kitchen table.

The attorney for the nameless new owners presented her with a letter outlining the change of ownership and her updated terms of employment. Her first reaction was to quit, but she tried and couldn't summon the will to follow through. She tells herself it's because of her obsession with Christmas but knows that's not quite right. When she tries to examine it more closely, her thoughts turn slippery and skitter out of reach.

She powers up the hated computer and waits for it to connect through the phone line. The faceless bosses insisted she learn this new technology.

Twenty-seven unread emails since she last checked a couple of hours earlier. Half a dozen are responses to her inquiries about Oliver: *He left a short note cancelling his newspaper; No, I haven't heard from him;* and *Please, let me know if he contacts you.*

No clues, just expressions of concern and requests to be kept updated. The balance of the messages bubble with praise from recent customers, a far cry from the hushed, worried voices of her Santas when they call to relay their uneasiness. Something is off, but none of them can quite put a finger on what. Like her, all are unwilling to document these concerns in writing.

Her concern for Oliver is tinged with anger and betrayal. He originally recruited her as Mrs Claus, but she soon took on organising and overseeing everything else. He often praised her leadership skills. Eventually, he trusted her with all facets of the business and started musing about retirement and flying off to other adventures.

He wasn't interested in selling her the enterprise and said she was destined for bigger things. She pushed, and they'd verbally settled on a price for True North Santa. After her diligent payment of installments, she still couldn't process that he'd run off with her money. It had to be a misunderstanding.

Ding. A new email.

With clammy hands, she opens it.

Dearest Gwyn,

The honour of your presence is requested at our holiday soirée this evening. A driver will pick you up an hour before moonrise. We are dispatching an elf to each of the afternoon events today. The elves are in charge and will provide further instruction to the Santas on arrival. And a reminder: make certain Santas Jim, Sean and Dave understand we expect perfect compliance.

The thought of finally meeting her new employers is accompanied by a thrill of excitement and a frisson of dread.

She phones each of the three Santas. The Santa-for-hire community is close-knit, and all immediately ask about Santa Eric.

"He'll be fine," she assures them, her fingers crossed. "Just make sure you take direction from the elf. Don't worry, it'll all be better next year once I get a handle on things." She grimaces as she speaks, but the Santas sound relieved.

There are still a few hours before moonrise, but the only fancy clothing she owns is her Mrs Claus outfit. She rips the plastic off the dress and smiles. It'll be good to go out. Working alone at home every day, her imagination gets away from her. Maybe she can convince the new owners to stop with the creepy, hooded elf costumes—she's had complaints. Besides, they're primarily a Santa business.

Thirty minutes later, Gwyn admires herself in the mirror. For the first time in weeks, she's humming her favourite Christmas songs. Perhaps they'll ask her to sing. She shivers in anticipation and slips a disposable camera into a pocket. The Santas hand them out at parties. It's always lovely to have a tangible record of happy events.

She's lacing up her scarlet Doc Martens when there's a knock at her apartment door. She grabs her down jacket and pager and opens the door to reveal a tiny man in a hooded cloak.

His face is shadowed. He bows slightly and intones in an odd accent, "Miss Gwyn, I assume?" Without waiting for an answer, he steps forward, and sniffs up at her.

And he's back in the hall before she can raise her hands to ward him off. "What the—"

"I'm to transport you to the soirée. Follow me." He turns abruptly and opens the stairwell door.

"We have an elevat—"

"Follow me," he snaps. She glimpses sharp teeth.

"I, uhm..." Her head feels fuzzy and her feet are already taking her down the stairs.

A silver sedan idles at the curb in the no-parking zone. Gwyn looks around for the building's doorman. He's usually quick to ticket infractions—so quick the residents joke that he probably gets a cut of the fines—but he stands impassively to the side of the entrance, not even glancing at the offending vehicle.

The elf-man holds the back passenger-side door open, and she settles into the pale leather seat. Opaque glass separates the back from the front.

The door on the opposite side opens and the little man takes the seat next to her before rapping on the barrier glass. He's not the driver, as she'd assumed. His face is wizened, and she feels sure if she could see his ears, they'd be pointed. She never used to be fanciful. The sedan glides away from the curb.

Gwyn makes a couple of attempts at small talk, but her escort doesn't respond. She gives up, stares out the window and hopes it wasn't a mistake to accept this invitation. A little voice in the back of her mind corrects her: you haven't really accepted. She thinks about it and decides she isn't sure.

The passing lights and low hum of the car lull her into a stupor. Sometime later, she startles and realizes they've left town, gone past the farm fields and are now travelling through the forest. The head-lights illuminate boughs of hemlock and cedar, heavy with snow and crowding the sides of the road.

"Where are we?" she whispers groggily.

The elf-man makes a noise she can't decipher. The car slows and turns into a narrow gap in the trees. It bounces along a rough road, branches slapping and scraping the roof. A claustrophobic panic builds, and by the time they emerge into a clearing, Gwyn is close to screaming.

The full moon illuminates snow-blanketed ground and the loom-ing form of a winter-bare tree. From the shape, she decides it's an oak, the largest she's ever seen. They pass underneath and she stares up into its silhouetted thicket of branches. Black shapes flit between perches. Her unease resurges.

Will they take her home if she demands it? She's afraid of the answer but decides to try. Straightening her back, she prepares to speak as the sedan rolls out from under the canopy of the tree. Near the crest of a large ridge, there's a sprawling mansion. The moon appears balanced atop one of the chimney stacks. It's a scene out of a dark fairy tale—her favourite kind—and Gwyn no longer wishes to go home.

As a child, she endlessly sketched Victorian brick homes like this one with its steep roof, turrets, arched windows and gingerbread trim. Every night she dreamed about another childhood spent in a home like this. Illustrating her dream house became an obsession, and her mother, having little patience with "fanciful notions", warned Gwyn to adjust her expectations in life if she hoped to find happiness.

She never felt welcomed by her dour, plain family. Once, Father wondered out loud if she was switched at birth. Mother shushed him but not before the memory was seared into Gwyn's brain. She found herself wishing it were true. Her siblings were as boring as her parents, and at an early age, she stopped sharing her drawings or talking about her interests. That was when the nightmares began. Dark dreams where the mansions she drew came to life and she ran through their pulsating, empty halls searching for horrors that never materialized. Always, she woke up disappointed rather than scared.

The mansion is done up for the holidays exactly the way she'd decorate it, with twinkling white lights, twisty garlands of evergreens, red-berried holly and pale Spanish moss.

Perhaps everything will work out with her new employer after all.

The sedan stops at the bottom on the front stairs and instantly the elf-man is holding open her door. Gwyn startles. He couldn't possibly move that fast, but the seat next to her is empty.

The air is sharp with frost. A tasseled rope dangles next to the intricately carved cedar doors. The elf-man pulls it and a muffled chime echoes. One side of the door swings open. Warmth from the house envelopes Gwyn in a muddle of happy scents: apples, burnt sugar, cinnamon and pine resin. Then, briefly, an undernote of spoiled milk. She wrinkles her nose and wonders why the entrance is dark—

She blinks. The sour odor is gone and the entrance glows with candlelight. An older man in a hooded blue cloak holds the door open, only his long, grey beard visible in the low light.

"Gwyn, my dear. I'm ssso pleased you could come. Welcome to my home."

Gwyn hesitates, sure it's the voice from the phone, but that doesn't make sense. She mentally chides herself. Lots of people don't match their voices.

Stepping over the threshold, the oddest sensation ripples through her. It's like she imagines a mother's warm embrace might be when a child returns home. Longing aches through her.

The man takes her metallic pink puffy jacket. He holds it away from his body and she hears a noise that sounds suspiciously like a snort.

A twenty-foot Christmas tree dominates the foyer. Twin staircases curve up either side and disappear into the gloom above. Silver and gold garlands spiral the tree, and hundreds, maybe thousands, of frosted pinecones are tied to its branches with red velvet ribbons. Reflected candlelight from an enormous chandelier sparkles the tinsel. Gwyn wonders at the logistics of lighting it.

"There's a pulley mechanism." The cloaked man points to a rope tethered to the far wall. The sibilant sounds have disappeared from his speech. "The chandelier can be lowered."

"How did you…?" Gwyn shakes her head. "Fascinating."

"You've always been attentive to how everything works. And good with details. Qualities we value." He gestures towards a coat rack. "A token of my appreciation."

Her pink coat is nowhere in sight. A long, snow-white hooded cloak hangs from a hook. *Expensive looking,* she thinks.

"Ermine," the man says.

She shudders. So many little white weasels slaughtered. She steps closer, trying to see whether he reacts, but his face is still hidden. A movement in the tree catches her eye. A slight shiver creates an odd rippling effect. The movements are small and randomly located. Reaching out, she touches a pinecone. The frosting is sticky and coats her fingertips. It's cobweb. She concentrates and squints at the branches. Dozens of spiders gaze back. Their long, black legs lift and fall like they are warming up for a sprint.

She carefully picks one up by a waving leg. "Your tree's infested."

"They're a sign of luck." The man pushes back his hood and smiles.

For a breath-stealing moment, Gwyn's sure it's Oliver. She drops the spider as the blood drains from her face. No, not Oliver. This man is far too old, the nose is wrong and his hair too long. Oliver only had a touch of grey at the temples and was always clean shaven. This man could be an elderly uncle or cousin. Still, the resemblance to Oliver is uncanny.

The man smiles, revealing crowded rows of slender, pointy teeth. Teeth like that can't be natural, and his skin's grey. Perhaps it's a costume or disguise?

The man continues to expose his teeth. Is he laughing at her? Is this an elaborate joke? She recalls that many years ago—after imbibing a few too many—she told Oliver about her childhood dreams. He's the only one who knows.

The sound of laughter and children's voices float out from an arched hallway. Likely, guests waiting to yell *gotcha!*—entertaining themselves at her expense. Humiliation burns through her, carrying dark, vengeful thoughts that fill her mind.

Her eyes narrow and her fingers curl into fists. They'll regret this. She lowers her head, scanning side to side as she stalks towards the hallway. The oak tree is visible through a sidelight window. A growl forms in her throat.

Thunder rumbles. Forks of lightning strike the oak. The urge to ride, to hunt, envelops her.

Gwyn stops and shakes her head. What is she doing? She remembers how once upon a time, she used to handle this kind of situation. Channelling her past self, she crosses her arms and turns towards the front entrance. "I'd best go."

The man is gone, and the storm continues outside. Roiling clouds resemble a herd of multi-legged wild horses. She can almost feel the enormous mare's saddle beneath her, the icy wind through her hair and the heat of torch-bearing hares at her back. Exhilaration fills her, then drains away.

The entrance doors haven't opened—she's sure of it—and the old man didn't go past her and down the hall. She looks up the stairs and notices a large painting on the wall at the back of the second-floor landing. It's the man, wearing his blue cloak, sitting astride a grey horse, a raven perched on his shoulder. The face is too stern to be Oliver, so maybe it was just wishful thinking on her part. The stress of the last few weeks is getting to her.

She peers out the window again. The storm has passed and the skies are calm. The car she arrived in is gone. There's no sign of a parking lot or any other vehicles.

The noise from the party is louder than before. *Best to get it over with.* She's only a few feet down the dim hallway when her pager goes off. Retrieving it from her pocket, she squints at the display—Santa Sean's number, and it's marked urgent.

An unsuccessful check of the foyer for a telephone and she returns to the hallway. The stone floor slopes down, and party sounds emanate from beyond a curve. Perhaps one of the closed doors leads to a quieter den or office where she will find a phone.

Rattling the doorknobs, she finds the first three locked, but the fourth opens into an inky-dark room. She pats the wall and locates a switch. Overhead, fluorescents flicker and crackle to life. Cold, flat light illuminates a powder room. Above a marble vanity, a shape that must be a mirror is covered with a tapestry. The scene the cloth depicts draws her closer: a stylized hunting vista in silver and blue, set against a stormy night sky.

With a finger, Gwyn traces a line of fine gold thread to where it disappears into the folds of fabric. Fascinated, she lifts one corner, and the cloth slips off the mirror.

Her reflection stares back, moon-faced, and not quite right. Her eyes are sunken and gleam with a gold sheen. Her skin appears stretched slightly out of shape. Her lips are narrower and a touch too wide. She grimaces and glimpses sharp teeth.

She gasps, hand pressed against her stomach. A carnival mirror? This place is a nightmare, more suited to Halloween than Christmas. She's not a fan of Halloween.

Anger sweeps aside lingering nervousness and she marches down the hall towards the party sounds. An odd rumbling catches her attention and she pauses in front of another closed door. It's unlocked. The windowless room within resembles a small gymnasium, complete with court markings painted on the floor and a couple of basketball hoops. Row after row of cots call to mind a disaster evacuation centre. On each, a slumbering adult covered in a red and green checked blanket. Gwyn wanders up one aisle. She recognizes some of the snoozing bodies as parents who organized the Christmas parties that should be taking place right now at other locations. She gently shakes a couple and their lips curve up but they don't open their eyes.

Alarmed, she heads back into the hall towards the party. Raucous laughter, childish squeals of delight and light leak around the edges of a double door.

Someone within needs to explain to her satisfaction what's going on and then either call her a cab or take her home. She pushes open the door. The cavernous, circular room is lit around the edges by burning torches stuck into holders in the stone wall. Two grey-cloaked figures turn spitted meat over an enormous fire pit in the centre of the room. It looks vaguely like a whole pig. The log underneath is enormous and will likely burn for weeks. A handful of very young children race by, screeching and laughing hysterically. The colour in their cheeks is high, their eyes glassy.

A clutch of men and women gather around a shallow bowl of blue flame. Taking turns, they reach into the fire and grasp an object, grimace and pop the flaming prize into their mouths. The rest cheer. A woman grasps a bottle with long, claw-like fingers and holds it high. A louder cheer goes up and she pours the contents into the bowl. The blue flames shoot higher.

Thumps and shrieks draw Gwyn's attention to the other side of the cooking pit. A blindfolded woman careens, grabbing at other laughing adults. She sends a couple flying and their bodies crash into both furniture and each other. They screech in glee.

It's a madhouse. Gwyn is about to seek help elsewhere when she notices two men in red suits leaning against the wall, watching the party. Santa Jim and Santa Dave.

She runs over, calling their names. They both look up. *Their faces!* The shock reverberates through her. Sunken, golden eyes, loose skin, wide and narrow lips. They're still recognizable as Jim and Dave, but there's an alien cast to their features and no carnival mirror to blame.

She touches her own face, recalls the man in the blue cloak and his resemblance to Oliver, then pivots on one heel and heads for the children. She recognizes some from client parties and they all appear normal.

Her skin is hot. Sweat trickles down her sides and her heart thunders as she searches the faces of the adults. Why are the parents in the gym napping? What's going on?

None of the adults at the party appear human.

A goat wanders by, bleating. The wreath of bells around its neck jingles. The children rush over, hands outstretched. Gwyn steps towards them, but the Santas block her way.

"Gwyn, great, we wondered when they'd bring you here." Santa Jim beams, sharp teeth reflecting the firelight. "We knew you'd make the cut. Sean and Eric identified too closely with the human, but you're a natural."

Santa Dave throws an arm around her. "Shame about those two. They're both gutted, and probably don't even know why." His laugh is high-pitched and nasty. "The glamour doesn't fully dissolve until you're properly here."

The initial shock is receding and the scene now appears oddly familiar. Long-ago memories nudge to the surface. She came through here as a child. Twice.

No, that's not right. She pushes Santa Dave away and pinches the bridge of her nose. *Think!*

Santa Dave smirks. "You really did embrace the other side—the human's Christmas construct. It's okay, though. We knew you'd be with us and the Yuletide Hunt, once you were here and remembered what it really means to be our leader."

Gwyn blinks. Now she recalls the scared child that wore her face. Gwyn didn't visit here twice as a child. It was only once and she encountered the girl she would replace as they passed in the lower hall. The girl handed her a candy cane and a Santa's hat... and left her to spend a lonely childhood feeling like an outsider.

She grabs Dave's wrist. "We must get the children out of here. Back to their parents before the other children arrive and it's too late."

"It's a good thing it's already too late then." Dave exchanges a look with Jim. They both narrow their eyes and press against her. "Man, you'd choose Christmas over Yuletide, forsaking the hunt we were born to?" They shake their heads in unison, eyes troubled. "Don't worry, the elves know what they're doing. The bloodlust will cure you."

More memories intrude. Gwyn's voice is flat, her tone no longer questioning. "Their parents will never know what happened because they'll be replaced by children who won't ever fit in..." Her voice trails off.

Jim pats her back. "Believe me, I know how that feels. It's worth it, though. All those years taught us what we need to know for the hunt. On the other hand, these ones—" He points at the laughing children. "The human young ones, they get the better part of this bargain. They'll have a life of candy, dancing, playing Snapdragon and never having to grow up." He looks wistful as he watches the adult changelings stuffing flaming tidbits into their mouths.

"Go. Enjoy yourself for a bit," Dave urges. Jim heads across the room.

Gwyn stares at the children. *Is it that horrible?* At least the human children will have each other. And fun and candy, as Jim points out.

She wonders if the real parents of the changelings have any idea what happens to their children. Do they care? She suspects she knows the answer. The idea of returning to Faerie fills her with both dread and sorrow.

"The man in the blue cloak? Oliver didn't really retire, did he?" She smooths her beloved dress and tries to think.

Dave shrugs. "Tomorrow, winter solstice, Yule, we join the host and ride at moonrise. It's been fun working with you at True North, but after we take our place in the hunt, none of that matters." He motions towards Jim. "Tonight, we celebrate."

Gwyn smiles and nods, hoping she looks convincing.

Dave wanders off, leaving her alone.

The lure of belonging exerts a powerful pull, but Gwyn cannot steer her gaze from the children. The glamour masking her memories is completely gone and she knows the mansion's a liminal space, but the lower levels, like this room, are Faerie proper. There's nothing she can do for the human children. There's no turning back for them and why would they want to?

It's the changeling children who need her. They'll be here soon. A love of Christmas sustained her, and with luck, makes it possible for her to choose her own fate now. It's a gift she can offer them too.

After a while, she backs out of the room and carefully closes the door. Perhaps she can slip out the front without running into the scary version of Oliver. It'll be a long, cold walk home but she's tough. Negotiating for ownership of True North Santa will come later, and if they can't come to an agreement, she'll start her own agency and True North will soon be history because they are missing the key ingredient: her.

She pats the instant camera hidden in her skirt pocket. The manor's a magical place. The images she captured should turn out well. This new Internet thing has possibilities. She'll make digital copies, upload them to a public site and ensure the photos are released if anything happens to her.

There are changeling children to save and, no matter what, she'll make sure they enjoy a merry Christmas.

About the Author

Surrounded by gnomes and gargoyles, KT Wagner writes speculative fiction in the garden of her home on the west coast of Canada. She loves to knit and is a collector of strange plants, weird trivia and obscure tomes. KT graduated from Simon Fraser University's Writers Studio in 2015 (Southbank 2013). She organizes writer events and works to create literary community. A number of her short stories are published in magazines and anthologies. She's currently working on a sci-fi horror novel. KT can be found online at www.ktwagner.com and @KT_Wagner

GOOD INTENTIONS

BY JESSICA FEATHER

It is certainly not my *first* time leading a soul to its eternal resting place in the afterlife. I have served as the humble guide to many, *many* souls as they traverse the paths of this labyrinthine shadow plane. Ten, at least. My success rate is most impressive, if I may permit myself to boast. So far, I have only lost one soul en route. I am basically a soul-leading expert.

You may have already surmised who I am. Yes, you are correct...

I am Death.

Or, well, that is a bit of an exaggeration. I am *a* Death. There are a lot of Deaths. With 107 people kicking their respective buckets every minute, you would hardly expect that only one of us could keep up with the job. And that is just taking into account human deaths. There are way more deaths than that when you consider all the plants, animals, extraterrestrial beings, civil liberties, hairstyles, fungi, *et cetera*. For instance, nearly all the souls I have led so far were that of rabbits. That is because training is primarily done with Leporidae souls.

For the record, being a Death is more like my job than my whole identity. I have hobbies. And, if I am being totally honest with you, my colleagues do not generally consider me to be a fully realized Death yet. I am more like an Associate Death.

But as an Associate Death, I do have my fair share of experience dealing with souls. There is very little the soul of a freshly dead being does that fazes me. Even when they are being weird and clingy, saying things like, "But I can't leave my family!" or "But my novel isn't done!" while desperately trying to clasp on to doorways and other corporeal objects—which they cannot do since they are immaterial. I am quite adept at dealing with that sort of soul. However, I am embarrassed to admit, I am feeling rather anxious about my most recent assignment.

It is just, well... I have never actually led a soul to *Hell* before.

So far, all my assignments have gone to "not Hell." Us Deaths rarely call it Heaven. In the biz, it is usually referred to as the Incinerator, because that is what it does to souls. Utterly and irrevocably demolishes them. I know it sounds a mite excessive, but honestly, it is a good thing. Souls experience this blip of euphoria—I have heard it described as going on an awesome mushroom trip at a giant candy store with their favorite celebrity. Of course, none of that means anything to me, since I am a Death and I cannot experience mushroom trips or eat candy—though, in my line of work, I meet more celebrities than I even care to. Anyway, whatever it is *actually* like, the soul experiences a nanosecond of the truest joy, and then, through the process of spaghettification, they are transformed into the eternal oneness, sometimes also called the nothingness. In that place, oneness and nothingness are the same thing. The official name is the Eternal Division of Cosmic Unmaking, but, like I said, all us Deaths just call it the Incinerator. That place is awesome. Souls *love* going there.

But no one wants to go to Hell.

In case you were wondering, in the afterlife, Hell is just called Hell.

Usually that is the first question most souls ask: "Am I going to Hell?" Or, that is what most *human* souls ask, anyway. Animals do not second-guess themselves as much as humans. Dogs *never* ask if they are going to Hell. Even the humans that honestly believed they were very well-behaved on Earth think they are bound for pits of lava and pitchforks the second they see me. Humans are all about self-doubt. That is kind of their whole thing.

But luckily, for every soul so far, I have the absolute pleasure of saying, "No, you are not going to Hell." They seem to warm up to me quickly thereafter.

I do not even want to meet a Hell-bound soul. I imagine they are likely to be deeply unpleasant. I just do not care for negative vibes, y'know?

I asked my colleague, a Senior Death, if it would trade assignments with me. It was on its way to pick up a massive fungus. One of those that lives under miles of dirt, communicating with trees, and doing other neat stuff like that. They live for hundreds of years, so it is fairly rare for us to even get to meet them. The other Deaths say they are astoundingly smart. Not wise, but smart. Like, they can do advanced math problems without a calculator. I thought they would be wise, because I assumed old things are wise. The more-veteran Deaths tell me that age and wisdom are not highly correlated. You learn a lot in my line of work.

It was for naught, anyway. The Senior Death would not give me its assignment. I am stuck picking up some crappy human and taking him to Hell.

Ugh. If I had eyes, I would roll them so hard.

Better get this over with.

I float effervescently (but also ominously) to the surface of Earth to meet my charge. The moment of meeting a recently deceased soul is rather tense. First impressions are everything, even in the great beyond. I see him bewilderedly standing next to his body, which is being mauled by the endangered African elephant he was illegally trophy hunting.

Wow, this guy *really* sucks.

"Am I having an out-of-body experience?" he wonders aloud.

"Well, yes, in fact, you are."

He looks up at me, startled. I guess he did not realize I was here and was just talking to himself a moment ago. I hope my appearance is not too shocking. To newly deceased souls, I generally appear as a spectral mist in the vague shape of a horned humanoid, though some souls have said I look more like a very tall rabbit (mostly the rabbits say that). Either way, my appearance tends to freak people out. This guy is calm, and merely pauses a moment before responding, "Are you also having an out-of-body experience?"

"No. I don't have a body."

"Hm." He considers this for a moment. "I am not going to lie to you, I have no idea what that means. However, I would like it if you could stop this beast from attacking me. That is a very expensive safari outfit I am wearing."

"I'm sorry, but that will not be possible. I am not here to help your body. Or your outfit."

"What are you here for, then?"

This is the awkward part. I still have not found the best way to soften the blow.

"I am here to take you to the afterlife."

"Oh, well, that's all right then."

This time, I am the one who needs a moment to process.

"All right?"

"Oh, sure. I am ready to get my just rewards. Live in my great big heavenly mansion. Fly or whatever cool things I get to do in Heaven."

"May I ask what makes you so certain you are heading to the Elysian Fields and not, you know, the other way?"

"That's easy: I give tons to charity. My foundation has donated billions to noble causes."

"Your foundation was primarily a front for your tax evasion."

"Obviously, yes, but it did still donate money to many worthwhile causes. Mostly to the puppies, but also to combat climate change."

"But your factories polluted the environment, contributing *to* climate change."

"Doesn't matter. I was named Philanthropist of the Year by National Geographic."

"Um... wow."

"Impressive, isn't it?"

"No. That's not... I just... You..." I sigh. Or, I would sigh if I possessed breath. I do not have it, or a corporeal form, but I do the metaphysical equivalent of heaving an exasperated sigh. "You have truly mastered the craft of self-delusion. No. Your money- and conscience-laundering, grandiose, philanthropic gestures did *not* win you a spot in Zion. You are going to Hell."

"Oh no! We'll see about that! I'll get my lawyer on the phone." He grabs for his pocket and attempts to pull out his phone. But his hand goes straight through his leg. "Damn!" He reaches down to what remains of his beat-up body, which the elephant has finally left alone, and tries to grab the phone out of that pocket. Still no use. "I am entitled to a phone call! I know my rights!"

"I am not arresting you. You are dead. Look, I know this is all very surprising, but if we could get started, that would be great. It is a long walk to Hell and I have a quota to reach."

The thing about souls is, they do not have a choice. No matter where they are going in their post-life journey, once they are dead, there is nothing for them to do but travel with their appointed Death. So, even though my new charge does not want to go anywhere without consulting his team of attorneys, as he looks around him—seeing his own dead body on the ground and the gray mist of the netherworld looming—he realizes that he *must* follow me. So, I guess, he decides to drop his privileged belligerence and try a new tack.

"Okay, buddy!" He walks up, and in an aggressively friendly manner, throws an arm on my shoulder—which is quite the charade considering we are both immaterial, so, in actuality, he is just holding up his arm in the place where my shoulders would be if I had shoulders. "Lead the way. It's a long way, you say. Well, if there is one thing I have learned from years of golfing is that a lot can happen on a nice, long stroll. Bitter business rivals can become the best of partners. I think you and I will see eye to eye soon enough."

"I don't have eyes," I grumble as the Earth world appears to melt around us into a spinographic array of colors and the path to Hell materializes.

We stand before an imposing iron gate with words scrawled along the top of it.

"Abandon all hope ye who enter here," my charge reads aloud.

"Yes, well, Dante Alighieri was a self-aggrandizing ninny, but he didn't get everything wrong in his book," I explain.

"Who?"

"Dante Ali—oh, never mind."

"What's all that other writing?"

"That's just the same phrase in every human language that has an official orthography. We're still working on a way to communicate it to people who use languages without writing systems. It's a work in progress."

I knock on the oversized doors. Even though I did not want to take anyone to Hell today, I am sincerely looking forward to this part. These folks are famous for putting on an excellent show.

"Who is it?" A thunderous voice shakes the doors and the ground below us.

"Death, escorting a damned soul."

"I see the soul of Upton Dobbs. Polluter. Exploiter. Tax evader. Money launderer. Poacher. Inside trader. Committer of fraud—*yeesh*, lots of kinds of fraud, actually. I'm not going to read off this whole list to you. If I did, we would be here all week. Okay, yes, he is also a cat-hater. You can't trust cat-haters. People hate cats just because they don't do well with others having boundaries, you know. Okay, yeah, this soul is the smelly sock drawer of souls. You may enter!"

The gates open and reveal five demons, their bodies completely ablaze. They run out and surround my charge, Upton, jumping on each other's shoulders and doing flips like the best acrobatic routine this side of Paradise. All the while they gnash their teeth fantastically, shouting "exploiter!" "fraudster!" and the other sins that were just listed. Except one keeps shouting "murderer!", which I did *not* hear the tremendous voice say. I do not know if that demon is a little overexcited or if they just really like shouting "murderer." In unison, and with impressive harmony, the demons cry out, "You are going to burn!" and then they disappear in five puffs of smoke, each occurring in fast succession.

"Bravo! Bravo! Incredible! Wow, they really are just as good as I heard!" I exclaim.

I glance over at Upton to see if he enjoyed the show and notice he is shivering and wailing in apparent agony. "Oh, god! No! What have I done? I'm really going to Hell!"

"Hey," I coo, trying to sound comforting. "Hey, Upton, buddy, don't cry. It's okay."

"Is it okay?"

"I mean... not really, since you *are* going to Hell. But don't forget, you've got me. And didn't you say you were going to try to talk me out of taking you to Hell? Yeah, aren't you a persuasive guy that could even bend the will of Death? You read lots of books about psychology and persuasion in business school, didn't you?" He seems a little cheered by this statement, or, at least he stops crying. "Yeah, see, you are a clever guy who knows how to manipulate any situation to your advantage, right? You and your circular logic are sure to trick me eventually."

"Maybe you are right."

"Of course I am. Come on, let's get going."

We start down the path together in what I would consider companionable silence. Just an Associate Death and its soul, doing the eternal dance. It is a special moment for me. I try to breathe it in (metaphorically speaking). I have been working on being more "present in the moment" recently. I think it is working.

It is a long walk to Hell, but at least it has some spectacular scenery. First, there is the Faceless Forest. The scraggliest dead trees you have ever seen line the road. The gnarled bark has this uncanny way of triggering pareidolia, so the trees look like they are simply covered in human faces—which really makes the forest's title something of a misnomer. Most of them appear to glower judgingly. I make a note to ask my supervisor why it is called "Faceless Forest" instead of "Forest of Faces" or maybe "Faceful Forest." Of course, the trees also whisper in disturbing detail everything your soul feels guilty about. Only the guilty-feeling soul can hear these whispers, so I do not hear anything. It is just a lovely stroll through nature for me, which, honestly, I could use more of. However, I imagine it is a bit intense for a recently dead soul. I glance back to see how my boy Upton is doing. He really did not handle the dancing demons very well, so I expect this to tear him up.

To all appearances, he looks cool as a cucumber.

"How are you doing, Upton?" I ask, thinking that he might just be putting on a brave face.

"What? Oh, I'm fine. The faces on these trees are a tad freaky, but honestly, what else would one expect on the path to Hell?"

"You... you don't hear anything?"

"Not a thing."

"You don't hear whispers reminding you of every sin you have committed? Everything you feel guilty about? The things you said or did that keep you up at night?"

"What? Certainly not."

"Do you feel guilty about anything? Anything at all?"

"Not a thing."

"Oh." I shrug. What can I even say to a guy like this? "Better keep up the pace."

"Why the rush? Is there time here?"

"No, time doesn't exist here. But there are still quotas. I know, it won't make sense to a mortal brain like yours. The afterlife follows a unique set of physical, metaphysical, and bureaucratic rules. Just trust me, I am behind schedule."

"Wow, these rules really seem to get you down, don't they, my boy?"

"I am a trans-dimensional spectral being, I do not have a gender."

"Of course not, my boy, of course I understand that. But what I am saying is I think this meta-popsicle soul quota balderdash is really taking the joy out of your work. Don't you wish you could just say 'damn it all to Hell!' and leave it behind?"

"I do damn it to Hell. That's literally what I'm doing right now."

"I don't think you are hearing me, my boy. I don't think this line of work suits you. I think you should quit. What is your passion? I bet you would make a top-notch start-up CEO, and I have the big bucks to invest and make your dreams come true. Let's just forget about this whole 'sending me to Hell' thing and you and I could be on top of the world!"

"Oh, I see what you are trying to do! You are trying to trick me into not sending you to Hell, just like you said you were going to do."

Upton stares at me for a moment, looking deep into my soul—which is impossible, really, since I don't have one, but it is still an effective figure of speech.

"You knew that's what I was doing, didn't you?" he accuses.

"Yes," I admit.

"Are you toying with me?"

"Oh no, no, not at all. I just want you to feel like you are succeeding. I know all this stuff along the winding path to Hell is designed to make you feel bad about how you lived your life, but that's just too much negativity for me. I figure you will have more fun if you think your plan to trick me is working."

Upton purses his lips, considering this, before saying, "My boy, you really are quite the clever ghost... demon... monster... thing. I can see that in the battle of wits, we are equally matched. I applaud the opportunity to spar with a worthy opponent. There is still a ways to go before we reach Hell, isn't there?"

"We are about a third of the way there."

"Then there is still time for me to convince you. 'Never say die!' That's what I always say."

"A bit ironic, since you are actually dead."

"Well, that's a bit beside the point I'm trying to make here. Anyway, no more dillydallying, let's see what else this *scary* path has to offer, shall we?" He says *scary* in a tone that would seem to imply that he, in fact, does not find the path to Hell particularly fearsome, which I find irksome. How quickly he seems to forget that he was quaking in fear at the sight of the fire demons. Humans are a strange lot.

But he is right, it is time to press on. Next, we arrive at the river of lava, sometimes known as Styx. I used to be close with Charon, but we had a bit of a falling out, so this is going to be a tad awkward for me.

"Hi Char, long time no see."

"Oh. It's you. What are you doing here?" Charon basically looks like a human skeleton in an oversized robe, except their eye sockets are filled with a void of the blackest black. The blackness of Charon's eye-socket voids is so deep and intense that it would put the feud to create the blackest black paint between Stuart Semple and Anish Kapoor to shame. Charon's eye sockets are quite pretty, actually; if you have the resolve to gaze into the void then you can really admire them. Of course, very few do have what it takes to look at something like that. Especially when that void is peering at you from a skull. That part is a bit unsettling, even for those of us who reside in the afterlife. I can already tell that Upton is deliberately casting his gaze a little off to the side, avoiding looking directly at my friend. Or, my former friend. My frenemy.

"I'm taking this soul to Hell."

"Ugh, I bet that's just a pathetic excuse to come down here and see me."

"That is so like you, Charon!" I exclaim, exasperated. "Here I am, just trying to do my job, and you have the gall to make it all about you."

"Whatever. Let's just get this over with," Charon spits back. "What will you give me in payment?"

"Oh, that should be easy, this guy is loaded. Hey, Upton." I turn to my soul charge, who has changed from merely averting his gaze to covering his eyes with his hands like a child during the scariest part of a movie. Charon tends to have this effect on people, even on fellow eternal beings. It is one of the things I used to like about them... their ability to make anyone act squirmy.

"What? Yes?" Upton responds a little too loudly, which I think is weird. He is covering his eyes, not his ears after all. But I guess that's just how nervous people get around Charon.

"I need a coin to give to Charon to ferry us across the river of lava."

"You want my money?"

"I mean, yes, I guess. But just one coin."

"What kind of scam is this?" Upton shouts. Forgetting his fear of the void, he uncovers his eyes to look right at me as his tone of indignation increases dramatically. "I knew it! This whole thing is just a ploy to get at my hard-earned wealth!"

"Your wealth was hardly hard-earned."

"I started with nothing, you hear me! My business was run out of my home office and I created it from nothing."

"I mean... your parents invested $500,000..."

"Don't all parents support their kids any way they can? Sure, my parents invested in my start-up, but that's not unusual."

"Yeah, and I'm sure you didn't use their network."

"Obviously my dad introduced me to some of his colleagues. It is not a crime to have good business sense. And now you are trying to take my wealth."

"We literally just need a coin."

"Oh no, not a single penny."

I turn to Charon, whose neck vertebrae make a slight creaking noise as they shake their head in disgust.

"I guess there is only one thing for it then," I respond. "We have to shove you directly into the lava."

Even though I am not corporeal and my charge is metaphorically in the same boat, when needed, us Deaths can grab onto a soul and pull it or push it where it needs to go. Of course, the actual mechanics that facilitate this grabbing are not friction, like on Earth. I cannot explain it to you unless you have a PhD in string theory and religious studies, so I will not bother trying. Suffice it to say, I held tight to Upton's arm and started pulling him toward Styx. I do not actually know what happens to a soul exposed directly to lava. Probably nothing, honestly, but Upton clearly did not want to find out.

"Fine! Fine! You can have one penny! But no more, you greedy devils."

"Not the devil," Charon and I respond simultaneously.

"Jinx," I say, momentarily forgetting that we are *not* friends anymore.

Charon almost smiles that toothy, skeleton smile, but catches themself and changes their expression back to a severe glower.

"Only problem is," Upton stammers, "I don't have any money on me."

"Check your pocket," Charon commands.

"I don't! I promise! And even if I did, I couldn't get it! I tried to get my phone earlier and my hand went straight through my leg."

"Check your pocket." Charon's tone does not give Upton an option. He promptly reaches into his pocket and pulls out a single copper penny.

"Well I'll be," Upton says, staring at the coin in amazement.

"Things work by different rules here," I offer up, trying to be helpful, but Upton's look of annoyance implies that he did not find my explanation particularly useful.

We step onto the small boat. Strategically, I get on first so that Upton will be standing between me and Charon. It is a long ride. There is just so much lava.

There is no time here, but it sure *feels* like there is—too much—when you are sharing a boat with your former friend and you can feel them seething at you. Fortunately, Upton is dense and does not notice the unspoken resentments. He chatters away, telling us about all the famous people that attended his parties on his private island back when he was alive. It is an impossibly dull topic of conversation. If I could die, boredom would take me now.

At last, we arrive at the far shore.

"Well," I hedge awkwardly, "thanks for the ride."

"Just doing my job," Charon responds gruffly.

"You do a good job at, uh, your job," I answer, hating myself for how forced my statement sounds. Before Charon has a chance to respond, I stalk off. Upton double-times it to keep up with me as we continue along the path.

"You are acting really weird, even for a spirit or whatever you are," he observes. But, because he is Upton, he does not dwell on a conversation topic other than himself for long. "I really think we are starting to be friends, don't you agree?"

"I don't agree."

"Well, even if we aren't friends, I can tell that we have an understanding. And I know that you really do not want me to go to Hell. Let's say we think of some other plan. Can I talk to someone about being reincarnated or something? Maybe with a second chance, I can prove that I'm not so bad. Give me a list of acceptable good tasks—besides donating massive amounts of money through my foundation, of course—and I will put my team to work making sure I do all of them."

"Reincarnation is not a thing."

"Oh, well, I'm still okay with the 'go to Heaven' plan."

"We're here."

"Really? Hell?" His normally upbeat, business-school-type tone shatters. "Already?"

"Oh, no, sorry to alarm you. We are at the pit. But it *is* the pit that leads to Hell."

"Oh, that's not much better."

Descending into the pit would be impossible if we had to climb. It is steep to the point of being all-but-vertical. Fortunately, in our current nonphysical states, we can glide along the side. You may wonder why we could not do that to get across the lava. Well, that is a good question. I do not know, actually—I just know that in my training they told me to take the boat. And, if I am being brutally honest with myself, I was glad of the opportunity to see Charon again, even if things are still weird between us.

The pit has a sludgy texture all along its sides. The sludge glops around—moving down the cavernous walls, but also upward and sideways, implying that the flow is not facilitated by gravity but by individual slime creatures groping about in the dim lighting. We are traveling downward toward a hole at the bottom, and as we descend, the walls grow closer. Even though I have no sense of touch, just *imagining* the feel of the writhing wall disgusts me. I think humans say things like "makes my skin crawl" which, I admit I do not fully understand, but sounds like an apt descriptor.

Upton is clearly not handling it well. He is shivering all over and looking around with wide-eyed revulsion. When we reach the small hole at the very base of the pit, we must condense our spiritual forms to the diameter of a quarter and slide through. Watching Upton become, essentially, a human noodle, is hilarious. I chortle a little, which clearly annoys him as he glares at me with his smashed-noodle face.

We land in a large, empty room. Almost like a living room, but bigger and mostly bare. There is a sofa with a small side table. Atop the table is a single vase with a brown, crinkly, dead rose. I guess they want it to feel homey.

Facing the couch is a large frame. Within the frame, one can see something that looks like static, like the snow on old TVs. I do not know if this description will make sense, but using human language to capture the complexities of things in the afterlife is never perfect: it looks like *otherworldly* static. One percent of the static on TVs back on Earth is composed of the cosmic background radiation—the waves emanating onto all matter directly from the Big Bang that gave rise to our universe. The static seen inside this frame is one hundred percent cosmic background radiation. And, when you look at it, you can truly see the difference.

"So that's the gate to Hell?" Upton asks.

"Yes."

Upton becomes, understandably, agitated. He paces, wringing his hands, and talking much too fast. "I was not a terrible person. I never hurt anyone. Sure, I knew my employees were a little overworked. So, sue me—*they* did! But does a little extra work kill people? Oh, I mean, sometimes it does. It did. I do remember seeing some reports to that effect. But it was all within the margin of acceptability. I just... I can't go to Hell."

"Upton, it is time." I motion to him and he hesitantly steps closer to the portal. As one approaches it, they hear the faint sound of agonized screaming. Like sitting in the waiting room of a dentist's office.

We stand together staring into the eternal static and listening to the wails of tortured souls. I can sense that Upton will not walk, willingly, into the portal. I might have to shove him.

He looks directly into a space where my eyes would likely be if I had them. "Don't do it, man. Don't make me go in there."

I will *definitely* have to shove him.

Upton Dobbs is irredeemable. I have no doubt. He has harmed so many people, animals, the environment, the future of his species. He is so self-absorbed and his logic so self-serving that he cannot see it. And yet...

And yet, I do not know if I can really send him to Hell.

This is not about *his* soul anymore. It is about mine. I mean... metaphorically. As previously stated, I do not have a literal soul. But I do have a conscience. And, by golly, my conscience tells me that I do not want to send anyone to Hell. Not even this moral waste dump of a human.

"I can't do it," I announce.

"Oh, thank you! Thank you! Merciful spirit!" Upton blubbers.

"We must move quickly. We are going to sneak you through the pearly gates. But first we need to go back the way we came, which means..."

"Going back through that terrible gunk in the pit."

"Oh, yes, of course we'll do that. I'm mostly worried about seeing Charon again. Things are kind of... you know, unsettled with us and it will be awkward."

"I'm sorry," Upton says in a way that does not sound even a little bit sorry, "but I'm confident you two can resolve your differences."

Even though I know he does not mean it, and is only saying it because he is a manipulative bastard that wants to convince me to take him to Heaven, the sentiment makes me feel better.

"Let's get moving!"

Since we can only float a little bit, I turn the couch on its side so we can climb up on it and reach the hole to the gross slime pit. We easily semi-float up the side and run all the way back to the lava river.

Time to face Charon again.

I do a spectral power pose to feel confident, then I signal for them to bring the boat around. Charon can sense the signal anywhere on their river. They arrive almost immediately.

"Again?"

"Yes, again. Look, Charon, I don't like the way we left things." *Yeesh,* this is hard. But it is time for me to be the bigger ethereal cosmic immortal being and apologize. "I am sorry I said that ferrying dead souls is not a real job. Now that I have seen you in action, I can tell how much artistry you put into your work. I hope you can forgive me. I want to be friends again."

Charon paused, a thoughtful expression crossing their skull face. Finally, they respond, "And I'm sorry I broke the tesseract that Anubis gave you. I think, in some ways, we've both been a couple of chowderheads."

"Friends?" I ask.

"Friends," Charon assures me.

We hug. Which, for non-corporeal beings, is a little like just meshing into a singular cosmic entity for a second. It is quite intimate. But, you know, not inappropriate or anything.

"Excellent, we're all friends again," Upton interrupts our moment.

"We're not your friend," Charon informs him.

"Compadres! Compatriots! Pals!" Upton continues.

"What is this guy still doing here? Isn't he supposed to be in Hell?" Charon quizzes me.

"About that... I decided not to take him to Hell after all."

"Why? He completely sucks!"

"I know, but *I* don't want to send anyone to Hell. You know?"

Charon looks at me kindly. "You are such a sweetie. Okay, so he's not going to Hell. What's the plan?"

"I'm taking him to the Incinerator."

"Wait, the *what*?" Upton shouts in alarm.

"Oh, don't worry, that's what we call Heaven," I explain.

"Oh, okay." Upton seems placated.

"You little rebel, you." Charon smiles mischievously. "I never knew you had it in you."

"Can you take us back to the other bank?"

"I'll do better than that! I know a shortcut. Jump in the boat."

We clamber aboard and Charon starts rowing us against the current. We catch up as we make the ride. I am so happy we are friends again. I feel a glow. Of course, the lava also glows. There is just a lot of glowing going on right now, and it is wonderful.

Eventually, Charon pulls the boat off to the side bank. "Here we are. Just go up this path a ways, it will lead you straight to the *escalier*. Just be careful, you need to go through the yard where the fire demons take their smoke break. Don't let them see you."

"Thank you," I say, before adding, "friend."

"Good luck. I hope they don't wind up throwing you to Cerberus for this."

We chuckle over this, though, truly, it is a mortifying prospect.

"Thanks, my number one bone man," Upton says, trying to give Charon a fist bump. Charon simply stares blankly at my soul charge with two eye sockets full of void. Upton shivers and scurries to follow me.

We come upon the furies, lingering in a large garden of sorts. All the plants are dead, of course, but they still manage to be attractive in a brown and crispy way. The fire demons are off duty, so rather than being engulfed in flames, they are covered in charred skin, still glowing slightly with the light of dying embers. Most of them are drinking black coffee, smoking cigarettes, or both. Somehow, they learned about coffee and cigarettes from souls of the damned. The fire furies *love* coffee and cigarettes. Of course, they are one of the only entities around here with a material form, so they are physically able to partake in such things, unlike the rest of us.

"How do we sneak past those guys?" Upton whispers. I guess I should have warned him that the demons' hearing is like a horned owl spirit from the eighth dimension. Or, well, that is to say, incredibly acute.

Immediately, they all turn and look at us.

"Oh look, it's the murderer," one of them calls out.

"Lottie, why do you call *everyone* a murderer? They aren't all murderers, you know. Just... most of them."

"You sure he's not a murderer? He looks like one." She gives Upton the once-over with her incandescent orange eyes. "I'm sure he murdered someone, even if it was indirectly."

Her interlocutor concedes, "Fair point," then they all go back to their cigarettes and coffees.

Upton and I stand around for an intergalactic minute, waiting to see if they are going to do anything. Finally, I figure the best thing to do is just ask.

"Hey, fire demons, do any of you have a problem with me sneaking this soul out of here?"

"What?" one of them asks. "You aren't taking him to Hell?"

"No," I respond, expecting them to react poorly to this.

"I mean, as far as I'm concerned, it's your call. You don't tell us how to dance in a blaze of righteous fire shouting sins at sinners, we don't tell you how to guide souls."

"Well, thank you. That's downright professional."

"No problem, buddy."

"Great show, by the way." I feel a little starstruck talking to the fire demons.

"Oh, thanks," one of them responds. "Always nice to meet a fan."

Upton and I stroll past the fearsome furies. Before long, we are standing at the base of an impossibly tall spiral staircase.

"It's really a stairway?" Upton queries.

"Why does everyone ask that? Even the rabbits ask that."

We climb. There are quite a few other people along the way, many more than on the path to Hell. It is a very long ascent, and it takes a very long time to get there—even if time is nonexistent here. Finally, we reach the top. A small queue has formed in front of the portal. The doorway to the Incinerator looks very much like the doorway to Hell, full of cosmic static. The only discernible difference is that the frame is made of pearl. Everyone in line is patient except, notably, my charge, who manages to fidget, wiggle, and look around himself in a most anxiety-inducing manner. He even asks the person in front of him if he can cut, which draws appalled stares from everyone within earshot. His inability to play it cool is definitely going to get us found out. I have no idea what kind of trouble I could be in if I am caught. I really am putting my metaphorical neck on the metaphorical line here. I hope that this crummy guy appreciates everything I am doing, but I sincerely doubt that he does.

There are only two people in front of us now, almost home free, when a Senior Supervisor Death meanders by, just keeping an eye on things. It makes a "hmm" sound, as if considering everything that is happening and finding it all to be quite fine. It nearly floats away when Upton clears his throat in that "I am definitely suspicious" way. The Senior Supervisor Death returns to our side.

"Hello, Eighty-Six Thousand Two Hundred and Eight," it greets me. Of course we all have numbers instead of names here. What else would you expect?

"Hello," I respond, trying to sound deferent and cheerful at the same time.

"How did your first Hell assignment go?"

"Oh, it went fine, just fine. He just, you know, hopped right in. Much less trouble than I feared."

"Really?" my superior asks suspiciously. It stands before us in silence just a little too long, and I know that it knows. There is only one thing to do.

"Quickly, Upton!" I shout, pushing the soul. "Jump into the gate! Before they stop us!"

Upton is not very quick on the uptake. He stands there looking overwhelmed.

"GO, YOU FOOL!" I shriek. A Death shriek is a truly horrific sound. Everyone in line covers their ears and all the nearby Deaths hiss. We have everyone's attention now. Upton finally realizes what is happening and makes a desperate leap for the door. Several Deaths standing with their charges on the stairs reach out to stop him, but it is too late. He is through. I can see him floating in the cosmic background radiation, a blissful, beaming smile across his face. For a second, I think he might shout a "thank you for everything" back out the doorway at me, but of course, he does not. People like that are not very adept at gratitude. And then he is gone. Demolished into the everythingness and nothingness. Entirely unmade.

"What are you doing?" the Senior Supervisor Death admonishes me. "That soul was supposed to go to Hell."

"I know! I know!" I lament. I regret my decision almost immediately. Why oh why would I risk everything for a guy like *that*? "I know I should have sent him to Hell. But I just couldn't! I couldn't bring myself to do it."

Many of the Deaths have gathered around me at this point. I do not blame them, I am making quite the scene, and Deaths, as a rule, love drama. They all take in what I am saying—that I snuck a Hell-bound soul into the Eternal Division of Cosmic Unmaking. I am a rebel and a criminal. And now they all know it.

Simultaneously, all the Deaths laugh. And they keep laughing. Some of them are guffawing. The laughing goes on and on for a long time. I really feel like I am missing something here.

"It's the same thing," the supervisor finally says.

"What?"

"Heaven and Hell," it explains, "they are just two different doors to the exact same place. That guy was going to get incinerated either way."

"Then... then why are there two doors? Two paths. With all the fire demons, dead trees, lava, pit, and everything. What's the point?"

Around me, the Deaths burst into new fits of laughter. Apparently, my ignorance to this one incredibly important detail of the afterlife is amusing to everyone.

"Some people were just really crappy while they were alive," the supervisor continues, "so we like it when they repent a little bit before moving on to the great beyond."

"Huh." I ponder this. "Yeah, that makes sense. So, I'm not in trouble?"

"Not at all, you did a perfectly fine job. But maybe next time you get a sinful soul, you will *actually* take it to Hell."

I respond enthusiastically, "Oh, hell yes!"

About the Author

Jessica Feather (she/her) followed her love of language through the secret tunnels under the University of Texas until it led her to a BA in Linguistics. For the past decade, she honed her narrative skills as a nonprofit grant writer, winning awards that provide affordable housing, teach arts, and save bats. She is part of the small creative team at KillerPartyGames.com, concocting thrilling plots and puzzles for murder-mystery dinner games. Jessica lives in the self-described Land of Enchantment with her husband, dog, cat, and surprisingly tall axolotl. *Good Intentions* is her first published short story.

WITH LOVE
JONATHAN

A Chronological List of My First Hauntings by Jonathan Chen

by Mei Davis

To the esteemed members of the Committee on Haunting and Possession:

I present to you this chronological list of my first hauntings with the sincere hope that my tireless studies and practicums, performed since my death and induction into Ghosthood one year ago, has provided me with the expertise, capability, and instincts worthy of earning a Provisional Certification in Haunting Basics, and one of the few yet revered recommendations for membership into the Haunter's Guild.

0000. JINGFEI CHEN

There's something a little extra wicked about haunting your own mother, isn't there? But chapter one of *Haunting for Beginners* states that when initiating our haunting careers, we ought to "Haunt what (we) know."

Members of the committee, there is no one that I know better than dear, old Mama. From her humble origins as a hostess working in San Francisco's finest mobbed-up restaurants, to an indolent trophy wife frittering away millions in a penthouse on Jackson Square, I was with her every step of the way, underfoot and cramping her style. "Nothing but a nuisance," was the delicate way she often phrased it. "And I was an idiot not to get rid of you when I had the chance!"

My familiarity with all the personal details germane to haunting, such as her crippling insomnia, heavy reliance on Xanax, and penchant for being easily triggered, made her undoubtedly my first choice as a hauntee.

At the onset of Fog Effect One (the simplest, yet in my opinion, the most efficacious of the Fog Effect litany), my drug-hazed mother tore screaming out of her bed. Her terror was such that I could have ended the haunt there. But in keeping with *The Quintessential Haunt*'s mission statement—"no haunt, whether poetic or prosaic in nature, is complete without the aroma of psychology"—I decided to go one step further.

I activated the Specter Detector, which allowed Mama a brief, yet crystal clear look at my incorporeal visage, into the very face of her selfishness and neglect; a single, purified glimpse into her failings which plunged her despair into unseen depths—and a broad kitchen knife into her belly.

As the gore spread across those expensive marble tiles, I admit I was not surprised. After all, she was the only person who mourned me in death.

Pity she never cared much for me in life.

0400. *ALEX WONG*

From his earliest years, Alex was an undisputed wunderkind. His combination of urbanity and brilliance quickly propelled him from the son of poor immigrants to one of Forbes "Top Twenty-Five under Twenty-Five."

From my oldest childhood friend to the man who later labeled me "a useless and predictable hack not worthy of a keyboard, much less fifty percent in profits."

Was it any wonder we parted ways? He to a vast, virtual empire, and I to a "useless and predictable" death. But once relieved of those shackles called life, I was resolved to eschew its concomitant weights of uselessness and predictability, to give Alex's haunt a true sense of individuality, what the authors of *The Original Haunt: How to Make Old Traditions Your Own* called, "that ineffable quality of horrific genius."

Alex once told me his particular brand of genius wasn't tied to the clock, that in fact he abhorred clocks above all things, as every young, virile man must despise the irrepressible passage of time. When I arrived, Alex sat lounging in his lavish, waterfront studio, replete with smart technology, minimalist furniture, and pretentious decor. Standard haunting practice would dictate malfunctioning appliances, accompanied by the poltergeist classic of a floating sculpture. Instead, I hearkened back to the neglected annals of *Archaic Haunting Methods, Volume 1*, and the nearly forgotten Clockleganger Effect, in which every object, no matter where the hauntee looked, would appear as a loudly and rapidly ticking clock.

Confronted with the relentless vision of the one enemy that can never be subdued, it was mere minutes before he was induced to self-enucleation, followed by a surprising act of self-defenestration—two of the rarest hauntee responses.

Alex was reduced to one of the many ubiquitous smears marring San Francisco's public sidewalks. But at least no one can ever say he was predictable.

0800. JENNIFER CHEN

"Congealed blood is thicker than poisoned water." This proverb, first recorded in the medieval *Filial Ob-ghoul-ations*, urges the vengeful spirit that even in death, "Family should fright first"—which is why I chose my dear half-sister as my next hauntee.

Born in the year of the dragon, *Jie-Jie* was preferred to me by anyone who knew us both, especially my mother and stepfather. It's why she attended costly, prestigious schools while I was relegated to Chinatown's public sphere. It's why she rode a golden elevator through the ranks of the Fushang Group to become its youngest and first woman vice president, while I was locked in the corporate basement, scrubbing the books, laundering the money, and polishing the less-than-legal side of the company's profit margins—an occupation I had little choice but to accept after my irrevocable break with Alex, and all my hopes of financial independence evaporated.

Jenny was the immaculate face of the company; I was the pair of dirty hands. "Your only job is to not get caught, and you couldn't even do that right," she was wont to say every time she posted my bail. "But at least Mama and Baba have one child they can be proud of."

Indeed, *Jie-Jie's* pride had been groomed and manicured since birth, and the one thing on which she prided herself most was being nothing like me, a sentiment echoed by the oft-quoted phrase from *Haunt Them Where it Hurts*: "The root of terror comes not from without, but from within, from looking into the worst parts of ourselves." My half-sister's relation to me was undeniably the worst part of herself, and why, for her haunt, I used the uncomplicated yet potent Reflection Deception:

When looking into a mirror, any mirror, her reflection appeared as my face.

Initially, her reaction was disappointing. She smeared every mirror in the house with dark red lipstick, put in a call to a therapist, and hopped into her Escalade to work. But I rallied under the fortifying advice of *Good Haunts Come to Those Who Wait*, and tweaked the Reflection Deception so that her reflection appeared as my face *at the moment of my death*:

Blood-splattered, brain-speckled, and an oozing maw of an exit wound.

It took many hours for *Jie-Jie* to crack, but in the end, my diligence was rewarded. There is no doubt that my parents now have two children in which they can be equally proud.

After all, that hole in the back of her pretty little head is a dead ringer for mine.

1600. *PENG "BIG SHOT" XUEFENG*

Haunting, as a moral obligation, was never better analyzed than in the exhaustive work done by the authors of *The Fault in Their Flesh: Why They Deserve It*.

Members of the committee, if ever a man deserved an unrestrained and gruesome haunting, it would be none other than my former boss, Big Shot. Known for bone-cracking, throat-garotting, and general humanity-terrorizing, he was the epitome of the hauntee those sage authors commissioned us to menace, "until the *schadenfreude* can be heard in their dying shrieks."

For a degenerate of Big Shot's pedigree, any sort of downfall would achieve *schadenfreude* as a matter of course. The challenge was how to maximize it. My previous haunts had employed the most powerful psychological tools in my haunting arsenal, and thereby overlooked the assertion set forth in *The Haunter's Manual of Style* that, "The lightest touch, the slightest fear, often leads to the greatest humiliation."

Big Shot himself was a purveyor of humiliation. A mountain of mass and muscle, he took every opportunity to showcase his physical superiority, much to the pain and degradation of others—particularly my own. "Clean this money till it shines, and lick my boots till they do the same," he often said to me, a request he meant only too literally.

But no one, however intimidating, is immune to a *bete noir*. In Big Shot's case, it was an inexplicable fear of dogs, linked, I believe, to an innate fear of capture. It was for this reason that I implemented the Surround Sound Hounds, a neglected technique considered little more than a mood enhancer, rather than the centerpiece of a haunt. But after an hour of relentless barking, heard only by him and which followed him everywhere, the mighty Big Shot was reduced to a mixture of anxiety, adrenaline, sweat, and urine, and willfully flung himself into oncoming traffic in an attempt to avoid his invisible, yet all too audible, pursuers.

"The bigger they are," so the old adage begins. Big Shot had fallen hard, and this time, he would need more than a cowering minion to clean the viscera off his boots.

2000. *YUKI CHOW*

Detective Chow, despite working for the other side of the legal divide, was at the time of my death, the only person I considered a friend. Born to a Japanese mother and Chinese-American father, in the insular community of San Francisco's Chinatown, she knew what it was to be an outsider, to be looked upon with tolerant disdain no matter how hard we tried to prove ourselves. Our shared struggle forged a bond of understanding between us, and perhaps that's why I became her criminal informant. Perhaps that's why I finally gave in to her insistence, and agreed to turn state's evidence against the Fushang Group.

Perhaps that's why we became lovers.

And perhaps, most pertinently, that's why I felt a tinge of reluctance as I watched her slim form hurry down the wharf. Garbed in a beige trench coat and sensible boots, she looked just as she did when I saw her last, at the grand finale raid on one of Fushang's gambling dens.

"Chen, you bastard!" Big Shot had yelled as the cops flooded into the warehouse.

Detective Chow had laid a placating hand on my chest. "Easy, Jon," she said in her cool, commanding way. "You don't have to worry about him anymore. We've got them now."

I never saw her betrayal coming. I lived in a fantasy where she meant something to me, and I to her. But one close-range headshot was all it took to undo me of every delusion. Her police report was a tidy affair, alleging that in the chaos of the standoff, I pulled out a gun and threatened her. Though my death meant she never got her star witness on the stand, I learned later that she did get something else in return.

Members of the committee, you will rightly understand the nature of my dilemma. According to FORM 146-7C: APPLICATION FOR ENTRANCE INTO THE CORPOREAL DIMENSION FOR THE PURPOSES OF HAUNTING(S), the one requirement of every spectral applicant is "that you haunt the person(s) who are, whether by intent, accident, or negligence, deemed the most influential and direct means of your demise."

Yuki, in fact my murderer, nevertheless had engendered nothing but affection from me until the very moment of my death, and was the one person I was both unwilling, and yet absolutely required, to haunt. In my hour of desperation, I turned to the wise counsel of the acclaimed *Overcoming Ourselves: How to Purge Our Remains from Our Remaining Sentiment.* "The yet-to-die," it reads, "are self-deceivers of the highest order, and it is our duty to force them to acknowledge what they refuse to believe."

Yuki made me believe we would be together when it was all over. Now, I would make her believe the same. My perfectly timed Seclusion Delusion gave her the illusion that she was trapped—with me—in an ever-shrinking steel cage, and her only means of escape was throwing herself into the sea.

It was only after her blue, stiff corpse washed onto shore that I noticed the coordinates entered into her GPS. Yuki had been on her way to the Fushang Group's headquarters.

On her way to visit my stepfather.

2400. *JIABAO CHEN*

Of all the people in a man's life, does any influence rank higher than a father's? Though Jiabao was not technically my father, he had all the trappings of one: severe judgment, palpable disapproval, and the uncanny ability to shape my life—and me—into whatever mold he desired.

Every event in my life, every desire of my heart, was somehow or other orchestrated by the long reach of my stepfather. "We are bound to haunt in death the one that was our greatest influence in life," so writes the un-living legend Sun Tzu in his groundbreaking *The Art of Haunting*. If those words are true, and my stepfather's haunt was a matter of destiny, then I was determined that it would eclipse anything I'd previously accomplished. That it would be a true showstopper, capable of garnering me a place in the Haunter's Guild with its nuance, creativity, and encapsulation of the very essence of haunting:

To bring one face-to-face with their greatest fears.

Detective Chow's payoff lay cold on the coffee table. "That boy has been an embarrassing stain on my life since the day I married his mother," he had told her weeks ago. "And now he wants to turn me in? Take care of him, Chow. Do whatever it takes. I'll make it worth your while." She would not be coming to collect it, though he didn't know that yet.

But what he did know was this: his wife had bled out on the marble floor of his home; his daughter's head was a thousand flecks smearing the wall of his penthouse; his top lieutenant was a heap of bones and blood outside one of his businesses; the investigations into all three deaths had the potential to strip him of his company, wealth, and freedom.

Everything he'd ever worked for all his life, gone in twenty-four hours.

Doubtless, his greatest fear would be knowing that he was the means of his own demise, which is why, for my *piéce de résistance*, all I did was scribble a simple, blood-inked phrase upon the wall:

With love,

Jonathan

Death is not an end so much as a new beginning.

This afterlife changing concept from *The Manual for First Arrivals* is something I have wholeheartedly embraced since my rebirth into Ghost-hood. During my lifetime, I dreaded rejection. I foolishly craved the acceptance and admiration of others, and strove by any means necessary to achieve it.

But all that has been eschewed. No longer plagued by the weakness of flesh and bone, I have ceased to hang my hopes on the opinions of others. Indeed, my only hope now is that you esteemed and lauded members of the Committee on Haunting and Possession have been convinced that I, by any means necessary, will passionately endeavor to earn your approval and regard forever, and ever, and ever, and...

About the Author

A child educator, Mei Davis maneuvers between managing fictional children and the far more troublesome tangible variety. She has been published by prairiefire, Sans Press, Translunar Traveler's Lounge, and Radix Media.

TINY
COMICS

THE SOUL STONE

BY ALY FAYE

Summer 1910—aboard *The Venturer*, three days out of Southampton, England.

"Spread the nets, lads. Get to the port side, grab the shrouds and chains; hold firm, don't let it escape, keep pulling it in!" The captain's shouts whipped the sailors as hard as the pounding rain and as fierce as the burn of the salt water on their skin.

The creature, entwined in *The Venturer*'s nets, screeched in fury and lashed out with a muscular tail.

"Keep a tight hold. You're looking at yer pension there, me lads."

The crew of twenty sailors, blinded by gobbets of water, swearing and shouting, hung onto the ropes, feeling the tarry fibres shred their flesh. Drops of their blood spattered into the churned waters; the netted prisoner shrieked, but this time in a higher tone. Blood leaked from the sailors' noses and ears as the notes rose up the scale to inaudibility.

"Hell's teeth, Captain! She's calling to 'em!" yelled First Mate Joe "Ironsides" Long. He rubbed the blood away from his face.

In the distance, the storm loured, whilst under the waves a squadron of dark, lithe shadows raced, tails and fins powering through the water.

"They're nearly upon us, Captain! We've gotta let her go, else we're done for!" Joe shouted towards the quarterdeck, voice frantic with terror.

Captain Jackson Moses swore, spat a wad of tobacco onto the deck and conceded defeat. *Damn it to hell and back.* "Right you are, First Mate! Release the nets! Let her go!"

The distressed pulleys and gears of the old whaling ship creaked and moaned, and the sailors staggered backwards, releasing their grips, spattering blood onto the decks. They collapsed, exhausted, lying on their backs.

The nets plunged into the chaotic waters, and the creature slashed at the mesh with long, cruel talons, whilst others of her kind swam to her aid, tearing with their razor teeth, biting a route to freedom.

The youngest sailor aboard, the new cabin boy, "Mighty" Billy Boy—as the sailors had jokingly nicknamed the scrawny child—crept across to port side, peering over the edge on tiptoe.

Below him, the ocean tantrumed; innumerable shadows circled the ship, tails appearing above the surface, and an unholy yowling reminded him of alley cats in heat in the Birmingham slums he'd run away from. He clasped his hands over his ears and prayed he'd see another dawn.

He jumped when a hand landed on his shoulder. "Don't be afeared, Billy Boy, the whole damned school of them will go now. They've got what they come for." Joe crouched beside the child. "I've seen this before."

"But, First Mate, sir, look—they're *not* leaving."

Joe followed the boy's trembling finger and noticed: a handful of the sinuous shapes circling, then re-circling the ship, scaly tails pushing their bodies underneath the waves, as they still clawed at the nets. He glimpsed a face, feral, inhuman, leering up at him. It stared directly at him and hissed, revealing razor-sharp teeth. A terrible fear coiled in his belly like a snake.

"Pull the nets up, lads!" Joe yelled. "Do it now!"

The sailors leapt to their posts, spurred on by the fear in the first mate's voice. Yard by painful yard, the nets were hauled back up. Unburdened of their catch, and therefore so much lighter, they rose much faster. To Joe's eye, they appeared empty, bereft of anything except seaweed, shells and other ocean debris.

Perhaps if they can see they're empty they'll swim away? he thought, his hand gripping the silver crucifix hanging around his neck, hidden out of sight. It didn't pay to talk religion on Captain Moses's ship.

For a long minute the nets swung in the air, before landing on the deck. The screeching from the ocean rose to a peak, and Joe saw the blood trickling from his crew's ears; he touched his own cheek. *Damn monsters.*

"Damn you all to hell!" he shouted into the night air.

Captain Moses threw back his head, humourlessly guffawing, and extracted his pipe and baccy from his pouch, though there was no chance of striking a flame with the wind and rain. It was his habit; a comfort ritual. The pipe had been his father's.

"They're g-going," Billy said, and sat hard on his bony backside with relief. He'd wet his pants during the attack, but hoped that in all the drama, no one would notice. The deck was awash with water anyway. A little more would make no difference.

Moses stomped below decks, to the muggy warmth of his cabin and the succour of the whiskey bottle. Joe envied him. As first mate he'd have to stay up on deck with the men, secure the gear and tidy up the nets. *One day,* he promised himself, *one day I'll have that old drunk's post and me own ship.*

"C'mon, lads, let's get the nets tidied away. Tomorrow we'll mends 'em."

Billy nudged his hip. "First Mate, sir, there's something caught up in them."

Joe brought a lantern over, lifting it high above the piles of snaky webbing. Something glinted in the orange light and twitched; a tiny movement, but he knew he'd seen it.

"Get back, Billy Boy. Keep away." Joe pulled out his knife and knelt. The sailors grouped around him, forming a semicircle, holding more lanterns up.

Joe cut away at the nets, careful not to slash. He reached in and pulled out a bundle, wrapped in sealskin, tied with seaweed. It was small, dark-haired, pale-skinned, with flippers instead of fingers and toes and... it was breathing, its tiny chest rising up and down.

"Bloody hell, Joe. We've only gone and caught ourselves a mermaid's babe. Be worth a fortune at the freaks and geeks show," said one of the sailors. A hum of agreement echoed the words.

"He's so—small and perfect," Billy whispered, "just like me mam's last baby." His eyes filled with tears at the memory.

"Yeah, but it don't half stink!" laughed one sailor.

"What's that around its neck?" asked another.

Joe reached into the bundle and, with one finger, lifted up the object tied around the baby's fragile neck. In the lantern light it glinted—soft, creamy and lustrous.

"It's a bloody pearl," Joe muttered. "A proper, natural oyster's pearl." In his head he was calculating how much this beauty would be worth back home in London.

At that moment the mer-baby opened his eyes and stared right up at Joe. The eyes were black as ebony, with no iris or cornea; inhuman, reptilian. The mer-baby opened its mouth, revealing rows of tiny, serrated teeth, and emitted an ear-splitting wail. It began wriggling, flapping its flipper and pissing black liquid, which dripped onto the decking. Where the liquid landed, the wood blackened and burned. When the flow reached one of the nearest sailor's bare feet, he screamed, jumping backwards, swearing. Two of the toes on the foot turned necrotic in a matter of seconds.

Every one of the sailors backed away from the mer-baby; one or two of the older men crossed themselves. However, Billy continued to gaze in wonder at the tiny creature. He seemed unafraid. He stretched out his right hand and stroked the baby's cheek. "Sleep tight, little one," he whispered. "Don't ye fret now. All will be well." They were the same words his mam used to say every night, before she'd died of the typhoid. He missed her every day. He carried a heavy burden in his heart for a ten-year-old.

The babe gazed up at him, gurgled and closed his eyes; blessed silence fell.

"You take him, Billy Boy, seeing as how you can..." Joe didn't know what had just happened, but no one else on board wanted to pick up the freak.

Billy smiled, like he'd been given a wonderful gift, and, carrying the bundle in his arms, crooned to it as he made his way below decks to the nook where he made his own bed.

Joe looked around at the crew. They were all waiting for the first mate to take the lead. They were all also staring at the pearl, as fat as an olive, still gripped in Joe's fist.

"Right, lads, well—er—I'll go report to the captain, and hand him this. It's ocean booty and every man here will get a cut when it's sold in London. I promise ye."

"Cap'll be in his cups, good and proper, by now Joe Long," said Horace, one of the most senior of the crew. "So, why don't we leave off telling the old man till morn?" He smirked through his thick beard.

There was a murmur of agreement and the sailors edged closer to Joe, who took a step back. Just as he was wondering how to react to the rising tension, the ship's keel reverberated with a series of massive thumps off the starboard side, which rocked the men off their feet. Above their heads flocks of seagulls appeared, whirling in a frenzy, landing in gangs on the foremasts and the mizzen. Joe had never seen such a vast avian gathering in his seafaring life, and, he knew, it was a sign of worse to come.

The masts and rigging began to crack and collapse under the flock's weight as the birds tore at the sheeting, ripping it to shreds, which drifted uselessly in the rising wind.

Captain Moses lurched, drunk and windswept, onto the bridge. His voice was furious and inaudible amidst the cacophony of the seagulls' demented shrieks, which were joined by others' voices but from below.

Joe watched Horace, a massive man, well above six feet in height, being dragged head first over the side of the ship, legs flailing, one boot flying off. The creature that crawled over the side after that was an apparition from one of Joe's drunken nightmares.

Around him, in every direction, the crew were under attack—above from the birds and below from the sea creatures arriving on board.

Joe had heard the tales, and the tavern talk, of gorgeous sirens luring sailors to their deaths with their singing. He'd laughed and jested with his mates, but he'd never believed mermaids were real. They were dreams conjured from the desires of drunken, homesick sailors.

The creature hauling herself, *itself*—Joe wasn't sure which—towards him, was nearly six feet in length, of which a good two feet was made up of a scaly, muscular tail that glinted in the moonlight. Its arms were long and thin, but ended in bony, coral-encrusted fingers and talons that scratched deep scars into the wood as it crawled nearer to him. Its dark hair streamed, sodden, crawling with bijou, glittering creatures, but its face did not resemble any woman's. Its eyes were dark holes, its nostrils mere slits, gills flapped in its neck and its lips were blue. It was feral and fearless and focussing on him. This was the face of a hunter. He was its prey. And the stink of rotting fish coming off it made him hurl a stream of bile onto the deck.

The night air filled with the screams of the dying crew, being eviscerated, gnawed and fed upon, whilst the foulness of their entrails, steaming in the cold air, added to the nightmarish scene. For no sooner had one of the mermaids finished its kill, than a cohort of gulls flew down, like white, feathery bullets, to feast on the flayed flesh.

Behind him Joe spotted Captain Moses high up on the forecastle, cornered, waving his arms at the gulls, whilst a mermaid crept towards him. As it reared up to its full six feet, jaws wide open, incisors on show, Moses screamed and threw himself overboard into the churning waters. He dropped into the arms of more of the mermaids, who fell upon his body in a feeding frenzy, turning the ocean red for a few minutes.

Joe closed his eyes, touched his crucifix and prayed. He knew his end would be unholy and messy. But his end didn't come. The decaying fish stink grew stronger and something wet brushed his face. He opened his eyes and found himself an inch away from the mermaid. So close to it that a tiny crab scuttled out of its hairline onto Joe's forehead. He flinched, but didn't retreat. The mermaid's lidless eyes blinked and its nostrils widened, inhaling his scent. It tilted its head to one side, and sounds came from its mouth, gentle, fluting.

Words formed in his head. *"The soul stone?"*

Its right talon scratched at Joe's chest pocket. Confused, horror-struck, Joe sat shivering, but when the talon pierced his flesh he yelped. "You mean, the pearl?"

His fingers ferreted in the fabric, pulling out the lustrous gem. Its shimmer entranced him. To his astonishment as the mermaid's claw touched the pearl, an image of the mer-baby bloomed in its heart.

"My son," the voice in Joe's head whispered.

Captured in the pearl, Joe beheld the babe, cradled in Billy's arms, curled up in a nest of bedding, sleeping. Both boys were oblivious to the turmoil happening above them. They slept like the innocents they were.

"Billy? Please don't hurt him," Joe begged, "he's lost all his family. He helped your son."

"Family?" the mermaid echoed, and again, its head tilted, black eyes scouring his face. Its fetor still made his chest heave, but he had grown somewhat accustomed to its hideousness.

It plucked the pearl from his hand, sliding it into its hair for safekeeping, and touched his face with its claw, before throwing back its neck. The gills were flapping double time. Joe guessed it needed to return to the ocean and soon. It wailed one long, eardrum-shattering note, and all its mermaid brood slithered, crawled and dragged themselves towards the sides of the ship, leaving behind a scene of utter carnage.

Entrails lay draped over posts, blood spatters decorated every surface diluted to pink froth by the sea water and the heads of Joe's crew were scattered around like obscene cannonballs.

Joe waited for his turn to die again.

The mermaid turned away and with powerful convulsions of its tail, and front claws, it reached the stairs leading to below decks. There it paused, and from its mouth flowed a song of such purity and sorrow, tears involuntarily poured down Joe's cheeks. He knew this was the song of a mother calling to her child.

Billy appeared from below, carrying the mer-baby swaddled in his arms. The lad's eyes were open, but unseeing; he was held captive in a trance state. The mer-baby opened his own eyes, looked up at his mother and smiled. She took her baby with gentle care from Billy, and, with strands of her long hair, strapped the babe to her bony chest.

She retrieved the pearl, *the soul stone*, Joe thought, from her hair. The babe grabbed at it, beaming. A double reunion.

An eerie, expectant silence had fallen. The hordes of gulls had departed, Joe realised, but the ship's crew lay massacred, and the ocean lay waiting. In the waters below, dozens of mermaids bobbed, faces looking upwards. It was as though the whole world was holding its breath.

The mer-mother slid to the side of the ship, turned back for a moment to stare at Joe. *"Family,"* floated into his head and, in the blink of an eye, she disappeared overboard. He heard the splash as she dived into the sea—then nothing.

When he looked offside the mermaid school were dark, fleeing shadows in the distance. At their departure the clouds lifted, the sun appeared and Billy waking called, "Joe, what's happened? Where's everyone gone?"

1915—aboard *The Soul Stone*, a small sailing boat, Southampton.

Joe lounged at the wheel, baccy lit in his pipe, anchor dropped and nets spread. He was a man content, doing what he loved, spending his life at sea, enjoying the fatherhood which had been a surprise but a gift nonetheless.

Billy climbed up the ladder from below deck, carrying two mugs of steaming hot tea with a tot of whiskey in Joe's. He was a strapping, muscular lad now, no longer scrawny and nervy, but tanned, confident in his work on the boat, and chatty.

In fact Joe sometimes wished his son would rein in the chat, cos he couldn't keep up. But at this time of evening the two men were in the habit of sitting in silence, shoulder to shoulder, drinking and watching the sea around them.

Billy spoke first. "Joe, what's that? Out there to the west?"

Joe squinted. "Dolphins?"

"Nah, don't think so, not like any dolphins I've ever seen. They're moving too fast, and they're coming right at us." His voice went up a notch. "Joe, I think, it's them. They're b-back." His old stutter, long gone, returning.

Joe didn't blame the lad. The sight of a half dozen mermaids ploughing at speed towards their small boat was terrifying. Long-buried memories of fighting, the horror and the scents of coppery blood and death, flooded him.

He touched his crucifix and prayed.

The mermaids reached the boat, and were circling, splashing, diving under the keel and reappearing, trilling high notes.

"They're playing, Joe." Billy gazed in awe at them. "They're so graceful. I'd forgotten that."

One of the mermaids swam right to Billy and, using its tail, pulled itself up out of the water, towering over the teenager.

"Take care ye," Joe warned, "keep back."

"It's her, Joe. Come back."

He was right. Joe recognised the feral face with the same dark stare, although there were fresh scars on her torso and arms.

The mermaid pointed down towards the water and beckoned. Into his head floated the words, *"My son."*

Joe joined Billy at port side. They watched the mer-boy frolicking, somersaulting and backflipping in the water, weaving in and out of the mermaids' tails and hanging off their long hair as they gave him rides. He shrieked with laughter, gurgling and chatting in the language of his kind.

Joe touched his cap to the mother, and Billy threw out his arms, laughing and waving to the boy. The sunset enveloped the ocean, gilding the waves tangerine and bestowing everyone, human and merfolk, with fiery halos.

About the Author

Aly lives in the UK, with her family and Labrador, Roxy. She is a tutor, editor, mum, dog-walker, avid old movie buff and wild water swimmer. Her fiction has been published widely – in *Space and Time* magazine #141, in Brigids Gate Press' #39 *Were-Tales, Musings and Daughter of Sarpedon*, Perpetual Motion's *Night Frights 2*, several stories can be downloaded at https://thecasket.co.uk, *Coffin Bell, Sirens Call* e-zines, *World of Myth*, and by Demain Press, who in March published the horror novelette, *The Night Visitor*.

Her work has been read out on BBC Radio, local radio and has won or placed in several competitions. She is a regular on the West Yorkshire, UK, open mic circuit. This summer her Gothic horror story *Night of the Rider* will be broadcast by Hawk and Cleaver and The Night's End podcast, at *The Other Stories*.

https://www.amazon.co.uk/Alyson-Faye/e/B01NBYSLRT

https://blackangelpressblog.wordpress.com

ROSEBUD

BY AMANDA CECELIA LANG

Nathaniel is late.

Deep in the undertaker gloom of Ashwood Hall, my husband's grandfather clock strikes two like a wicked heartbeat. *Too late, too late.* Midnight has left us far behind. Moonlight cuts an abandoned path across my snow-frosted window. Seated upon the sill, a carpetbag swelling at my feet, I shiver. Despite my heavy velvet cloak and the mink muff cocooning my restless hands, an omen of terrible cold conspires to overtake me.

Nathaniel is never late.

Has he changed his mind?

Our train, beyond vast woods and frozen mist, will depart in just over an hour. If we miss it, others will venture along, as they always do. But I've seen it in my dreams, other trains will never deliver us to our intended destination. Other trains will prove empty of devil-may-care devotion and carry instead a corrosive luggage of doubt and hesitation. Delay will lay a curse upon us. Already we've been brazen in our temptings of fate.

No, it must be tonight.

While the season of snow is still an early breath. While my husband remains entranced with the secret machinations of his beloved cadavers, too consumed with exploring the dead to heartily pursue my absence.

I trace sigils of hope across the icy window. If not tonight, then what have these many months been about? A spring dalliance that blossomed in forbidden moonlight, a summer tryst that swam deeper than the nude waters of our hidden pond, an autumn passion that burned heady as the leaf-smoke woods where we whispered plots for a life together. New identities, a faraway horizon.

Nathaniel promised winter would never cool his heart.

And on countless stolen midnights—save for tonight, our most vital of nights—he's appeared faithfully below. Signaling our hour using the same sweet salutation...

A rosebud plinks my window.

"Oh, thank you," I whisper, gathering my skirts and my bone-deep relief. I peer down at Ashwood's winter-bare gardens. A lacework mist eclipses the skeletal briars. Another rosebud taps the glass, and I cannot imagine where Nathaniel still finds them, free of the season's frozen kiss. Yet such joy they ignite within me.

With practiced hands, I silently open the pane. I'll scold him for his tardiness and my aching relief once we're seated victoriously on our train. For now, I hoist my carpetbag and lean out, eager to drop it down. The crisp silver-blue night tastes of freedom and possibilities—even as my breath becomes an icy phantom inside my chest.

"Nathaniel?"

The snow-dusted gardens stand empty, virginal.

No telltale footprints.

No leather-cloaked, sure-eyed savior gazing up at me.

Only a pair of rosebuds, wilting upon the unbroken snow.

Where is he? Playing one of his amorous hiding games—with our train so soon to leave the station? I whisper his name again, let the freezing air solidify my desperation. Empty silence eddies from below, possesses my breath, fills my marrow with an arctic dread.

And I know.

Even before the servants in the north wing begin their ragged, horrified screams, even before the wild-blooming firelight haunts the snowdrifts with flickering shades of bloody gold.

I know.

I stand beside his open casket, a prisoner of my secret grief, unable to properly mourn. I should be shrouded in tears and black veils, clasping his cold hands and guiding his spirit into the smoky channels of the next world.

"Madam Ashwood, a bit to your left, a shade closer to your husband," the photographer says, rising from beneath the black curtain of his camera.

Lachlan hooks a steely arm around my hip, his touch scarcely warmer than the grip of the dead as he tugs me near. The faithful wife supporting my bereaved husband, that's my role now. Tarnished daylight opens up behind me, shining from the parlor windows, casting Nathaniel in radiance below us. I dare another glimpse, capture every heart-torn scream in a deep, echoing well inside myself. My brilliant, sensual, rapturous Nathaniel! He doesn't look asleep, as the dead sometimes do. The spectacle of his left side prevents it. Lachlan saw to the embalming himself, down in his lab, his secret tonic of flesh-immortalizing chemicals. Yet there was nothing he could do about the damage done by the fire.

"That's lovely," the photographer says. "Our angles are all lined up. Ready to hold, sir?"

"Is this truly necessary?" I whisper, voice ghastly small.

"*Memento mori,*" Lachlan responds, gripping me tighter against the casket, as if I don't know of tradition and fate. "Remember you must die."

He nods at the photographer. The man readies his hand upon the camera. "Just ninety seconds, madam. Perfect stillness, then you'll be rid of me."

The camera whines and opens its eye.

I keep rigid, my expression lax, empty. This *is* unnecessary. Portraits of the brothers hang all throughout Ashwood Hall. Yet Lachlan insisted, humoring death rites he's made a career of mocking. Every clock frozen at the hour of demise, black crepe shrouding the mirrors. I wonder if he'll study this photograph for the intrigues of his brother's mortality or the secrets veiled behind my unflinching countenance.

And devil take me. Am I at all convincing? And what of my husband's mask? I've cursed myself to this theater we now perform. I've known it since the servants found Nathaniel swinging from an alleged suicide rope, a toppled candlestick igniting the bedchamber around him. They managed to douse the fire and save him from the flames—but only for burial.

Yet there will be no burial. Not yet, not with the grave soils frozen winter-solid, not with my husband ever-zealous to make our home a crypt.

"There now, all done," the photographer says. "Don't look so fretful, madam. All my years, never captured anything ghoulish. No phantoms, only the quiet after-moments of life."

"Pity," Lachlan says, lording over Nathaniel's casket like a hunter mounting a slain beast. "Norah fancies a good ghost story. Believes in all folly of séance and superstition. Don't you, dear heart?"

"Perhaps there's more to death than what we see."

"What do you see now, wife? Is my tragic fool brother present to commune with us? Why was self-murder his final endeavor? Can your dreams and charms answer us that?"

I lower my chin—fearful if I speak again, I'll wail. Lachlan thrusts free of me, busying himself with the photographer and ordering the servants into the parlor.

I allow myself a soft, shuddering breath and lament this stony man.

He scarcely resembles the groom of my tender youth. True, the striking gray eyes and handsome jaw remain the same. Three years haven't turned him haggard. And true, the young doctor had never been a particularly warm suitor, though he proved pleasant and mysterious during our courtship. My mother promised the wedding bed would ignite him. And perhaps, for a short spell, it did. Yet then came the clandestine experiments in Ashwood's basement catacombs. What began as the occasional cadaver sent up from the university became too many to ponder, and less than a year into our marriage, a newborn ghost walked our cold, stone corridors. The man I swore to love had transformed into a specter of bleakest obsession.

The dead have secrets.

Lachlan believes those secrets can only be unlocked through the flesh. His folly, perhaps. Yet on this tortured day, I, too, am obsessed.

I dare another glimpse into the sun-streaked casket, aspiring not to see the ruin. Nathaniel would never hurt himself—such isn't the question upon my heart. *But was that you below my window, tossing rosebuds, come to bid a grim goodbye?*

"Open the parlor windows," Lachlan orders the servants. "We must keep it frigid to mask my brother's odor. And bring more lilies, pile them high. It haunts of cooked ham in here."

"How much longer must you keep vigil?" I let my words shiver, as if the prospect of his brother's corpse in my velvet parlor, night after night, tortures me ill. It does not. Once he's under soil, I might only ever see Nathaniel in dreams—and how will that sustain me?

"Until all have mourned him," Lachlan responds.

"Who else are you expecting?" I raise my head. Nathaniel was less than a year home from university. He had but a few acquaintances in the nearby township, and falsities of self-murder have stained him. His mourners have been a trickle. Servants mostly, and the dredge of medical colleagues Lachlan has yet to isolate with his theories. The latter offered stiff condolences then exited the chill of Ashwood as promptly as was polite.

"Nathaniel's fiancée, naturally," Lachlan says with a twitch of a phantom smile. "I've sent word. She should be here within the week."

"Fiancée?" My heart leaps even as I recognize a ruse for a ruse. "He never spoke of a fiancée."

"Men make wise habits of speaking apart from women." Lachlan narrows steel-cut eyes upon me. Behind him, the servants slink lower, dropping chins as they arrange perfumed lilies around my dear Nathaniel. "He swore himself to the girl while at university. They've exchanged letters since his return home. Yet, it seems Nathaniel's recent writings grew disturbed, as though a dark stone sat upon his heart. The poor fiancée's last response sounded positively vexed. Dare I say, she fretted for his very life."

"You have them? These letters?"

"What care are they of yours, wife?"

"I simply thought..." I swallow, scrying for a convincing fiction. "If I knew this fiancée through her writings, perhaps I might better soothe her grief when she arrives."

"The servants found her scribblings in the rubble of his bedchamber," Lachlan says. "Though it's hardly appropriate to pass them around like vulgar erotica. If you wish to portend the girl before her arrival, perhaps consult your fickle spirits."

"Forgive the thought." I glance at Nathaniel, shrouded to the chin in a snowdrift of lilies. Has the heaven-swept slant of light shifted from him? Surely not.

"Matilda will sit with my brother through the night, keep the rats away." Lachlan orders the maid into a chair beside the casket then offers me the sharp point of his elbow, continuing our morbid dance. "Now, wife, let us feast on supper before I return to my work. You're looking rather gaunt beneath the eyes."

"Matilda," I whisper, breath fogging in the snow-dusty parlor. "Wake up."

The maid startles in her chair, rising from a slump, face aghast in the trembling light of a dozen midnight candles. "Forgive me, Madam Norah. Sleep caught the better of me."

"It's of no worry. Come now, rise, I'll sit with him."

"Are you certain?" Her gaze drifts toward the south wing where my husband keeps his private laboratories.

"Yes," I whisper. "Go warm yourself, get some good rest. Return before the dawn."

"Thank you, madam."

I take my rightful spot beside Nathaniel, then conspire bolder. "Matilda?"

She pauses in the arch doorway. "Yes?"

I sense she'll play her role. Several times these many months, she's washed telltale stains from my skirts and bodices, though never spoke of it. Not even the night of the late spring chill when she came to ignite my fireplace and found me unlacing muddy boots, the blush of passion still upon my cheeks.

"Is it true about the letters?" I ask.

She hesitates. "Yes, madam. I saw them pull the stack from Mister Ashwood's charred wardrobe. The blaze scarcely touched them."

"And where are those letters now, do you suppose?"

Silence. The wind blows glinting whorls through the open windows.

"Matilda?"

"I might suppose Doctor Ashwood's private study, madam."

"Thank you, Matilda." I listen as her footsteps fade toward the servants' quarters, letting the silence of Ashwood descend like snow, wretchedly hopeful Nathaniel will at last open his eyes. We shouldn't still be here. We should be on a train to some faraway forever.

I clasp his hands beneath the lilies. Impossible cold marble, unyielding, these hands that used to entwine me and lift me to the peaks of ecstasy.

"I won't believe it," I whisper. Candlelight betrays the mottled bruises snaking his throat. I won't believe our future perished so easily. I won't believe Nathaniel took himself to rope. Won't believe in a fiancée nor her flame-spared letters. Our love lightened us. It wasn't a stone weighing upon Nathaniel, yanking him into death. "I won't believe it…"

This is my husband's theater. And I grow so weary of my role.

Heart blackening with frostbite, I lean over Nathaniel.

The air cloys of my husband's foul embalming tonic, yet the offense of death remains absent inside my breath. My tears wet Nathaniel's face. With a soul-torn sob, I press fevered lips against his.

I love you, I love you, I will forever love you!

I want to shriek it and hear it echo. And when my husband comes stomping, perhaps I will follow Nathaniel into the misty channels of death. Grief like mine pulls widows off turrets. Grief like mine inspires lovers to cast themselves under carriage wheels. Yet such an act, so deep into our stage play, would only elicit my husband to villainous laughter.

I'll refuse him the pleasure.

I'll see him suffer for all he's wrought upon us. I've witnessed it in a lucid dream. Soon he'll come for me, as he did for Nathaniel. We thought his fascinations with the dead kept him blind to the exploits of the neglected living. We should've been more cautious in our untamable deceits.

Yet transgressions of love pale against murder.

Exposed in the parlor's golden-frost candlelight, I part my lips against Nathaniel, kissing him fuller. If only I might stir him like in grim fairy tales.

I cannot say how long I stay upon him. My lips melt the rigid chill from his own until, by my own warmth, I imagine him alive. Here again, to waltz beneath starlight and caress my throat with whispered poetries. Here again, to laugh and run breathless toward our smokestack train and evermore exotic destinations. I cannot say how long I dream. With the clocks silenced at 2:13, there's nothing to mark the passing of time.

Hours, eternities, mere heartbeats.

Nathaniel doesn't wake.

With an aching shudder, I break our kiss. The insidious ghost of embalming tonic lingers upon my lips. Perhaps Lachlan means to poison me. I wipe my mouth with the pale of my wrist and wait. My only gag of illness rises with the image of him manhandling Nathaniel then plying him with copper tubes, draining him of his vital fluids, replacing life with giddy concoctions.

I cup hands over my face, muffling wretched sobs.

A finger taps my knee.

Gasping, I drop my hands, ready to find Lachlan's shadow against the candlelight.

There's nobody. Nobody at all, yet...

A rosebud plinks off an open window and bounces to the rug, rolling to a stop beside the first. The rosebud that tapped my knee.

A curious shiver possesses my spine. Not quite a thrill of passion, but a bracing against a rush of marvelous heartache.

Gripping my skirts, I fleet-foot to the window.

And for the briefest pulse-beat, I'm the girl of several days prior, the girl swelling with secret desires and wildest joys. The girl with the warmth of a lover waiting below.

I lean out, his name the echo of a whisper, even as my heart portends the peculiar truth.

Not a soul waits in the snow below.

A day has passed. Another day without the shelter of his arms. Another day without the arrival of this mysterious fiancée, though the servants have prepared a bedchamber. Never mind the roiling gales of ice overtaking the woods and countryside. Lachlan assured me at tonight's quietly hostile supper that the girl is on her way.

Now, I stand in the frigid corridor of the south wing, clasping sublime rosebuds in a prayerful hand. *Oh, Nathaniel, do you walk with me now?*

I creep forward with my candlelight trembling, every footfall echoing. I despise this corridor with its endless chill and gloom, its eternal reek. It suffocates of human decay and depraved chemicals, the scent of my husband.

I pass door after forbidden door. His bedchamber, his library, the iron stairwell twisting down to his underground crypt of laboratories. He's there now, naturally, performing a lover's waltz with his experiments, searching for existential truths using methods I shudder to imagine. How can one so faithfully probe the mysteries that animate the human heart, while refusing to understand the nature of hearts themselves?

Every door I pass proves firmly locked.

Every door except his private study.

The heavy oak moans inward at the twist of my hand, and it's as if the spring of a trap pulls taut, waiting to snap. Heedless, I cross the threshold with my candlelight.

His study is a shadow-cave of mahogany furniture buried in manic clutter. Dusty research journals, open-spine medical tomes, copper hoses and varied conical apparatuses I cannot name. His obsession occupies every murky corner, even the chilly stone recess of the fireplace. Fires are forbidden here, warmth is forbidden. Cadavers fare better in the cold.

The fiancée's letters wait prominently atop Lachlan's desk, a thick stack tied with twine. Bait. *My dearest Nathaniel...*

I thumb the pages, heart shivering a riot, knowing Lachlan has led me here, a puppet on strings. Yet I cannot resist this hideous curiosity.

My dearest Nathaniel...

I sit in my husband's chair to read by candlelight, wondering if he'll gloat or rage when he catches me.

The letters display lovely, windswept handwriting. I examine each slant and whorl for betrayals of my husband's stiff penmanship. Yet any forgery eludes me. Perhaps Lachlan retained a calligrapher? My heart sticks in my throat as I read. This fictive fiancée speaks of kind, spring weather, of missing Nathaniel's handsome laughter, of the sweetness of his parting kiss.

Her name, signed in a flourish, is Eleanor Chastain.

As I delve deeper into her writings, I confess—*I confess*—my certainty begins a slow, icy plummet through the darkest pit of me.

Spring, summer, autumn, Eleanor's letters dance parallel to my stolen months with Nathaniel. My chest grows tight, breathless, though it's Eleanor who prattles on. Oh, how she aches for Nathaniel's raven eyes, the sure passion of his touch. She boasts of lace and flowers for a March wedding at her father's manor, soliciting Nathaniel's opinion, delighted to hear roses are his favorite. Delighted to speak of a long honeymoon on a foreign train. And with every letter she includes a sonnet. The same poetries he breathed against my throat while easing himself ever-deeper into my soul.

Her words blur, tears like snowflakes upon my lashes. I should end my torture with her spring ramblings, but autumn was the season Nathaniel confessed his love. Would I take a train with him? Yes, I promised, a winter train. Winter, when Lachlan could keep his dissections on the slab longer; winter, when he would be less likely to hunt us.

It's autumn time in Eleanor's letters now and she's losing her light. She fears Nathaniel is having second thoughts, fears he's hiding some great darkness, fears some melancholy demon peers out at her from his ever-sparser replies. By the first days of winter, her frantic scribblings have me very nearly convinced. She promises whatever ills Nathaniel is hiding, she forgives him. She'll forgive him a thousand times for any stray path—as long as he doesn't bring himself to harm.

...please, Nathaniel, hemlock and rope won't mend whatever shadowy deed darkens your conscience...

A rosebud drops onto her final page.

My heart leaps.

The room slants with shadows, yet is empty.

I touch the wilted rosebud, realizing it fell from my own hand as I dabbed my eyes.

I expel a ghastly, humorless laugh then let the loose letters cascade from my lap and across the rug. Perhaps they aren't a fiction of my husband after all. Perhaps they're true, and his cruelty was simply letting me find them.

"Please, Nathaniel, tell me it's a lie." My voice in the stillness startles.

My eyes dart to the arch doorway, bracing for a shadow, not truly expecting to find one. Yet there...

The silhouette of a man.

Black as coal, his face thwarting my candlelight.

"Nathaniel?" I gasp. *Lachlan?*

The door slams shut. A heavy sound like thunder, chased by a frigid draft.

The candles gutter and blink out.

Blackness.

Before I lose my direction in the dark, before the silhouette escapes me, I rush for the door, slipping on loose letters. For a terrible, mad instant, the doorknob doesn't turn. I tug and tug. A heartbeat before my third tug, the door pulls inward as if on its own.

The corridor beyond stands dim and vast, utterly empty.

I hurry to the nearest doorway, the iron stairwell to the laboratories.

Locked.

Over the tempest of my pulse, I can faintly discern the baritone of my husband's voice commanding the catacombs below.

He cuts off, a sudden breath-held silence. Bated.

And a softer voice responds.

"Please, Nathaniel, speak to me..." I trace my fingertips along his jawline, brush my lips against his cool ear as if he might better hear me. A séance of quietest passion. He tastes of silence and my toxic husband. "Is she real? *Were we real?*"

Snow swirls through parlor windows, dancing candlelight. I wait, listen, scry the flickering void. Voices haunt my thoughts, yet they belong to Lachlan and his visitor, unseen. *Who?* The tepid voice spoke only a few muffled words before the hateful silence of the south wing resumed and elongated and chased me away.

Praying I imagined it, I drift to the window. The ashy storm blusters the nightscape, vanishing the moon, smoothing the bony shapes of the garden.

Smoothing Ashwood's winding drive.

The snow appears uncut by carriage wheels. Matilda assured me, when I overtook her post, that the fiancée had not arrived. Truly, only fools would travel in this weather. With a shiver of defiance, I close the windows. Returning to Nathaniel, I tighten my cloak, certain I'll never find warmth again.

I brush wilting lilies aside and drape myself across his chest, closing my eyes like when I used to divine his heartbeat. "Please…"

Yet he doesn't answer.

I wait, fade, his silence sweeping me under.

Hours, eternities, mere heartbeats pass.

I lift my slumber-fogged head, stirred. Heart knocking. Something… Is someone here?

A rosebud plinks the parlor window.

And another.

Another.

I rise, stiff from repose, and chase the breath of his name to the window.

As I unhook the latch, a final rosebud hits the pane. Icier, harder.

The glass cracks, spiderwebbing outward, becoming a rose in bloom.

I've seen this in a dream, I'm sure of it.

As if in a fairy-tale trance, I touch the glass and prick my fingertip on a thorn. Tasting the bead of blood, of life, I remember what called me here.

I reach again for the latch, only to discover the glass smooth and unshattered.

Gasping, blinking, I open the pane, lean out, brace for virgin snow and empty whorls of mist. I'm a fool to presume disappointment.

Rosebuds constellate upon the snow below, the rough anatomy of a heart.

And a path.

I blink against wind and ice, but yes, my vision is true.

A path of rosebuds leads away from Ashwood Hall, into the woods where our hungers cycled through the seasons.

Now comes the season of passage. Of truth.

Do I dare follow a spirit into the storm?

I tighten my cloak, racing the corridors and out the main door, certain when I regain my spot below the parlor window the rosebuds will have vanished like the fractured glass. Or worse, that I'll race around Ashwood in an eternal swirl of ice and heartache, never finding the window or the rosebuds, only running, madly forever, my husband's laughter echoing on the wind.

The rosebuds and windows are where they should be.

As is the path into the woods.

Gritting against the cold, I follow. The rosebuds remain untouched by the gusting storm. Whether they're corporeal or ethereal, I dare not touch them, lest they disappear.

The snowfall lightens inside the hawthorn woods, the treetops form-ing a skeletal canopy. The path of rosebuds continues, hundreds of passion-ruby blooms dot the white-glowing snow, thousands, infinity.

I watch for Nathaniel between the passing trees, a coal-black silhouette standing ready. Yet for now, all he reveals is the path onward, the journey which will end in us meeting.

The rosebuds ramble near the Ashwood family graveyard. Stone crosses and winged angels loom between haze and distant trees. But I pass it by.

Beyond the frozen pond that once rippled with our laughter and the snow-crystal meadow where we first made love, gasping together in a wild bed of bluebells. On and on, the path snakes forward, deeper now than we ever journeyed. The winter cold at last glances my marrow.

The hawthorns begin to thin, the snowfall to thicken.

A rosebud drops from the sky.

It falls like a dream and joins the path ahead.

Another falls, and another, laying the final bend. The trees part as curtains, revealing a meadow I've never known.

In the center, where the path ends, waits a brick and glass hothouse.

The door stands open a crack.

Even before I reach the threshold, I feel the mystic warmth emanating from inside, taste the sweet perfume of roses.

My breath disappears as I step inside, and a small mystery answers itself.

Rose bushes line the long room, vibrant despite the dead season. Lacework silhouettes decorating the dim, branches and thorns, trembling leaves and buds.

And the shadow of a man...

Strong shoulders, wind-wild hair, waiting in the farthest corner.

"Nathaniel?"

"This was our mother's hothouse," comes a voice, so insidiously familiar yet unexpected that for a heartbeat I hear Nathaniel speaking, I do. "Seems my brother revived it."

Lachlan steps forward. The shadows don't leave his face.

"You followed me here. Why, Norah?"

The words gag in my throat. "I... You left a path."

"A path?" Lachlan's teeth glint, and he closes the hollows between us. Devastating and handsome, horribly so, razor-edged angles and clever, storm-fierce eyes. "You chased my footprints through the dead of night?"

Any whisper of rosebuds freezes inside me. I lower my chin. "What are you doing here?"

"I came to pluck flowers for our guest."

"Our guest?"

"Arrived just tonight—*Miss Eleanor Chastain*," Lachlan says with a flourish. "Come, wife, wouldn't you like to meet her?"

Upon returning to Ashwood Hall, all warmth abandons my bones, vanishing as the path of ethereal rosebuds vanished from the snow—as the tracks of carriage wheels faithfully appeared. Have I gone mad?

In the foyer, Lachlan stomps snow from his boots then extends his elbow. "Come, I'll make introductions. Let's hope the girl is fit for conversation."

Our footsteps echo. Yet Lachlan doesn't lead me into the grieving parlor, nor the north wing where the servants prepared a bedchamber.

By candlelight and waking nightmare, he escorts me into the south wing.

Leads me to the forbidden door and the iron staircase twisting down.

"Why is Nathaniel's fiancée in your laboratory?"

"Come, let the girl explain."

Exhaustion pulls me along behind my husband.

So weary of this theater, so weary of it all. If this is the role I must live, let the curtain fall upon me like grave lilies.

Like rosebuds.

I grit my jaw to keep my teeth from trembling. It's colder than the storm here in the catacombs. As Lachlan's new bride, he allowed me, on rare occasion, to tour them. Though, after his first enigmatic breakthrough, I was quickly forbidden. Happily so.

Now, he guides me through his stone labyrinth of operating chambers. Each room stands equipped with steel operating slabs—several currently occupied with naked cadavers, diseased, wretched men. When the correspondence arrived from the university, informing Lachlan that his request for medical cadavers could no longer be satiated, I never asked where else he gathered his dead. Graverobbers, or worse.

My footsteps slow the deeper we walk, until he grabs my wrist and tugs me forward. "She's ahead, in the master suite."

An iron door looms like the cell of a dungeon.

And I'm so exhausted. So endlessly exhausted. I've forgotten my lines.

As Lachlan unlocks the door, I know I'll step inside. Whatever lurid fate awaits, I'll embrace it. I've dreamed this moment too.

Jaundiced torchlight illuminates the operating theater beyond.

A nude corpse rests upon a slab.

A young woman.

Lovely once. A thing of strawberry curls and elegant, supple breasts—and satin flesh mangled with bruises, bones oddly crooked. The gruesome whiteness of a femur juts from one mottled thigh. Yet fractured bones aren't the spectacle.

"What have you done to her?" I gasp.

Lachlan approaches the girl like a ringmaster unveiling magnificence. "Not what *I've* done, wife. The girl went and died by carriage accident. The countryside isn't fit for travel in this weather. Now she's a sight."

"You know that's not what I'm asking." I step closer, bile burning my voice. An obscenity protrudes from the girl—a thick copper pipe lodged between her teeth and down her throat. It connects to a snaking tube ending in a copper cone like the sound horn of a phonograph.

"What have you done?" I say again.

"I've spoken to her!" For the first time in years, I watch my husband come alive. "The dead talk! They do indeed! My embalming tonic fills her, preserving not only flesh, but the mind, saturating her brain, reinvigorating every thought that ever passed through. A chemical imprint, a verbal photograph that will call out from my Mortuis Communica! The ultimate *memento mori*."

"You're mad," I say, unable to look away.

"Madder than *you*, wife?" He loops a curved, copper clamp around Eleanor's dead chest. Coiled wires twist to a boxy iron mechanism of clockwork gears and levers. "Let us see."

He vigorously cranks a lever. The mechanism hums, whines, invoking a marvel of sparks. The cadaver twitches, stiffens, bites down on that hideous copper mouthpipe.

A foggy voice whimpers from the Mortuis Communica.

Eyes enflamed, diabolical with passion, Lachlan leans close to the cadaver's ear. "Tell her, Eleanor, tell Norah who was in your thoughts as you died. To whom do you belong?"

"Muh-mmmm-mmmuh-lllooooooovvve..." The snaking words scrape through her, resonating, chilling me. *"Myyyy loooovvve... Nah-nah-Nathaaaaaaaaniel..."*

I wake from shattered dreams to wrenching darkness.

My bedchamber distorts around me, every blackened shape the silhouette of my husband. I remember running from Lachlan's operating theater with my soul in pieces, sobbing openly and true, and I remember voices chasing me.

"Nah-nah-Nathaaaaaaaaaniel..."

And Lachlan laughing. "Wonder what my brother will have to say..."

I reclaimed my stolen place, guarding his casket from rats and fiancées, and from there the remnants of the night blur into utter despair. My husband's work proved true. Eleanor spoke my heart's faithful name.

Now, I sit up in bed, unsure how I arrived.

A blanket of funeral lilies cascades from my chest.

My husband did this. A grave omen.

I must rid myself of Ashwood tonight, run to the train or to a grim, white-storm fate—here my vision eludes me. Here, I'm numb.

I unbury my carpetbag, still plump at the seams with old ambitions.

I won't leave without a final kiss.

Draped in dire cloaks, I tiptoe to the parlor, every clock forever frozen at 2:13, every doorway haunted with the prospect of my husband.

In the parlor, nobody sits beside the casket.

As I approach, snow and rosebuds fall outside the windows and a final death knell tolls inside my chest.

The casket stands empty. Nathaniel is gone.

"He wouldn't..." I whisper of my husband, certain he would.

Swiftly, before my own clock freezes, I must decide. The train or...

The door to Lachlan's laboratories stands unlocked.

It swings inward, and the spiral staircase swallows me down. I shadow-stalk the catacombs and rediscover the operating theater. Heart pounding, I hesitate on the threshold.

Nathaniel's voice shudders out to me.

Nathaniel's voice! An obscene distortion reminiscent of carnal passions, a moaning that even now stirs currents inside me.

"And how many times did you have my wife?" Lachlan's voice booms, maniacal, giddy.

"*Aaalllwwwaaayyysss...*"

"And how did she feel, was she sweet, was she worth it?"

"*Mmmiiinnne...*"

"And how did my rope feel around your throat, *brother?*"

"*Nnnooorrraaahhh...*"

And oh, the sickness of this theater—and oh, the sickness when our masks drop free. A thousand screams well up inside me.

"Monster! Murderer! Stop this cruelty!"

I sweep inside, refusing to let the obscenities I find slow me.

A forced reunion on the slab, Nathaniel and Eleanor, hip to pale hip and nude. Their stiff fingers intertwine around a rose bouquet. His other hand cups one breast, hers his manhood.

An oversized copper mouthpipe protrudes from the lips that once fevered me in kisses, splitting him at the red-raw edges, drawing a grotesquely false smile.

The smile bleeds onto my husband's face too.

Before Lachlan can stop me, I rush to Nathaniel and grasp the copper pipe. A sharp tingle sizzles through me as I tear it from his mouth.

Lachlan bellows. Yet as I prepare to heave the Mortuis Communica aside, a deep, ethereal vibration echoes from its sound horn. A voice.

"Norah..."

Nathaniel. Clear and true outside the folly of his cadaver. Nathaniel. Clear and true and utterly disembodied.

"Norah... I'm here..."

"I feel you—I do!"

"I'll never leave you... my only love..."

A rosebud tumbles from the ether, and another, another.

One bounces off Lachlan's shoulder.

He scowls at it, and at his Mortuis Communica, a direct line to a misty realm he spent his fetid life denying. Debauched glee sharpens to a thorn of rage.

"Then have her forever, brother!"

His hands clamp my throat. With a brutal thrust, he slams me to the stone floor. Savage-eyed, fury-faced, he mounts me, pins my arms with his knees, crushes my breath with his iron grip. Cartilage grinds inside my wheezing scream.

"I spied you with him, wife, saw every whorish passion!" he spits and squeezes. I thrash beneath him, chest burning, heart and spirit thundering. "And when he posted his spring letter, ending his engagement, I intercepted it, invented my own, strung the fool girl along just like I strung up—"

Lachlan's gloat strangles short.

With a red-eyed bulge of astonishment, he coughs up a rosebud.

And another, another. Choking, gasping. Blood-red rosebuds flood his mouth and throat, filling him like grave soil. His hands loosen from me, and he thrashes onto his spine, clawing at himself now. His fingers rake bouquets of rosebuds from his mouth, yet still they fill him.

Nearby, the Mortuis Communica's copper sound horn echoes with Nathaniel's laughter. The laughter of the seasons, the laughter of the woods, the laughter of our love.

I stagger to my feet and stand vigil as my writhing, blueing husband slowly succumbs to the bitter cold he brought to Ashwood Hall; stand vigil as our theater nears its final black curtain.

If only I could capture a photograph. Yet this gift will forever be enough.

The ultimate *memento mori*.

Shadowing over him, I smile. "Remember, husband, you must die."

On a soul-swept train destined for faraway exploits and newly imagined horizons, I sit beside the window, staring out.

At my feet, my carpetbag swells with a glint of copper.

In my chest, my spirit swells with the warmth of good omen.

The sun will rise soon upon a new day, a new season. And as the darkness begins its faithful melt from gray to golden, his rosebud taps my window.

About the Author

Amanda Cecelia Lang is a horror author and aspiring recluse from Denver, Colorado. As a die-hard scary movie nerd, her favorite things are meta-horror, 80s nostalgia, and the rise of a fierce final girl. Her stories haunt the dark corners of many popular podcasts, magazines, and anthologies, including *NoSleep, Cast of Wonders, Tales to Terrify, Uncharted, Dark Matter, Darkness Beckons,* and *Mixtape: 1986.* Her short story collection *The Library of Broken Girls* will debut in Spring of 2025. You can stalk her work at amandacecelialang.com—just don't be surprised if she leaps out at you from the shadows.

FORTUNE OF THE TÉMÉRAIRE

BY DJ COCKBURN

"He won't." Charles Stowe raised his voice over the carriage's creaking springs.

"Ask him," said Harry Buckland for perhaps the twentieth time.

"I've been asking him for years. He never answers."

"You were a boy last time you asked. Now you're a fellow officer."

Stowe's service as a midshipman had involved two weeks swinging at anchor in Portsmouth Harbour. He doubted that his grandfather, a lord of the Admiralty, would regard him as a fellow officer.

Buckland pulled his card box from his coat pocket and sent kings, queens and knaves flying between his fingers.

Stowe groaned. "We've been in this carriage not twenty minutes, Harry. Can't you keep your cards in their box that long?"

"Lady Luck's a sailor's best friend. The cards are my way of courting her."

"My grandfather was at sea for fifty years without a scratch and won't touch a pack of cards."

"He must have a more direct acquaintance with the fair mademoiselle." Buckland hunched over the cards to protect them from the rain blowing through the carriage window. He shuffled again and offered the cards in both hands, a parody of a supplicant making an offering. "I draw the high card, you ask him."

Stowe could not suppress a laugh. "Very well. And if I draw the high card, *you* ask him."

Buckland's smile faltered. It would be an impertinent question for a midshipman to ask an admiral on first acquaintance. Yet Stowe knew Buckland could no more box his cards without drawing than he could calculate his longitude, which the sailing master said he could no more do than walk across the Channel on his arse cheeks.

Stowe took a card. Ten of clubs. Buckland looked him in the eye and drew his own. Four of diamonds.

Buckland swallowed. "Very well. I *shall* ask him."

Before Stowe could think of a reply, the carriage lurched to a halt. Stowe and Buckland dashed through the rain to the townhouse door, which swung open to reveal a blue-coated butler with a weatherbeaten face and white hair braided in a style the navy had left in its wake before Stowe was born.

"Why it's young Mr Stowe," said the butler. "You look very well, sir, very fine in a blue coat. The Admiral was hoping you'd call before you sailed and, well, so was I."

The North Country accent Stowe had known all his life kindled a warm glow in his breast. "Thank you, Clough. You look very well yourself. How is Mrs Clough?"

"Hm." Clough's lips twitched downward. "Her joints still ail her, and her tongue still ails others, so I'm certain she's well. May I take your cloaks? And if I may enquire as to your companion, sir?"

"I beg your pardon, Clough. This is my friend and messmate, Mr Midshipman Buckland."

"Honoured, Mr Buckland." For Clough, a messmate was a serious matter.

Clough led them out of the parlour to the drawing room, where they found the Admiral pouring a glass of wine.

"Young Mr Stowe and Mr Midshipman Buckland, sir," said Clough. "And there ain't no sense in having a butler and pouring your own wine."

"Quite so, but an old addlepate like me cannot be expected to show sense all the time. Especially when you're at the door, the rest of the staff are still in Sussex and the wine is under my nose."

The Admiral's sharp blue eyes showed no sign of being addled as he advanced to shake his grandson's hand.

"Well, it does me good to see you, Charles. And Mr Buckland, Charles mentioned you in his letters. Both in the *Odin*, are you?"

"Yes sir."

Stowe hid a smile at Buckland's falsetto. Having his hand pumped by one of the navy's most senior officers left Buckland looking like a frightened rabbit. Stowe took pity on his friend and engaged the Admiral in small talk while Clough seated them in armchairs, poured wine into glasses, put coal on the fire and left the room with the precision of the topman he had once been.

"You'll find a good berth in the *Odin*," said the Admiral. "A well-found ship and officers who know their business. A frigate's just the ticket for a midshipman to learn his ropes."

"Thank you, sir." Nothing had been said, but he was certain he owed his appointment to the Admiral's influence.

"Then you'll be off to fight the Russians, along with the French and the Turks. At Navarino, we fought with the French and the Russians against the Turks and in the Great War, we fought with the Turks and the Russians against the French." He drained his wine. "Well, our masters in Westminster propose and the Service must dispose."

"Yes sir," said Stowe and Buckland in unison.

"Ha! I see someone already taught you how to answer prolix officers. That's something. In my day, it was off to sea when I was twelve and flogged over a gun if I spoke out of place. I'd try saying it differently next time and if I wasn't beaten, I'd know I'd got it right."

The Admiral busied himself refilling his wine glass. Stowe nodded across at Buckland with a glorious sense of mischief. Buckland took a deep breath, as though he'd just been ordered to the *Odin*'s masthead.

"Admiral Stowe, sir, I beg your pardon, but Mr Stowe mentioned you were in the *Téméraire*?" His confidence was already reasserting itself.

The Admiral frowned at Stowe. "Been telling family tales, has he?"

"No sir," said Buckland. "I was merely wondering, well sir, I was wondering if you could perhaps tell us about Trafalgar?"

"Trafalgar, eh?" said the Admiral.

Stowe stared very hard at his wine glass. He did not need to look to see the hard line his grandfather's mouth assumed whenever the Battle of Trafalgar was mentioned, or to watch his eyes focus on something no one else could see.

"I daresay young Charles put you up to asking."

Stowe looked up. "Sir, I..."

"Haven't they told you about Trafalgar in the gunroom yet?" The Admiral cut him off. "Used to be the first story a midshipman heard when he came aboard. Must have been a much bigger battle than I remember, for at least half the men in the navy were there. Or say they were."

"Yes sir," said Buckland. "But sir, I mean to ask, that is to say..."

"Belay speaking, Mr Buckland. Now decide what it is you wish to say and say it."

Buckland flushed crimson, but his voice was under control when he spoke. "They told us of the *Téméraire* at Trafalgar, sir. They told us how she was yardarm to yardarm with the *Fougueux* on one side and the *Redoutable* on the other and took them both. I would very much like to hear it from someone who was there. Sir."

"Yardarm to yardarm, they said? Hardly a yardarm between the three of us by the end of it."

The Admiral's hand strayed to his fob and pulled out an unadorned iron locket. He turned it over but his eyes were unfocused, as if his hands were at liberty while his mind was elsewhere. Stowe waited for him to say something dismissive and change the subject, as he always did when someone asked about Trafalgar.

The Admiral blinked and looked directly at Stowe. His hand closed on the locket and returned it to his fob as though commanded by a bosun's pipe.

"Charles has been asking me about Trafalgar since he first read that fellow Marryat," said the Admiral. "I've not said a word. Now you're off to sea yourself with the Russians preparing Lord knows what to welcome you."

Stowe held his breath. Had Buckland's comment about fellow officers been closer to the mark than he had thought?

"I was on the foretop," said the Admiral.

Trafalgar was a damn slow business. Hardly any wind at all and the sea so calm you didn't even notice the sway of the mast. When we beat to quarters, we were chipper enough. We were English and they were French so one of us was worth three of them. Mulcahy, one of the marine sharpshooters, said we needn't bother ourselves with the other two because they'd be poxed and set himself to calculating prize money.

Did I say we were English? Well, close enough.

Mulcahy made us laugh, and we set to persuading ourselves that the men pointing their guns at us were less than us. We managed to believe it for a time but we had too long to think. Soon enough, I wasn't calculating prize money so much as counting their guns. We were second in our line and heading straight at the middle of theirs so when they started lobbing iron there'd be the devil to pay and no pitch hot, and damn all we could do about it until we got in among them.

I swear those ships got bigger the longer I looked at them, and not just because we were getting closer. Then they opened fire on the *Royal Sovereign*, leading our other line a mile to leeward. I'd never seen anything like it, and never have since. She must have had two hundred guns pointed at her. We could hardly see her for the spray, but she stood on as though she were running up the Solent to Southampton. Spars and rigging were tumbling down and no one aboard minded it more than a spot of rain. It would have made me proud of the Service if I didn't know it would be our turn next, and the foretop was nothing but a few planks some sixty feet up the foremast. A twelve-pound ball would smash it to kindling under our feet.

"Pacing, pacing, pacing," said Mulcahy. "Never stops."

I had no idea what he meant. I'd forgotten there was anything beyond the mauling the *Royal Sovereign* was getting, which was a poor show for an officer.

Remember that, boys.

Mulcahy was looking at Lord Nelson, marching up and down the *Victory*'s quarterdeck no more than a hundred yards ahead. He looked like a dwarf next to Captain Hardy, but nobody said it. Can't imagine any of us even thought it at the time. Not about Nelson.

"He'll lead us to victory." It was a damn fool thing to say, and I knew it as soon as the words slipped out. The three marines and two sailors all grinned at each other. More fun to make game of me than to watch what was happening to leeward, but I didn't think of that at the time. I went to the edge of the top and looked ahead so they couldn't see how red my face was.

"Not to worry, sir. We're next to this 'un." Clough slapped the other swivel gunner's shoulder. "He's got the luck o' the devil, he does."

Julius Fortune frowned. He was always frowning. He smiled even less than he spoke.

"Dodged the noose two year ago, didn't you Julius?" said Clough.

Fortune's frown deepened.

"Don't fret," said Clough. "Mr Stowe won't tell no one. There's no evidence anyroad."

"What're you saying?" Marine Hazlett was a Cornish giant, towering over all of us. It was easy to forget that he was barely older than me.

Clough and Mulcahy were both about ten years older than me, which made them old men in the tops. It didn't occur to me that they'd never headed straight at a French fleet any more than I had, or that they were burning with the same need to believe in their luck.

"Go on, mate," said Clough. "You tell 'em about it."

Fortune looked around, at all of us watching him. He seemed more worried about us than the French.

"I won't tell," I said. "Whatever it is, I give my word."

"There you go," said Mulcahy. "He's a young gentleman, he is. If he gives his word, it'll not go further."

The idea of luck had taken hold of us all, but Mulcahy most of all.

Fortune shrugged and sat down, his back to the mast where it came through the middle of the top. "You tell 'em."

His accent reminded me what he was. A son of a gun, born at sea with a whore as a mother and every man before the mast for a father. His "o" came from London, his "r" from Bristol, his "a" from Norfolk and every other accent in the isles mixed in his words. He was a veteran topman and not yet twenty. All land was a foreign country to him.

"That I will," said Clough. "Well, young Fortune here, he were on the *Scorpion* gun brig, weren't you?"

Fortune stared ahead at the French line.

"She were in Plymouth when his shipmates find out he never had a woman. Talks too much, don't you Julius?"

Fortune said nothing.

"So off they sneak to find one for him. They don't mean no harm. They're planning to sneak back before dawn and the officers don't mind as long as they don't miss their watch. Only a man can't just march up to a woman and ask her. Not if he's never done it before, can he, Mr Stowe? Wouldn't be natural."

They all laughed at that. They knew I hadn't had a woman either. I laughed with them. I didn't have to know about women to be an officer.

"A man has to get ready for something important like that," Clough went on. "Only young Julius, he got so ready he were three sheets to the wind before his mates got him sorted out. Next morning, he wakes up behind the pub, all on his own. The bint's stolen everything but his drawers and scarpered."

We laughed loud enough to drown the guns pounding the *Royal Sovereign*.

"Oh, mate!" Marine Lockwood leaned forward to put his hands on Fortune's shoulders. "Women! Didn't they warn you?"

You don't get a lot of Londoners in the marines. I often wondered if Lockwood had chosen the name himself when he joined. Some sort of private joke about having known more about locks than was good for him. It was the sort of thing that would have appealed to him but even then, I knew it was the sort of question best not asked.

"It gets worse," said Clough, when we'd calmed down. "It's already daylight. He can't get back aboard without someone seeing. That's two dozen lashes if he's lucky. So he scurries down the docks to get it done with, but the *Scorpion* ain't there. She got orders in the middle of the night and sailed with the tide. So now young Julius is a deserter. He's standing there, nothing to his name but the cloth to cover his arse and it's the gallows as soon as he gets caught."

I tell no lie, I nearly fell off the top for laughing.

"So what's he do? He swims over to the *Swiftsure* and signs up while he's still dripping on the deck. He's picked the biggest ship he can see cos he knows she'll be shorthanded an' they won't ask too many questions. So he's been a free man for all of four hours, and already he's sworn hisself back in."

"'Tis a good story," said Mulcahy," but I don't see where the luck comes in. He can't remember his first woman, he's lost his money and his clothes and now he's down as run. I can't see the luck in it."

He was a Peter Pipeclay, d'you see? Needed things spelled out.

"You like to tell him about the *Scorpion*, sir?" Clough didn't have the stomach for that part of the story.

"The *Scorpion* ran on to Chesil Beach the night she left Plymouth." Even I knew that. "She went down with all hands."

"And her muster book," said Clough. "But Julius was on the *Swiftsure* by then, and there's nothing to say Julius is a deserter what ain't at the bottom of the Channel."

Mulcahy whistled. "That is luck. That really is."

"Weren't so lucky for the *Scorpion*." Hazlett said what the rest of us were trying not to think about.

"No, it weren't," said Clough. "But they left him ashore and we ain't going to leave him nowhere, are we?"

We all murmured in agreement. I still don't know if Clough had meant it the way we took it, but with all of us standing around the top and Fortune sitting in the middle of us, it felt like an oath.

Three ships ahead all gave the *Victory* their broadsides at once. So much powder smoke I swear I could smell it, even from more than a mile to windward. The *Victory*'s rigging shivered as though she'd been taken flat aback by a gale.

"Still bloody pacing," said Mulcahy.

Every man on *Victory*'s upper deck was lying flat, trying to get some cover behind their guns. Except the officers of course. Nelson strolled up and down as though nothing was happening, even as a couple more ships joined in shooting at him. I knew I'd never look as nonchalant as Nelson if I lived to be, well, as old as I am now. And it would be our turn in the next few minutes.

I didn't understand then that men don't look to a midshipman to act like an admiral, and perhaps they don't need to when the admiral's right in front of them.

"Not to worry, sir," said Clough. "If you can't see the shot, it ain't coming at you."

I'd heard that before, but I didn't know if it was true. Not that I was going to argue as long as I couldn't see any shot. Nor was I going to point out that if a shot knocked down the foremast, it could kill us all without coming anywhere near us.

A line of splashes showed a ball skimming the surface. It must have hit the base of the mast because I felt the quiver through the planks of the foretop. I shared a look with Clough. It had started.

Some of the Frenchers were firing pell-mell, no order to their gunnery at all. Not so the *Redoutable*. Her gunners knew their business, firing timed broadsides. I didn't know her then, but I would soon enough. I remember her with every gun out and could swear every one of them was aimed straight at me and close enough to touch. At the same time, she looked so far away it would be past sunset before we could fire a single shot back. Then she fired at the *Victory*. We were close enough to hear the rending timber, the ring of shot hitting cannon barrels. Close enough to see two men knocked off her mizzen top when the mast gave way.

"Why'd they call you Fortune?" Lockwood couldn't stand to watch it any longer. Can't say I blame him. "They know you was gonna be lucky?"

Every time I looked at Fortune, his frown was deeper. He was only a few years older than me, but when you're fifteen, nineteen looks as far away as the Japans. At that moment, Fortune looked like the old man of the sea himself. I thought he wasn't going to answer, but perhaps he needed to fill the silence as much as the rest of us.

"Me mother died bringing me into the world," he said. "They had to cut me out of her. The surgeon said 'twas a miracle I lived. Called me a child o' fortune. Then they christened me Julius, cos they said there were some Italian by that name got born the same way and done right for himself."

That shut us up. We didn't want to hear about, well, cutting and woman things. I felt quite sick, and that made me realize I needed to piss. That's a problem with being in the tops. The men on the deck won't thank you if you just let go, so you have to tie a hitch in it.

"Nelson's signalling." Clough broke the silence, much to everyone's relief.

"Can't see the flags," said Mulcahy.

Victory's rigging, or what was left of it, was between us and the signal flags but the frigates relayed it smart enough. I didn't have the signal book, but I knew it better than the Lord's Prayer. What midshipman doesn't?

"Engage enemy more closely," I said.

We heard a cheer rising from the deck below us even as the mast shuddered to another hit on the hull. We were close enough to the *Victory* that their cheers mixed with ours. More than a thousand men *huzzah*ing their lungs out. No doubt that cheer was rolling down the line astern of us. Nelson had that effect.

"That's Nelson," said Mulcahy. "Never close enough. I was in the *Culloden* when we followed him at Cape St. Vincent. By the time we caught up with him, he'd already taken two Spaniards. Damn good prize money that day, so there was."

"Didn't know you was there." Clough's voice held the respect due to a veteran of a major battle. "Never served with him myself. Met plenty who have o' course."

He looked around and dismissed Lockwood, Hazlett and me. We were all in our first berth and didn't have any Nelson stories we hadn't all shared.

"What about you, Julius?" asked Clough. "Ever served with Nelson before?"

A howl and a bang opened a hole in the foretopsail, not three feet from Clough's head. He'd been right. I hadn't seen the shot.

"Ever served with our Nel?" Clough asked as if nothing had happened. Except he wouldn't have asked again if nothing had happened.

I saw Clough was just as afraid as I was, which cheered me up more than a double tot of rum.

Fortune hadn't flinched. He sat there as though all the iron the frogs were throwing at us would go away if he ignored it.

"Aye," he said. "I were in the *Vanguard*."

"At the Nile?" Clough's voice carried a hint of awe.

"You was on Nelson's flagship at the Nile?" Hazlett's eyes were round. "You really are the lucky one."

"Hold up." Mulcahy didn't sound as impressed as the rest of us. "I think I heard of you."

I'd thought Fortune's frown was as deep as it could be. I'd been wrong.

"Aye, from a friend I ran into at the Nore a year back," said Mulcahy. "I'd forgotten till now cos we—well, we'd had a drink or two by the time he told me—but I remember now. You don't hear a name like Julius Fortune every day."

"You don't want to listen to a drunken bootneck," said Fortune.

"He wasn't a marine, he was a matelot like you." There was an edge to Mulcahy's voice. Sailors and marines, it never changes.

Fortune stood up and glared at Mulcahy.

"You don't want to believe no bog Irish marine," said Fortune, which would have started a fight if we were on deck even with a few thousand Frenchers trying to knock us all on the head.

Even on the foretop, I think Mulcahy would have thrown a punch if the *Redoutable* hadn't fired another broadside at us. We felt every hit thrum up the foremast while shot howled around us. Three years I'd been skylarking in the *Téméraire*'s rigging and I felt as secure on the ratlines as on the deck. The stays were made of oakum woven thicker than my leg. The masts were hewn from oaks that were old when Drake chased off the Armada. Now, I felt we were held up by matchsticks and string. I was wiser than I'd been a few minutes ago, so I could see Clough and Mulcahy thinking the same. None of us mentioned it of course. Not done. But Mulcahy let the insult pass without hitting Fortune, which said it all.

"What I heard," said Mulcahy, "was you'd just come from being rated *boy*." He emphasized the word, implying the nineteen-year-old Fortune was still a boy from Mulcahy's perspective of twenty-five or six. "Still hadn't drawn your first rum ration, but you were working a gun. Shot and splinters flying all around you, and not a man hurt. Do I tell a lie?"

Fortune said nothing.

"You were running out of shot and not a powder boy to be seen, so the gun captain sent you off to find more balls. So off you went to fetch some shot from a gun knocked off its carriage. You probably didn't know what happened no sooner you turned your back. 'Twas night by then, and the gundeck must've been full of smoke and noise. But my friend was on the next gun. He seen your gun burst. Kilt every man of your mess and a few of his. Then you come back. Just a figure he could see by the gun flashes, standing there with a twenty-four pound ball in each hand."

Mulcahy raised an eyebrow, inviting Fortune to answer. Fortune glowered silently as though daring Mulcahy to say more.

Perhaps Mulcahy hadn't forgotten being called bog Irish. Perhaps it was the French fleet, which we could hardly see for powder smoke by now. Perhaps it was just the need to have something to listen to other than French guns. Whatever the reason, Mulcahy said too much.

"What my friend said was, nobody wanted you in their mess after that. It got so you had to be transferred out when the *Vanguard* made Genoa. Strange that. Anyone can have a stroke o' luck like being away from a bursting gun. What else had happened before that? Hm?"

Fortune stepped toward Mulcahy, which made us all move round. Not a lot of room on a foretop. A couple of minutes before, he'd been our lucky charm. Now none of us wanted to be any closer to him than we had to be. Only Mulcahy didn't move. He couldn't have stepped back without falling off the top.

I should have said something. I was the officer and the last thing we needed was a fight. But I was fifteen and I had no idea what to say.

Where I'd moved put me almost next to the mast, looking over Fortune's shoulder at Mulcahy. Beyond them both, I could see mast after mast towering out of a cloud of powder smoke. It was as though the French had joined to make one colossal ship. It made what was happening right in front of me seem so small. The truth was I had no idea what to do about what was happening on the foretop, so I told myself it wasn't important. I had a lot to learn about being an officer.

"It do look like your luck ain't that lucky for anybody else," said Hazlett.

"Don't choose it meself." Fortune's voice was so low I could hardly hear him.

"Neither did your messmates in the *Vanguard*," said Mulcahy.

"Don't talk about them!" Fortune's voice was suddenly loud, and shrill enough to remind us it wasn't long broken. "They was good lads! And the scorpions too. Captain to powder boy, good shipmates all! And the others."

"Others?" Lockwood leapt on the word.

"Aye, what others?" Mulcahy looked like a card sharp who'd thought he held an ace and found himself holding a hand of twos and threes.

By the way he was glaring at Fortune, Clough felt the same.

"You want my luck!" Fortune shouted. "They all do at first. I'd give it to you in a moment if I could. If I could make a friend without being the death of him no sooner I turn my back. The Devil take my luck! I wish it were... were..."

His hand clutched at thin air, groping for the word he needed.

Something blurred behind Mulcahy. Like the sun reflecting on a piece of sky. Don't know how else to put it. I'd only had time to notice it before it thundered over his shoulder and then I couldn't see a thing. A warm wave burst over me, which made no sense as it was a calm day and I was sixty feet above the sea. Funny the things that go through your mind when you don't know what's happening.

I pawed at my eyes. That was the most important thing. I needed to see. I once saw a man fall from a mast, hurt so badly he didn't understand why he couldn't stand up. Kept apologising to the lieutenant of the watch. Died a couple of hours later. I thought something like that had happened to me, and it was suddenly very important not to die blind. I flailed at my face until I saw daylight.

I hadn't fallen off the foretop. I was still facing Mulcahy, and the frogs were still blasting away at us. Mulcahy was soaked in blood from head to foot. I looked around and there were Clough, Hazlett and Lockwood, all painted red. So was I. I could taste salt even as I realized it was blood in my eyes that had blinded me.

Time slows down at moments like that. I spent an age thinking Fortune was missing. Gone. A gap in the circle we'd made around him. Looking down was as slow a process as tacking the *Téméraire*. There was Fortune, lying on the top. Or at least his body. The shot had taken his head clean off. No sign of it. No wonder there was so much blood. It was gushing out of his neck, pouring off the foretop to the deck below.

Lockwood nudged the body with his foot, about to knock it off the top and on to the netting that protected the deck from falling tackle.

"No." Clough put a hand on Lockwood's shoulder. "We'll not be leaving him. Not today."

I don't know what was going through anyone else's mind as we looked down at Fortune. I just didn't want to look any more. I believe to this day it was the sight of his headless body that finally made me an officer. Luck aside, Fortune's blood had given us a problem to solve when we needed something to do.

"Clough," I said, "we need to sponge out the swivel gun. Mulcahy, Lockwood, Hazlett, check your flints. Change them if you can't clean them. Nelson's about to give you a Frencher to shoot."

The Admiral drained his glass.

"That was then. The French will be on your side this time, and they do make the best wine."

His hand returned to his fob and moved inside, feeling every surface of the locket. Stowe exchanged a look with Buckland.

"Sir?" said Buckland.

"Hm?"

"Beg your pardon sir, but what happened then?"

"Well, Clough became my coxswain and then my butler when I went ashore. You know that. Mulcahy and Lockwood went into the coal trade when the *Téméraire* was paid off. I always buy from them when I can. Hazlett stayed in and got himself commissioned. He was my captain of marines when I had the *Blenheim*. Lives in Plymouth now. Somehow we all stayed in touch. As for Fortune, well. He spoke more in that last minute of his life than I ever heard him say in a day. Yet, here we are, fifty years later, still talking about him."

The corners of his mouth turned down in a suppressed smile.

"Oh, you mean the battle? You told me yourself. We were yardarm to yardarm with the *Redoutable* and the *Fougueux* and took them both. All I remember is a lot of smoke and noise. That's what usually happens in a battle."

His eyes focused on something further away in time than in distance.

"That's more than I've ever said to Charles about Trafalgar, and he's been pestering me about it for nearly ten years. I fear when I next see you, you may understand why I don't speak of it."

Buckland shifted in his chair. "Thank you, sir."

The Admiral turned his head to Stowe. "I told you this today for a reason."

He put the hand holding the locket in his lap and turned it palm up, so he could look at its smooth surface.

"We lost more than a hundred men from *Téméraire* that day, and twice as many wounded. None of us on the foretop had a scratch. Even when the foretopmast came down and took half the top with it, it didn't touch us. We were lucky that day. Damn lucky. So we each cut a section out of our shirts that were soaked in Fortune's blood, and we kept it. We used our prize money to have five of these lockets made from one of the *Redoutable*'s balls. One of hundreds that didn't kill us."

He turned the locket over, though neither side had any engraving.

"We'd probably lost our senses of course. It's difficult to remember what was going on in our heads. But I've always kept this with me. And who knows? We've all done well, all kept our health, had children to be proud of. You know, when the Admiralty board meets I can barely hear myself think for the cracking joints and rattling lungs. I bound up the stairs like a midshipmite. Clough's past seventy but doesn't look a day over fifty. I swear ten years of that's down to his wife."

He stood up and held out the locket. Stowe and Buckland were on their feet in an instant.

"Take it," said the Admiral.

Stowe felt a tremor at the feel of cold iron at his fingertips. A cannonball fired at Trafalgar would be a holy relic in the *Odin*'s gunroom. He could not take his eyes off it as he heard the Admiral sink back into his chair. He fumbled the clasp twice before he got it open. The blood-soaked cotton inside was black with age and as hard as teak. Stowe snapped the locket shut.

"Sir?" Buckland's urgent tone jerked Stowe's eyes from the locket. "Are you unwell, sir?"

Stowe crouched before the Admiral, who stared at nothing. No man could be that still while he was breathing. "Sir! Sir!"

"Clough!" Buckland shouted. "Clough, there! Come quick! The Admiral is ill!"

Clough flew into the room and shoved Stowe aside. He felt the Admiral's pulse. His head sank forward. Stowe stared at Clough's white braid for what could have been a moment or an aeon. When Clough stood and looked to Stowe, his face was composed. He appeared unaware of the tear on his right cheek.

"Your grandfather is dead."

Stowe stood to face him. Clough's eyes darted down to the locket in Stowe's hand. "He gave you that?"

"Yes." Stowe reached forward to return it to the Admiral's pocket.

Clough caught his hand. "No! No sir, you mustn't. If he give it you, don't ever part with it."

Stowe felt a weight in his stomach. It was impossible to believe the Admiral was gone while he sat there, eyes focused yet again on something no one else could see.

"We'll need to make arrangements, sir," said Clough.

"Yes, yes of course. I'll write to the captain of the *Odin*. I'm sure he'll understand." He turned to Buckland. "Would you take it aboard, Harry?"

Buckland's face was white. He shook his head. "I think, Charles, that I had better stay with you." He swallowed. "Very close to you."

"Harry?"

Buckland forced a smile as brittle as his voice. "I believe, Charles, that we have made the lady's acquaintance."

He took his card box out of his pocket. He opened it and shuffled the cards once, twice and a third time. He put them back in the box and threw it on the fire.

About the Author

DJ Cockburn funded his unfortunate writing habit through medical research on various parts of the African continent and drinking a lot of coffee. Earlier phases of his life have included teaching unfortunate children and experimenting on unfortunate fish.

In between a steady drizzle of rejections, he's seen a few stories in various venues including Gardner Dozois's *Year's Best Science Fiction* for 2014.

His website is at http://cockburndj.wordpress.com/ and he has occasionally been caught twittering as @DJ_Cockburn.

Helping Hands in the Acreage

by Chris Kuriata

Plump human hands sprouted from Auntie Sandra's acreage field. Hundreds of them, as clustered and weather-beaten as wild mushrooms. Young Katie pinched her shirt over her nose while the disembodied fingers waggled in the breeze. She thought the field smelled dirty and moist, like a neglected chicken coop. Auntie Sandra walked fearlessly between the rows of hands, but Katie stood in the grass, afraid one of them might grab her ankle. She thought the hands looked alive, and pictured grown men down there chilling beneath the soil, paralysed, trying with all their might to claw their way back to the surface.

"They can't hurt you," Auntie Sandra claimed.

Using the long blade from her apron, Auntie Sandra grabbed one of the fingers and sliced it off. No blood came. The hand didn't curl to protect itself. Katie saw nothing to indicate the hand experienced any pain.

"Now you try."

Although city-born and raised, Katie understood the important function a blade played on the farm. On Auntie Sandra's command, Katie could behead a chicken or use the axe to release a pig runt from the process of starving to death, but cutting off a finger from one of the field hands felt different—needlessly destructive, like some shitty boy who likes to catch snails and hold a match against their extended eyes.

Auntie Sandra wouldn't take no for an answer. "Please, I insist."

Katie peered around the edge of the barn for her mother, who stayed behind in the shade of the fieldstone chimney to spare herself from the sight of the hands. Katie wanted to apologize and promise to behave like a good girl. Problem was, Katie had promised her mother to change too many times already to sound believable.

Fed up with her stalling, Auntie Sandra forced the blade into Katie's hand. Not knowing what else to do, Katie gripped one of the waggling fingers tight and jerked the knife up. The skin felt rubbery like a rooster comb, and the blade sheared cleanly through the joint.

The wilted digit thumped into the dirt. Auntie Sandra scooped it up, perhaps worried it might crawl away.

"Can't let this go to waste." She tossed the fingers into the chicken pen, and the yellow-feathered babies swarmed, pecking the skin down to the bone. The fingers continued waggling even as they were being devoured. "You've done it once," Auntie Sandra said. "That means you can do it anytime you need."

The rest of the afternoon passed quietly. Auntie Sandra invited Katie and her mother to sit on the porch of her crumbling manor house. The iced tea she served tasted bitter and granular, as though the leaves had been steeped in muddy water filled with drowned worms.

Auntie Sandra puffed her cigarette to blow smoke rings. She opened her mouth wide and puckered her lips like a fish. Her throat looked cavernous, wide enough to swallow young Katie whole.

"She's darling," Auntie Sandra said, and Katie wondered if the old witch meant as someone to look at or as someone good to eat.

"She's quite the troublemaker," Katie's mother said, lifting her skirt for the breeze to cool her thick legs.

"Wonderful. My acreage is where troublemakers belong."

The implied threat chilled Katie to the bone. When the time came to catch the bus back to the city, she'd never felt so thankful.

"It's a hard life living on the acreage," her mother said.

Katie shut her eyes and tried sleeping during the bumpy trip through the winding dirt roads of Pelham. She thought Auntie Sandra's acreage an awful place, reminding her of a series of disgusting European paintings she saw in a book at school. The boys laughed, pointing to the genitals of the little naked people wearing crow's beaks who tumbled screaming from the tops of windmills. With its dark skies and seemingly endless tracts of land, Auntie Sandra's acreage would have looked right at home in one of those ghoulish paintings.

"If you continue misbehaving, you'll have to live on the acreage with Auntie Sandra."

Outside, the dusty road kicked up tornado-shaped clouds, hiding the awful countryside from sight. Katie now understood there were worse places to live than beneath her mother's roof. She pledged to be different from now on. No more running wild with the neighbourhood boys, stealing mail and smashing windows. She would behave.

At least for the next few years.

Katie's mother grabbed her by the hair, literally jerking her out of bed by her scalp.

"Where have you been?"

Katie stank of smoke, incense and sweat. Less than twenty minutes had passed since she snuck through the basement storm window, surrendering to sleep beneath her smooth, clean sheets.

"God," Katie's drowsy lips slurred, "what's wrong with you?" Mother probably thought she was drugged up, which in her mind justified whatever steps she took to correct her daughter.

"This is it, Katie. This is the last straw."

Before Katie knew what was happening, she stood at the bus station. Her phone was gone. She didn't even have her debit card. Her sole possession was the forty-seven dollars Mother stuffed into the top pocket of her pyjamas—the exact amount to pay the fare to Auntie Sandra's acreage.

Katie noticed people at the bus station staring. Some of them smirked, seeming to enjoy the sight of a young lady being punished. Head held high, she crossed the platform to board her bus. She thought the driver might kick her off, telling her she couldn't ride in slippers and pyjamas, but he collected her ticket and jerked his head towards the coach, inviting her to find a seat.

No phone, no music. At least she had two seats to stretch across. Katie regretted coming home at all. She should have camped out in Zack's basement, pretended to have gone missing for a couple of weeks. That would have taught Mother a lesson about snooping through her private things.

Hours later, Katie disembarked along a lonely stretch of road. The end of the line. Once the pneumatic doors shuttered behind her, the bus made an impossible U-turn across the narrow dirt highway and shrank into the horizon.

The path to Auntie Sandra's acreage was easy to find. Every tree leaned in that direction, the branches seeming to stretch for Auntie Sandra like they wanted to hug her. Losing your way was impossible. Any time Katie strayed from the road, thorny brambles scratched and tore at her skin, forcing her back onto the path.

She searched the reddening sky. By now, all her friends must be assembled at Wild Rose Tattoo, likely wondering where she was. Her hand kept flopping to her thigh, reaching for her phone, still not trained to remember it wasn't there. Back in the city, her real phone must be dancing across the nightstand as messages from Zack poured in; first curious, then annoyed by her nonresponse, by now concerned.

The acreage came into view as night fell. The wooded fields on either side of the road began to swirl with activity. The countryside came alive in the dark, rousing animals both to feed and be fed upon.

Auntie Sandra lounged on the porch, as though expecting Katie's arrival. She'd aged in the ten years since Katie saw her last. Cracks and wrinkles covered her face, like a clay bust about to fall apart.

"I haven't a room prepared."

Katie took a load off on the steps. She could see the dirty soles of her feet through holes in her slippers. "Whatever. I'll stay out here all night. I don't care."

"Get up. Don't be stupid."

A percussive clang rumbled across the acreage, sending animals scurrying and birds flapping from their trees. Heavy water flowed through the brambles, flooding the road where Katie had walked just minutes before. She wondered what would have happened had she dawdled along the path. Would she have been washed away?

"Come inside. It's bedtime."

Auntie Sandra showed her to a corner room on the second floor. Dusty bookcases on the verge of collapse struggled to support moldy tomes with torn jackets and faded spines. Katie kept her arms to her sides, afraid of touching the books, which she knew were filled with dangerous knowledge.

"You can sleep here."

She sniffed the stained blankets covering the floor. Surely, a sick dog or goat had slept on them previously, but she didn't dare criticize Auntie Sandra's hospitality.

With no lamp or candles, the library turned pitch-dark once the door shut. Katie curled up in the filthy blankets, amazed at the difference a day could make. Unable to fall asleep, she tapped at the air, composing text messages to Mother on an invisible phone.

> how dare U violate my privacy?

A minute later, she added:

> don't pretend you were any different 😤 I know about all the shit you got up to

Katie was just getting warmed up, but a square of light came through the library window, sliding along the wall, changing shape and direction once it hit the corner. Someone's car pulled up the narrow pathway onto the acreage.

For a moment, she thought Mother decided to brave the watery roads and bring her home. She kicked off the sheets, ready to fling herself into Mother's apologetic arms. She'd be reunited with Zack in the city before lunchtime tomorrow. This foolish trip to the acreage would soon be forgiven, forgotten.

Katie reached the landing and peered through the bannister rungs as Auntie Sandra opened the front door. She had changed from her frumpy gown into high heels and a lacy, black dress that in its day would have been called "scandalous".

A gentleman caller stepped into the house. Auntie Sandra celebrated his arrival by cranking her record player and filling the air with music. Corks from ancient bottles of wine popped. The bottles were so old

Katie could smell the French Revolution wafting in the air. The vintages of wine Auntie Sandra served could never be purchased, only killed for.

Katie watched the happy couple drunkenly race up the stairs and tumble into Auntie Sandra's luxurious bed. Together, they moaned like squeaky train wheels. Katie plugged her ears, but the roar of the gentleman caller penetrated her head. He was having the time of his life. Every last desire of his little heart fulfilled.

The gentleman caller announced his finish by bellowing like a moose. The bed went silent before a new rhythm rocked the bedsprings, this one more aggressive. The gentleman caller began to cry. His fun times had come to an end. Auntie Sandra tried to muffle him, but his shrieks rattled the house. Katie was grateful when he finally went silent, if only so his suffering ended.

With trembling fingers, Katie resumed texting Mother on her invisible phone:

Satisfied the truth would sting, Katie swaddled herself in the sheets and went to sleep. She awoke a few times in the night, disturbed by the gnawing sounds coming from Auntie Sandra's bed. Moist chewing, like a dog with a fresh butcher's bone.

On her knees, Katie felt along the floorboard, searching for wires. A wire would lead to a landline.

"Where's your phone?"

Draped in a burgundy robe, Auntie Sandra tossed a handful of herbs into a glass jar and set them in the morning sun to steep.

"I have no desire to talk to people so vulgar as to call me on the phone."

Katie looked out the window. The gentleman caller's car had disappeared, perhaps seized by the nighttime waters and carried away. A lone chicken ambled past the tire treads, pecking the ground. The animals must be expecting their breakfast.

"Are there morning chores?" That's what happened on a farm, right? You fed the chickens, milked the cows, whatever earthy shit was supposed to build character and make you worthy of returning home.

Auntie Sandra grinned, the first bit of mirth Katie had seen since her arrival. "Yes, time for your *mourning chores*." Katie didn't like the look on Auntie Sandra's face. Her private joke was clearly a laugh at Katie's expense.

Putrid odours made the master bedroom unendurable. Katie couldn't believe Auntie Sandra slept amidst all that pollution, or that the gentleman caller didn't turn around and run at first whiff. Animals know better than to enter a cave with unwelcoming smells; what was it about men that made them incapable of heeding a warning?

Katie gagged. Burnt candles, armpit sweat, baby oil, dirty underwear, tooth decay…all these items formed into a super funk. The bedroom had no windows, and Katie's mouth tasted dirty.

The intensity of the smell momentarily distracted her from the gentleman caller's remains scattered across the bed. Auntie Sandra had worked him over well. Barely anything was left in the sheets, not even stains, only his clattering bones.

"Take these to the field behind the barn and bury them with the others."

Katie guessed which field Auntie Sandra referred to, where the hands sprouted—a place she did not wish to return.

"Quit dawdling. You need to earn your keep around here."

"Can't we put them in the fireplace and burn them?"

"The only smoke I want filling my house comes out of a pipe."

Katie yanked the sheets off the bed. The gentleman caller's remains broke apart when they hit the floor. His bones behaved delicately, as though they had lain in Auntie Sandra's bed for hundreds of years. Katie didn't want to touch them, but her curiosity got the better of her and she tapped a long bone that might have once been a leg. The femur crumbled like a roll of birch.

She sucked every last drop of moisture, Katie thought. *Even the marrow.*

Having seen proof of Auntie Sandra's appetite, Katie hustled, dragging the remains outside. At the barn, she heard the field hands waggling, rippling the air like a swarm of butterflies—too quiet to be heard alone, but in legion they drowned out everything.

"You will bury them here," Auntie Sandra said.

Katie didn't need a shovel. The rich dirt behind the barn was soft like talcum powder. While keeping watch over the hands to make sure they didn't grab her, Katie opened a wide trench in the soil. After she dumped the remains, the dirt sealed itself like the mouth of a Venus flytrap closing over its prey with a satisfied smirk.

The hands stopped waggling. The fingers went erect, exposing their palms, standing with perfect posture. Katie wondered if the hands were feeding, sucking the remaining nutrients from the bones, but she didn't dare ask.

"You've done it once," Auntie Sandra said. "That means you can do it anytime you need."

"Will I need to do it again?"

Auntie Sandra tended to a trampled hand lying broken in the dirt. "Yes. You will need to do this every morning."

Barbed thorns covered Katie's arms and legs. The sharp pricks broke when she tried pulling them out, leaving poisonous stubs stuck behind. Her skin turned red and itched.

Katie searched for the road for hours. She didn't know how often the bus came. Every day? Every four days? She would wait. She had no money, but refused to stay at the acreage with Auntie Sandra until Mother decided she could come home.

She failed to find a path off the acreage, only dead ends. Thick brambles clustered together, three different breeds tangled into intricate knots. Defeated, she returned to the house where Auntie Sandra had prepared dinner; roots and wildflowers swirling in a watery brew the colour of rain puddles.

"Open wide," Auntie Sandra said, alternating between spooning brew into Katie's mouth and dribbling broth over her ravaged arms and legs.

"That's good stuff," Katie said. The soup tasted bitter, like weeds, but the water filled her stomach and restored her energy. It also softened the barbs, which detached naturally from her skin.

"What's the boy's name?"

Katie hadn't breathed one word of Zack to Auntie Sandra. She didn't know if it was safe to mention him. Mother only ever uttered his name like profanity.

"There's only one thing that would make you so desperate as to try crawling home through the brambles. There must be a boy."

Was it that obvious? Sent to the acreage over boy trouble? Katie felt ashamed to be such a cliché.

"If I can offer you some wisdom: it is always better to divide your love amongst many boys. A boy loved too much will eventually hurt without conscience."

Katie shook her head. Auntie Sandra didn't know what she was talking about. "I'm only the second person he's ever slept with."

Auntie Sandra set down the soup bowl, unimpressed. "Is that why your mother sent you here?"

"She found a receipt in my pocket."

"From a drugstore?"

"No. A motel." Between meddling mothers and unemployed older brothers, neither Katie nor Zack had much in the way of privacy. Intimacy was expensive.

"You must be very important to him, then."

Katie spoke across the table in a hushed voice, as though she and Auntie Sandra sat in a busy restaurant and needed to fight for their privacy. "The first person Zack slept with shouldn't even count. Some gross hockey coach who took advantage of him when they made trips to play in Scarborough. And Etobicoke. And a few more times at her house when Zack was supposed to be practising."

Katie felt so proud to be Zack's first, she cried when he confessed the truth.

"But I'm the first time he wanted. Being wanted counts a lot more than being first."

"And what about you? Was Zack your first?"

Katie didn't like Auntie Sandra's question. It sounded like an accusation of hypocrisy.

"It's all right," Auntie Sandra said. "After you've done it once, you can do it anytime you need."

The arrival of the next gentleman caller awoke Katie.

While Auntie Sandra bid the man welcome with her enchanting voice and crackly old music, Katie rolled a cigarette from a bushel of dry weeds she found outside. She made lopsided smoke rings, listening to the squeaking of Auntie Sandra's bed, waiting for the gentleman caller's screams of unbridled agony to begin.

She tapped her fingers across half a potato she found on the kitchen floor, pretending the desiccated spud was her phone. She sent message after message to Zack, telling him she loved him, that she didn't mean to abandon him and that she would be home soon. She trusted the universe to deliver these communications. A bird might pick up one of her messages and sing it into Zack's bedroom window, or by some incredible coincidence her words would find their way into a fortune cookie he'd open at lunch. A lover's cry could not disappear. Eventually, Zack would come for her. He'd hack the brambles apart like cotton fluff.

The gentleman caller moaned in ecstasy. Katie lifted the sleeve of her pyjamas and rubbed her bicep tattoo. The ink looked fresh enough to smear. She remembered how Zack leaned close to her, squeezing her hand while the tattoo gun punctured her skin, drawing a pair of winged hands pressed together as if in prayer.

After his orgasm, the gentleman caller wept. His broken voice confessed his weaknesses, as though he looked to Auntie Sandra to grant him absolution. Auntie Sandra barely listened to his jabbering. She hummed, still riding waves of pleasure, looking forward to what always came next.

"Ow!"

The tattoo was sore. The skin puffed up, as if infected. Her winged hands now looked like they were in a struggle, the bigger hand violently subjugating the weaker.

Katie hadn't been alone with Zack when she got the tattoo. Hailey had also been there. A niece of the artist, Hailey worked at Wild Rose. The whole time Katie was being inked, Hailey rested her chest on the counter, watching Zack kiss the sweat beads from Katie's forehead. She knew exactly what Hailey was doing: looking for weaknesses.

Auntie Sandra thrashed the gentleman caller in her bed. Katie heard the sound of bones cracking and skin tearing.

Katie fumbled in the dark for the old potato. Never mind the late hour, she didn't care if Zack was sleeping. This was too important.

The devouring noises from Auntie Sandra's bed sounded to Katie like Zack and Hailey laughing, their mouths stuffed full of one another's flesh. Katie punched her filthy sheets, imagining the lies Hailey spun. "Forget her, Zack. She doesn't count any more than your old hockey coach."

Alone, Katie wept in her ramshackle bed, helpless while Hailey schemed. If she didn't get home soon, Zack might find someone else he'd had been his first.

Each morning, when Katie dragged out the pathetic remains of the latest gentleman caller, the field hands turned towards her, moving with the synchronization of a flock of birds. The fingers touched the palms, presenting their nails like a row of eyes. She felt like the hands were studying her, but whether they looked for strength or weakness she didn't know.

A shrunken skull lay in the sheets. Katie turned it over, trying to imagine the face that once lay overtop of the crumbling bone. How old was this man? Did he wear a beard? Glasses?

"Do you feel pity for them?" Auntie Sandra wheezed. Her breathing had been laboured the last few days.

Katie dropped the skull into the soft dirt. The hands set upon it, busting the cranium apart, sending shards flying like smashed China.

"Don't their wives miss them?" Katie asked. "Or their mothers? What do the people left behind think?"

Auntie Sandra squatted, dragging her fingers through the dirt, letting the field hands caress her wrist. "Do you think there ought to be a search party? Men with dogs tramping through the acreage? Sniffing bloodhounds?"

Katie did. She thought the newspapers should be full of stories detailing the mysterious vanishing of hundreds of men from the city. "People can't just disappear. There's always going to be someone, at least one person who'll come looking for them. Right?"

Wearing her years of experience across her weary face, Auntie Sandra said, "Honey, the sad truth is people are forgotten more easily than you can ever imagine."

In Katie's dreams, Hailey stood hand in hand with Zack, her stomach fat, the skin rippling as Zack's baby squirmed underneath.

No, Katie thought. *That could never happen.*

Hailey dropped out of school. She named Zack as the father of her child. Instead of scowling and calling Hailey a liar, Zack held her close and caressed her fattening stomach. Zack was eager for their baby. He told lies, claiming Hailey was his first, and everyone believed him as if their coupling was destiny.

Katie woke physically ill. The sheets roped over her body like a straightjacket. She paced the library trying to regain her sense of balance, but the acreage house listed like an abandoned ship, knocking her into the bookshelves.

Headlights shone through the window, gliding across the wall like lazy ghosts.

Katie felt like she might pass out, or have a heart attack.

"Can't you assholes leave her alone for one night?"

Although Katie could not leave the acreage, walled in by the brambles, the gentlemen callers had no trouble arriving night after night. They parked their cars and went inside to their doom, confident no one would ever come looking for them.

Just like no one is looking for me, Katie thought. Her isolation was an illusion. Nothing stopped Zack from coming to the acreage to find her. Maybe he didn't get her messages, or maybe he actively ignored them, but the results were the same: Katie had been forgotten more easily than she ever imagined possible.

The potato's face was mashed in from the hundreds of messages sent to Zack. Katie thought she must have looked like a madwoman, carting around a rotten spud, holding it to her heart like a sacred totem. Auntie Sandra probably laughed her ass off this entire time.

"Damn you."

Katie bit the potato. Her teeth ached, but she forced herself to chew. The potato was leather-tough, but she persevered. Her throat strained to swallow such large chunks. She hoped she would choke.

The potato burned, splashing waves of acid in her stomach. Katie burped and the fumes burned her nostrils. The stupid phone was gone forever, and Katie collapsed to the floor, wondering how she would keep her hands occupied now.

Down below, the gentleman caller pounded the door, knocking aggressively, as though an audience with Auntie Sandra was his birthright. Katie hated him. Tomorrow, before she shook his bones from the sheets, she would spit on them.

The library door opened. The bright hallway light blinded Katie, and she shielded her weeping eyes.

"I'm exhausted," Auntie Sandra said, shaking and chilled. "I need to take a bath."

Katie nodded. She could no longer imagine returning to the city, facing all those who had forgotten her. Walking into Wild Rose Tattoo, Zack and pregnant Hailey would look at her with perplexed faces, overcome by déjà vu. "Do we... know each other?" Zack would ask.

No, going home would be more terrible than staying on the acreage.

"Have your bath," Katie said, brushing the tangles from her hair, and swinging her arms to get the blood flowing. "I'll take care of him."

"Are you sure?"

"You deserve to rest."

Without hesitation, Katie went downstairs and opened the door. The gentleman caller looked surprised to see her, but pleasantly so. He smiled as the record began playing, and Katie urged, "Please, come inside."

That Katie hadn't washed in weeks made no difference. She felt confident in her desirability as she crawled into Auntie Sandra's luxurious bed. Beneath the sheets, the gentleman caller looked grotesque, all the wrong parts of his body swollen up; thighs, belly, even his forehead bulged. The contrast between his bloated guts and Zack's tight, muscular belly made her snort derisively. The gentleman caller didn't notice her mocking him, too blinded by his delight.

Although the gentleman caller's face contorted with ecstasy, Katie's expression underwent no such change. She did her best to consume the man as Auntie Sandra would have, but when Katie finally crawled off his shredded body, there were still large chunks of him thrashing around in the sheets.

Panicked, not knowing how to put him out of his misery, Katie ran downstairs and broke open the bathroom door. The tub sat empty, only silt in the basin, as if ancient Auntie Sandra had finally crumbled to dust and washed down the drain.

Katie was all alone now.

Eventually, the gentleman caller went still. Hunks of flesh dangled from his bones. Katie grabbed the sheets and hauled them downstairs.

The heavy load strained her back, so different from the bones left by Auntie Sandra which were hollow, light as wafers. Katie's sheets were weighed down by meat and dripping blood. The floor and the stairs would need to be scrubbed.

She dumped the remains into the dirt, and immediately the hands swooped upon the offering. They stripped every last piece of meat until the bones gleamed pure white.

She wrapped the stained sheet over her chilled body, watching the hands frenzy. The taste of the gentleman caller lingered on her lips.

Next time will be better. Next time I'll make the bones as good as Auntie Sandra.

"Now that I've done it once, I can do it anytime I need."

The field hands waved back and forth, charging the air with their energy. Katie lay back and the hands caught her. Long, dexterous fingers and smooth, sensual palms roamed all over her body, massaging her legs, caressing her cheeks. She sensed individual personalities within the hands. Each had a different way of touching her, some gentle, others desperate for her affection.

A beam of white light rolled across the acreage. The next gentleman caller had arrived. He did not see the abandoned car of the previous gentleman caller. The ground had already opened and swallowed the car whole, dragging it down with all the others. What a museum of automotives must be hidden beneath the acreage soil, stretching all the way back to the very first model.

The gentleman caller's headlights blasted Katie in the face. Her pupils shrank to pinholes. She looked positively feral—knotted hair, eyes swollen, mouth smeared with dirt, teeth pointed and bits of the previous gentleman caller caught between them.

Without hesitation, the gentleman caller leapt from his car and approached Katie. He had travelled for ages, years perhaps, uncertain the acreage even existed, but he kept the faith and his persistence had paid off. He longed for Katie to take him to her bed and make him a part of the acreage forever.

"Welcome."

Katie believed the acreage was the best place for her, where her youth and wildness could be put to practical use making the bones. Perhaps in time, when she grew as grey and wrinkled as Auntie Sandra, she would see Zack again. Exhausted by Hailey, distanced from his children, confident no one would ever come looking for him, Zack would feel the magnetic pull of the acreage, and follow the trees and the brambles to Katie's bed. Denied her place as Zack's first, Katie would dwell in his heart forever by one day being his last.

She took the gentleman caller into her arms, offering him music, wine and company. She carried him swiftly across the dips and waves of the acreage, scrambling up the porch steps like she was climbing the gangway of a ship casting off on a voyage to the promise of a new world.

About the Author

Chris Kuriata lives in and often writes about the Niagara Region of Canada. His first novel *Sacrifice of the Sisters Lot* will be published by Palimpsest Press in October 2023.

REST STOP

by John Haas

Taillights flashed in and out of view, the car's wipers pushing sheets of rain aside. The downpour had started only minutes ago, quickly reducing visibility to near zero. Steve followed the pickup ahead, his only company other than the rhythmic *swish-kathunk* of the wipers on their most frantic setting. If Steve could see where road ended and ditch began he would have pulled over.

"Just water," he said, forcing his hands to ease their stranglehold on the wheel.

The pickup's taillights tilted right, and before Steve could question it, his own car did the same. For one panicked moment he was sure they were heading into the ditch. Then a path crunched under his tires. Trees lining either side provided a brief respite from the storm before passing into a wide parking lot where the rain resumed its assault on the windshield.

"A rest stop?" Steve laughed.

Since his one east coast trip thirty-five years ago, there'd been an effort to modernize these places. Gone were the dirty, menacing areas, replaced by coffee shops, restaurants and clean bathrooms.

Steve declared the pickup driver a genius and his new best friend. Already he saw himself inside, a fresh cup of coffee in one hand, watching the rain beat its fury against the glass.

The pickup led him across six car lengths of lot until the lights flared brighter and disappeared. Steve steered left to roll into a spot two over. A wooden overhang cut the rain off like an umbrella, giving immediate visibility.

"Aw, crap," Steve muttered, hopes of fresh coffee vanishing.

Lurking on the other side of the overhang was a rest stop from his childhood memories. A dark, wooden hut maybe twenty feet square. Two windows flanked a solid door, giving the impression of a face staring back at him. Steve shivered.

Smaller shacks to either side would hold bathrooms that Steve didn't care to visit, but the constant sound of rain emphasised his need.

"Okay, fine. Any port in a storm. Literally."

The pickup's interior light came on revealing a beefy driver, hands gripping the wheel. Beside him, gazing straight ahead as if awaiting a signal, perched a thin woman. Two teens in back completed the picture of an all-American family. An animated discussion was underway.

Steve exited the car, scanning the surroundings. "If Patty could see me now."

When Steve told his wife he planned to drive cross-country for his new position, she'd looked at him like he wanted to swim to the moon. Except for one annual hunting trip at a warm, secluded cabin, Steve was a homebody, preferring his comforts. Yes, the car could have been shipped as part of his transfer—the bank would've paid for it. This way, he'd explained, he could take items the movers wouldn't take, like the propane tank. Thin reasoning but Patty accepted it, assuming he just wanted alone time.

True enough.

The pickup's back door opened, the teenage girl popping out.

"Tina!" the beefy man called, opening his own door.

"God, Uncle Ted. I need to go."

Fifteen or sixteen with shoulder-length black hair shaved to the scalp on one side. A nose ring looped through her right nostril and another through her lip. Somewhere under that white sweatshirt would be a tattoo.

What Steve's mom would call a "naughty girl".

"You went an hour ago."

Uncle Ted stepped from the truck. The man was a six-foot-tall gorilla, half as wide, in blue-jean overalls. Wife and son followed, eyes on the man, waiting for orders. She was thin and nervous while the boy was a clone of dad down to his close-cropped hair. Everything about them screamed farm.

"Well, if you must know," Tina said, "I'm on my period."

Checkmate. Nothing shuts a guy down quicker than that topic. Ted's eyes skimmed over Steve who smiled, knowing he—a short, skinny guy in wire-rimmed glasses—would be dismissed as harmless.

"Rosie," Ted said, "go with her."

It was the command of someone used to being obeyed.

Tina rolled her eyes and stomped off for the women's bathroom, her aunt a pace behind. "I'm not going to run away you know," she called over her shoulder.

I'm not going to run away? Steve considered. *Interesting thing to say.*

With a shrug he headed for the opposite bathroom, unable to delay the inevitable.

"Nice day for a drive," he ventured, passing the remaining two.

Ted made a point of ignoring Steve. The son gave a brief smile before glancing at his father and adjusting his reaction.

Well, fuck you too, buddy, Steve thought. So much for his new best friend.

The bathroom was dim, cramped, and Steve was done as quickly as possible, touching as little as possible. He passed Ted and son at the door. The two acted like he didn't exist.

Whatever.

Returning to the overhang, Steve watched rain dance off the parking lot pavement, contemplating what to do next. Lights had come on inside the hut and he scanned with vague curiosity for the motion sensors that had activated them. Now that the place was awake it gave an impression of warmth and invitation. Drier than out here for sure. One counter was covered with maps and brochures.

What had he found so menacing?

Footsteps brought him around. The girl, Tina, returned, no chaperone in sight. Steve gave her a smile then turned away as the uncle came back into view.

"Where's your aunt?" Ted grumbled.

Tina cocked a thumb towards the bathroom, not looking at the man. Annoyance crossed Ted's face and he opened his mouth to reply when the son returned in a rush, glancing over his shoulder. Ted looked at the teen with one raised eyebrow.

"The lights went off and—"

The aunt screamed, one high, panicked shriek. The family rushed for the closed bathroom, Steve dragged along in a wake of curiosity.

"Rosie!" Ted called.

"The door won't open," came her muffled voice, "and the lights went off."

The son seemed about to speak when Rosie screamed again. "I can hear breathing."

Ted pushed on the door with no result, then gave it a shoulder only to bounce off.

"Get back," he commanded.

He brought one heavy-booted foot up like a TV cop and kicked the door, connecting above the latch and slamming it inward. His wife rushed out and Ted caught her by the arms, looking ready to slap her. Instead he moved her aside and stepped into the restroom.

"I heard something," Rosie said, forcing herself under control.

The women's bathroom was as spacious as the men's and took Ted all of two seconds to search. "Nothing in there," he said, stepping out. The words carried an accusation of overreaction.

She glanced at the bathroom then at Ted before focussing on her shoes. "I thought..."

Steve turned away, unable to watch this scene of the perpetually bullied. Ted ruled his family with intimidation and probably worse, just as Steve's own father had.

What was the full story though? Tina hadn't been with them long, not with that attitude. Had her parents given her over to Ted as a last resort? A wild girl, out of control with smoking, drinking, drugs and promiscuity? In need of a firmer hand?

Yes, that fit.

With a sigh, Steve eased back behind the wheel, one foot still outside while considering his options. He slipped the key into the ignition, thinking he could head to the far side of the parking lot to wait out the storm. There, he could get what he wanted from the trunk and relax in privacy.

Ted lumbered back into the area, paces ahead of his family, wearing the red face of someone righteously pissed. He stopped, noticing the interior lights of the shack.

"Someone *is* here," he said, pointing.

Ted was going to be disappointed when he discovered it was all motion sensors. Steve followed the other's gaze then leaned forward at what he saw.

"Well, shit."

Someone *was* inside, an expressionless man behind the counter tidying brochures.

Where had *he* come from?

"Get in the truck," Ted ordered the teens. "Rosie, come with me."

The son scrambled in while Tina leaned against her door in an insolent slouch only teens managed. Ted crossed to the hut's door and jerked it open. Inside the man continued his tasks, oblivious to their presence.

Lantern fish, Steve thought, without knowing why.

Ted stormed across the floor towards the man, boots making hollow thuds against the wooden floor. He waved one hand at Rosie, stopping her in the doorway, then slapped a meaty paw on the counter.

Silence filled the world, broken only by the rain's constant drone, slower but still steady.

Then reality flipped.

The man tipped backward, the counter splitting into a wide, mouth-like opening. Ted stepped back as the mouth-counter shot forward, biting his outstretched arm and severing it at the shoulder. He screamed. He spun, spraying windows and wife with blood.

One prolonged heartbeat later, Rosie turned in the doorway.

Yes, that's right. Run, Steve thought, his own mind bugshit with shock.

"Aunt Rosie!" Tina yelled.

Jagged knives of dull metal sprouted from the doorframe around the hapless woman.

No. Not knives. Teeth.

The teeth clanged shut on her like a vault door on a sack of hamburger. Rosie was bisected front to back in a spout of blood that would have been gratuitous in any movie. Her front half slid down the teeth, an expression of dying surprise on her face.

"No!" her son screamed from a million miles to Steve's right.

The teeth opened and what was left of Rosie splattered against the doorstep. A runner of carpet snaked forward to collect her remains, flipping them through the opening. The teeth clanged shut and it chewed.

Steve twisted the key and threw his car into reverse, hitting the gas without a glance in the rear-view, muttering the word *no* over and over, without knowing it.

Pounding rain beat the windshield and through the still-open door, drenching his left side. The cool water against his skin dampened his fight-or-flight. He flipped the wipers on and hit the brakes, watching the son bull his way across the truck's back seat and out Tina's open door. She struggled to hold him back, a losing battle that brought her closer to those teeth with each step.

"No," Steve repeated, slamming the car into park and jumping into the pouring rain. "Run, you idiot."

"Come on, Teddy," Tina said.

Steve wasn't surprised he'd been named after his father.

"No!" Teddy screamed again.

The wooden hut continued chewing, a thin trail of pink oozing from between the teeth.

Teddy could have jumped into those shredding teeth for all Steve cared, but Tina deserved a better fate. Steve rushed forward and grabbed Teddy's other arm, stopping him for the moment.

"Dad!" Teddy sobbed.

"Come on, Teddy, get your shit together!" Steve shouted in his best authoritarian voice. "Your dad would want you protecting Tina, wouldn't he?"

Steve had no idea if Ted Senior would have given a shit about the girl but those words seeped through. Teddy stopped struggling.

"That's right, Teddy," she said. "I need you."

Steve knew Tina didn't need Teddy in the least. She did care for him though.

No accounting for family ties.

Teddy considered a moment before grabbing her wrist and doing an about-face, dragging her into the rain. Steve rushed ahead before Teddy got the idea of hijacking his still-running car.

"Get in back," Steve said, sliding behind the wheel.

They did and he stomped the gas, spinning the car in a tight circle that headed towards the exit. In the rear-view, he watched the unthinkable horror receding.

"Stop!" Tina yelled.

Steve did and shifted focus to the trees he'd been about to plow into.

"The exit's gone," she said.

"How can an exit disappear?"

"How can a building come alive?" Tina responded.

No answer for that. Steve switched on the high-beams, twisting the steering wheel to the left and letting the car inch forward. Headlights followed an unbroken treeline until it had them facing back towards the shacks.

The exit *was* gone.

They sat in the now-unmoving car, rain drumming in a steady, percussive beat. Steve wiped the windshield with his sleeve then turned up the defogger. He focussed on the hut, half expecting it to shamble across the parking lot after them.

How long could they stay ahead of that?

It hadn't moved though, just stared back at them with its warm, inviting lights. A haven from the storm.

Lantern fish, Steve thought again, understanding. *What were they called? Angler fish? Something like that.*

"It's a lure," he said.

"What?" Tina leaned partway into the front seat.

Steve could smell her teen too-young-for-perfume scent. The rain had plastered shirt against skin, making it translucent in spots.

"It can't move," he said, turning his attention back to the hut. "It needs to lure people in."

Tina considered, head cocked to one side. "Maybe it's an illusion inside, showing us what we want to see."

Ted *had* been looking for someone to tell off when the man appeared.

"Illusion," Teddy blurted, mania to his voice.

The door flew open and Teddy leapt out, pulling Tina along.

"Son of a bitch," Steve muttered, involuntarily following them.

The rain had slowed from hammering storm to heavy downpour. Still enough to soak them in seconds. Steve was already sick of being wet.

What could he do anyway? Teddy outweighed him by at least fifty pounds of farm-boy muscle. Steve's toolbox in the trunk had a hammer but he doubted Tina would be okay with her cousin getting brained.

She solved the problem herself, jamming one foot in front of Teddy's. As he tripped, dropping to the soaking pavement, his grasp on Tina slipped and she pulled free. Teddy flopped over, glaring.

"Don't you get it?" he screamed. "It's *all* illusion. The exit, the trees, the rain that forced us here."

"I've got wet clothes that say the rain is real," Steve said.

Tina nodded.

"I'll show you." Teddy jumped to his feet, rushing for the treeline.

"Teddy!" Tina called.

Steve returned to the car, Tina following and slipping into the passenger seat. He spun the car around so its headlights landed on Teddy. The kid's idea was desperate, but all they really had.

He stumbled twice before reaching the trees and glared back at them, an expression saying what assholes they were.

Steve itched to hit the horn.

The kid reached for the first tree, moving his hand forward quickly and colliding with solid wood. Shaking his head, he moved to the next tree and touched that one. Then the next. And the next. With each, he deflated more until leaning his forehead against the rough bark in defeat.

Tina sighed. "Now what?"

Steve shrugged, realizing he'd been holding his breath.

"We could hike through the trees," she suggested, "get to the highway."

It couldn't be more than a couple hundred feet but the darkness in those trees made Steve hesitate. If that horror could make the exit disappear, what else could it do?

Teddy raised his head and looked into the trees, as if hearing Tina's idea. He stepped deeper into the gloom, towards the highway. After a few paces he stopped, then scrambled to retreat.

"What did he see?" Steve asked.

The boy stared at the movement weaving through the shadows.

Tina opened her window. "Teddy, get back in the car."

Shapes moved from darkness to headlights, one on Teddy's left and another to the right. Even in the light they were little more than animated shadows, humanlike in that they had legs, arms and a head.

"Oh, Christ," Steve said.

"What's in their hands?"

"That *is* their hands."

Each shadow had one arm which ended in a weapon. The one to Teddy's left had a sword starting at its elbow, the other had what appeared to be a mace.

"Teddy!" Tina yelled, this time pressing the horn.

Teddy didn't need prompting, already retreating.

Two other shadows glided past the car, one on each side, and Tina stabbed at the button to roll up her window. The four shapes focussed on Teddy, ringing him in a semicircle with the open side facing the shack. Teddy mopped rain from his face with one sleeve.

"No!" Teddy screamed. "You're not real."

He rushed the one between himself and the car, ramming it with his shoulder. The creature gave one step, raising its axe-like appendage.

"No," Tina whispered.

The flat of the weapon caught Teddy across the face, knocking him to the pavement. He jumped up, shaking off the blow. The four moved forward in formation, weapons raised. Teddy retreated in the one direction left to him.

"They're herding him," Steve said.

"Ram them."

Steve looked at the steering wheel as if surprised to find he was in a car. He stepped on the gas, revving the engine high but going nowhere. One shadow broke from the group and rushed the car.

"Idiot," Steve said, shifting to drive.

He stomped the gas pedal, aiming for the approaching shape. With the few feet between them there wasn't time to gain any speed. A moment before impact the creature raised its hands, one ending in a hammer, and pounded them onto the car's hood. Their movement stopped though Steve had the pedal to the floor.

The thing faced them through the windshield.

"Oh god," Tina said.

The face was a gaping hole rimmed with sharp teeth. Above this were two golden, glowing eyes.

Steve flipped the car into reverse and hit the gas again, tearing out of the monster's grip, hammer claw gouging a deep furrow in the metal. It made no movement towards them.

Because we're too late.

Teddy's back was to the hut's door, the other three creatures giving no avenue of escape.

"Shit!" Tina gasped. "Look."

The man was gone, replaced by Ted Senior. His lips moved. Teddy turned in surprise, relief spreading across his face.

"He can't believe..." Steve began.

Teddy stepped through the open door without hesitation.

"Oh, Teddy. No," Tina said.

The teeth clanged shut behind the boy and the shapes returned to the shadows.

Tina's eyes locked on Teddy, not letting her cousin die alone. Steve didn't watch. The sound of his dying screams were enough, carrying over the rain and through the car's closed windows.

"That fucking thing needs to burn," Tina said, her breath short and shallow.

Getting close enough to set fire to *that fucking thing* scared the shit out of Steve, but he was a realist. They were trapped, without options, and surrounded by predators that could wait.

"Okay. Any idea how?"

"Um... there's a gas container in the back of the truck. I saw it every time we stopped."

"Full?"

Tina shrugged.

"Yeah, too possible for it to be empty."

Tina stared out the windshield. "How about the truck? There was like a quarter tank left."

"What, blow it up?"

Tina shook her head. "Cars only explode in movies. It's not impossible, but without gas fumes and a spark they just burn until nothing's left."

"You seem to know a lot on the subject."

Tina ignored his comment. "A fire could work though."

Steve examined the building. The wooden walkway, two side bathrooms, all under an overhang keeping it relatively dry.

It could work. But how did they get it burning?

The answer hit him. "I have a full propane tank in the trunk."

"They don't explode either."

"Maybe not, but we could light the gas..."

"Yeah! And throw it through one of the windows?"

"To throw a twenty-pound tank we'd have to get closer than I want to be. No, I was thinking more along the lines of using the tank inside the truck. Turn it into that fire you suggested."

"Fire," Tina whispered. "Yes."

"We have nothing to light it though."

Tina smiled, showing teeth that would have taken years of orthodontics, and pulled out a Zippo lighter.

Steve returned the smile. "First thing's first. We need the tank."

"I'll get it."

"No!"

She rolled her eyes. "Ugh! I'm no helpless girl, okay?"

"No, it isn't that." Steve shook his head. "I just have something... embarrassing... in the trunk."

"A secret shame? Must be huge to care right now."

You have no idea.

Steve scanned each direction, then before Tina could argue, popped the trunk latch and jumped out into the rain.

"I'll hit the horn if they come," Tina said.

He rushed to the back, his "secret shame" pressed in deep towards the back. He ignored it and grabbed the propane tank, grunting with the weight of it.

Twenty pounds? Feels like a ton.

He put the tank on the ground next to him. The trunk's toolbox was on its side. He flipped it back and unlatched it.

Gotta be something to use as a weapon.

The horn blasted and he jumped, slamming the trunk closed. The entire operation had taken less than twenty seconds, but in that time two of the monsters had come within a foot of the car's front.

"Dammit!"

Where the hell had they come from?

He spun left, searching for the other two, and staggered in a panicked effort to retreat, almost tripping over the propane tank.

Hammer-hand advanced, close enough to touch, eyes glowing.

"No!" he screamed, hating the high-pitched fright he heard.

It moved forward, mouth huge, razor-teeth snapping. Steve grabbed the propane one-handed and backpedaled, ready to swing it like a weapon. Behind him, the ones with sword and mace cut him off from the car. The fourth came from the shadows to Hammer-hand's right.

Steve zagged left, trying to keep them all in view. This close he could see they weren't made of shadows at all, but the same dark wood as the hut.

The wood of their bodies. The glowing eyes.

They're extensions of the building, tools to push its food around. Animated forks.

And the forks had left him one avenue to follow, just like Teddy.

"No. Not like Teddy."

Teddy had resisted his herding, tried to fight the shadows. Not Steve. He backed away, swinging the tank onto his shoulder. The things stepped forward and Steve bolted for the pickup. The sudden action gave him a short lead, but the truck was so far and the tank weighed so much.

His lead couldn't last.

The growl of his car's engine grew to his right. He glanced over and saw the closest pursuer veer off. As it closed on her, Tina shifted to reverse and cut around in an arc, coming up on the opposite side to get another one's attention.

Man, can she drive.

Rain beat against his face, flowing into his eyes to distract him. Steve forced his feet forward, slapping against the pavement, knowing the silent creatures could be reaching for him right now.

"Stop it! Almost there."

He approached the truck, headed for the back door Tina had left open, and swung the tank back one-handed. On the forward swing he launched it into the back seat and scrambled to follow, grabbing for the door's handle, certain he'd been too slow.

The door clicked shut, something ramming into the outside.

"Almost had me. They almost had me."

Spinning in his seat he tried to see every direction at once, icy fingers of panic caressing his heart.

"Losing my shit."

The turn of phrase came from a hitchhiker he'd given a lift to years ago and that memory calmed him. Panic receded, enough for him to focus anyway. He could see the bed of the pickup and its mad jumble of unrelated items.

Those horrors were nowhere to be seen.

A horn played a double tune and Steve scooted to the opposite window. Tina sat behind the wheel of his car giving him a thumbs-up. She'd stopped so the two vehicles almost touched.

Steve returned the gesture then pantomimed searching for his pursuers. She made a motion of smoke dissipating.

Gone? Like after Teddy. But why? With those hands they could get into any vehicle.

Steve stared at the demon building, feet away from him now. His mind churned, grasping at ideas and not liking what it found.

"Oh, son of a bitch. You're playing with us."

Playing with its food.

"She's right. That fucking thing needs to burn."

But he didn't have the lighter.

The car's horn sounded again, returning his attention to Tina. She waved the Zippo back and forth then brought her window down. Steve nodded. Ted Senior had the keys so opening this window was out.

Do they even make cars with manual windows anymore?

He popped the door open the few inches possible, ramming it into the side of his car.

Another scratch in the paint. A giggle escaped him, but if he started laughing now he wouldn't stop.

The gap between cars was wide enough for Steve to push his arm through to the shoulder; jamming himself against the door he waved around, searching for the lighter.

"Stop moving," she called.

A mental picture of slapping the Zippo to the ground stopped him. One of her soft hands grabbed his and gently maneuvered it palm up. He felt the cool metal of the lighter pressed into his hand and closed on it. Then her touch was gone and he pulled back.

Steve glanced around. That hadn't been enough to bring them back. The building was still playing. If it had any idea what they were planning...

He tested the Zippo, confirming it would work. Where could he place it though? Somewhere the flame wouldn't get snuffed when he opened the door, or fall over when he closed it. He leaned across the front seat and placed the lighter in the driver's cup holder.

"That should work."

The propane tank wouldn't explode, but it held enough gas to turn the truck's cab into an inferno. Was it enough? Would the fire spread? Steve twisted in the seat, wishing he could get at the plastic gas container.

Beside the truck, Tina watched his every move with appraising eyes. He popped the door open again.

"Pull the car over a few feet. When I open the door again, lower the back window."

Whether she understood his idea or not, Tina repositioned the car a couple of spaces over.

Steve spun the tank around so it faced away from him then surveyed the simple setup, wondering how he'd fallen into the role of hero.

No, I'm no hero. I just want control back. I got a taste of being the hunted and I don't like it.

Tina's Zippo worked on the first try and stayed lit. Before twisting the wheel on the tank, Steve took a deep breath, unsure how quickly propane could overcome him. The hiss of escaping gas whispered, telling him to move his ass.

He opened the door and jumped out, watching the flame inside as he carefully reclosed the door. Still lit.

Quick movement came from the shadows as he turned. Two of the creatures got between him and the car, the others came from the sides, weapons raised.

"Goddammit."

He was trapped with his back to the truck. No opening in the semicircle this time.

No!

Tina flipped the car into reverse and peeled away. Steve never considered she might just bolt.

The monsters were feet away now.

Can I get around them? Then what?

The car's horn sounded. Steve glanced at the far side of the truck with relief. She hadn't deserted him. The car was parked backward in the spot he'd chosen when he'd come in.

Steve saw her plan and dropped to the ground as Mace-hand swiped the air where his head had been.

Shit! They aren't fooling around.

He rolled under the truck, hammer and mace beating into the ground as he escaped.

Had it understood their plan, or was it just bored with playing?

He didn't think about it but kept moving until he came out the other side. There would be bruises and scrapes later... if he was lucky enough to have a later.

Jumping to his feet, Steve started for the car then spun back and grabbed the gas container from the back, smiling at the three-quarters full weight. In one motion he spun the cap off and threw it at the shack. It bounced off a wall in a splash of gasoline, hitting the wooden walk and spilling in an amber river coursing back towards the truck.

His pursuers skirted the pickup on either side, moving fast. Steve prayed his trick with the gas hadn't gotten him killed and sprinted for the still-opening back window.

"Son of a bitch!"

Not *still* opening. Half-open. The back windows didn't open more; he'd forgotten the child safety feature. Mace-hand took another swipe at him and he ducked in time to avoid getting his brains scrambled.

Tina flipped the driver's door open and scooted into the passenger seat. The car moved forward at idling speed while Steve dived inside, landing in Tina's lap. He pulled himself up using the steering wheel as Mace-hand drove its weapon into the open door, shattering the window.

Steve hit the gas, not bothering with the door.

Axe-hand thunked the cutting edge of its blade into the hood and was jerked forward as the car took off, the open door smacking it as they passed.

"They aren't disappearing this time," Steve said.

"Yeah, they're done fucking around."

The ones with hammer and sword had gotten in front of the car and Steve rammed them. They braced themselves and were pushed backward but didn't go flying as he'd hoped, digging in their heels and slowing the car to a crawl.

"Here they come," Tina said.

The rear-view mirror showed the other two approaching.

"If they stop us we're dead," Tina said.

Steve knew it. One could take their time dragging them out while the others held the car.

"No," Steve said, shifting into reverse and hitting the gas. He twisted the wheel right and cut around them in a tight arc, sending the car hurtling across the lot backwards.

"Shit!" Tina said. "They can move."

The four chased the car as one. With infinite space Steve could outdistance or outmaneuver them, but hemmed in by trees as they were...

"Trees!"

Steve stomped the brake with both feet, but the car's trunk end collided with one tree. The impact first pressed them into the seats then threw them forward.

Well, so much for what was in the trunk.

Across the lot the pickup was a raging blaze, growing as more propane pumped into the cab. Flames had reached outside now, lighting the trail of gasoline. Fingers of fire stretched up the wall of the building.

The four creatures approached, emitting thick smoke as though on fire themselves. Then the rightmost one burst into flames, the others following one after another.

And still they came, flaming weapons raised.

"I thought the fire would end it," he said.

"It will," Tina said in a quiet voice.

Steve shifted back to drive. Maybe he could get around them, keep ahead until...

The explosion was sudden, loud and devastating. A blinding flash became a widening fireball heading towards them. Steve threw himself sideways, pulling Tina down at the same moment. The dashboard provided some protection, but still the heat was incredible.

Pieces of truck rained around them, colliding with the car in sharp, metallic blows.

What had Tina said? Gas fumes? Had the truck exploded after all, or was it the hut itself?

An inhuman shriek of rage and pain blasted through their ears and minds, rising above all else before receding like the siren of a passing ambulance. The dying bellow of a monster that should have never existed.

As the metal rain ended, Tina moved to get up and Steve reluctantly did the same. They peeked over the edge of the dash through a spider-webbed windshield.

The building was a flaming ruin, its four shadows nowhere to be seen. What was left of the monster itself sagged inward, more like wax than wood and glass. The car rolled towards it at a steady pace and Steve threw it into park.

Around them trees burned, though the steady rain would soon control that. Tina slipped out of the car and moved to the front, leaning against the hood, mesmerized by the flames.

Steve was lost in his own thoughts.

If someone passing had seen that explosion they would already be here. He glanced behind at the exit which had reappeared. The smoke might bring people, but with the rain it might not.

No, he decided, *no one was coming.*

Steve stepped into the rain and made his way to Tina, resting against the hood next to her.

"It's beautiful," she said, watching the flames.

Steve said nothing, watching the girl.

"I have a… problem… with fire," she said. "It's why I was going to live with Uncle Ted… well, one reason."

She breathed in deep, holding it before letting it out in a shuddering release. Steve watched her breathe.

"Good thing I managed to keep my lighter," she added.

He nodded. "So. What next?"

"Next?" She shrugged. "I find a phone and call my parents, I guess."

"They'll never believe this."

"Nope."

"You could come with me," he said.

She looked at him with a hint of wariness—only a hint though. They had, after all, been through some fucked-up shit together. Steve leaned farther back, placing an arm on the hood behind her but not touching.

Not yet.

"You know what?" he said. "You told your secret, I should tell mine."

Tina glanced back at the trunk then started leaning forward, moving away. Steve snaked one hand out and placed it on her opposite shoulder.

"See, I'm driving cross-country to my new home," he said. "I could have flown with my family, but I wanted some time alone. Like my yearly hunting trips."

Tina didn't move, glancing towards his hand. He started to caress her shoulder.

"Hunting trips," she repeated.

"Yep," he agreed. "Oh, not animals. No. See, I like the company of girls. Like yourself. Naughty girls."

The car had enough damage that he could get pulled over. He would say something fell off a truck and hit him, tell them he was headed for the next garage. Yeah, that could work.

Tina would be in the trunk by then.

A grin, one recognizable to his victims, flashed across Steve's face. "You can be my... what did you call it? Secret shame?"

Tina moved forward but Steve grabbed one wrist and pulled her to him. He could smell her fear *and* his own excitement.

"Tina..." he began with a laugh.

Then pain screamed into his head like a bullet and he pitched forward, grasping at Tina and falling face up at her feet. Rain beat against his open eyes as he struggled to understand. The muscles in his legs refused to obey. His vision wavered.

What the hell?

Two Tinas stood in front of him.

His vision focussed.

Not two Tinas. Two girls for sure, but separate ones.

The one on the right had zip ties around her wrists and ankles. The duct tape was gone from her mouth though, and in her hands was the hammer from his toolbox.

"Michelle."

Memories flooded back of the two days since he'd picked her up. She was a naughty girl too, he could see that right away.

The trunk must have popped when they hit the trees.

"Bastard," Michelle spat.

Tina looked from her to Steve and back again, understanding in her eyes. "Finish him."

Michelle raised the hammer above her head and brought it down. As it crashed into his skull, Steve smiled.

He'd been right about both of them.

About the Author

John Haas is a Canadian author, born and raised in Montreal before moving to Calgary where he lived for twelve wonderful years. Now he lives in the nation's capital of Ottawa, but misses those Rocky Mountains in the distance. He lives with his two wonderful sons who continue to give him lots of motivation, support and time to write.

John has been writing for most of his life but only became serious about being published in the last decade or so. In that time he has had more than twenty short stories published in various excellent publications, including Writers of the Future volume 35. He has seen his first three books, a humorous fantasy trilogy beginning with The Reluctant Barbarian, published by Renaissance Press. Cults of Death and Madness kicks off the next trilogy, a Lovecraftian-inspired series, published by Wordfire Press.

For more information and a chance to join the newsletter, check out John's website at: https://johnhaas.ca/

THE YAKSHI OF ASTHIKAAVU

BY NEETHU KRISHNAN

Benny arrives a mess of run-on sentences and open wounds, puncturing the silence in the car with his desperate slapping of bloodied palms on the window by my side, stippling the clean glass with ruby handprints and causing Arjun, seated to my left, to heave a whistling sigh of relief. Despite there being an empty seat next to the driver, who only cursorily glances at the new joiner before retraining his intense black eyes at the shadow-gathering path ahead, Benny, much to my unease, chooses to cram himself beside me as soon as I unlock the door.

"Arjun! We made it, man! Scaled *Asthi mala*!" Benny trills, proffering a grimy, rust-wafting hand to Arjun over me, who clasps it limply with his gloved hand for a beat, the right of his moustached upper lip twitching into a wry smile.

Sickeningly averse to blood, I recoil, pressing myself as far back as the velvet-cushioned seat allows.

"I dressed poorly for this trip, man!" Benny continues, gesturing to the spectrum of cuts, scratches and nasty gashes on him, sucking on the swollen slit on his lower lip as he speaks, still addressing Arjun, bypassing me, as if I were an inanimate accessory to the seat.

"And the bones?!" he exclaims, shivering. "Whoever knew there'd be so many bones. The hill is practically more bone than ground!"

"That's why it's called *Asthi mala*: the hill of bones," Arjun and I reply at once, the double voice of admonishment causing Benny to close his mouth for a beat and blink slowly, to register me for the first time. Bemusement and confusion crease his wide forehead as he scans me briefly before letting his mouth run again.

"Hi, I'm Benny. The drone guy," he chirps, offering his blood-slicked hand for me to shake, which I decline, nose scrunched. He doesn't seem to mind.

"Tara," I say with a perfunctory smile.

"Hello, Tara!" he greets, his tall, white pills of teeth on display. "My drones procured the leaf samples for Arjun, who, after analysis confirmed they contained insane amounts of gold nanoparticles, which only proves the stories about this place aren't mythical yarns but facts. *Asthikaavu* is definitely a gold mine, or ginormous treasure chest, or both," he explains, his small eyes widening with childlike wonderment. Arjun sucks at his teeth, presumably irritated at Benny's blabbering of purported insider intel.

"What about you, Tara? What's your claim to *Asthikaavu*?" he asks, registering none of Arjun's bitterness—his tone earnest, unlike the latter, who'd questioned me pitifully, like I was a lost child strayed into the wrong ride.

"Its map," I say, disinclined to elaborate.

Benny smiles toothily, clapping his blood-caked palms with approval.

"That's incredibly impressive! How in the world did you manage to score a map when no one who enters *Asthikaavu* allegedly ever returns?" He shakes his head with amazed disbelief.

Before I can answer, the driver, who's remained mute all this while, raps his bony, burnt umber knuckles on the steering wheel, commanding attention. Arjun holds out a leather-gloved hand to shush us, leaning forward, face tense.

"It's time," the driver says, addressing us through the rearview mirror, his unsmiling eyes piercing. "Anyone who wants to leave, should. For once I deposit you at the thorny arch, the only entrance to *Asthikaavu*, there's no turning back. Once you enter the *kaavu*, the arch sews impenetrably shut behind you. Saudamini decides your fate thereafter," he cautions, his onyx eyes locking with mine in the mirror.

"Saudamini?" Benny interrupts, incomprehension scrunching his face, as if the rest of the driver's warning was commonplace knowledge, nothing of concern.

"*Asthikaavu* belongs to Saudamini, the *yakshi* who resides in the *kaavu*, the sacred grove. One of the most powerful of magical entities. Shape-shifter. Ruthless protector and guardian of what's hers. She allows not even a grain of sand to leave the perimeter of her abode, so, any human entering her *kaavu* offers themselves up to her will and mercy, never to return to the outside world again. Though *Asthikaavu* translates to 'the sacred grove of bones', you'll find not a single splinter of bone in there, such is Saudamini's elemental power. A funereal pyre might spare you some bones and teeth, but at the hands of Saudamini, your erasure is absolute, without even a refuse of bones."

"What's your name, driver *cheta*?" Benny interrupts again, addressing him as elder brother in Malayalam, oblivious to the fact that he's the youngest looking of us all.

"Bhairava," he replies, the deep brown of his angular face clouding with impatience.

"Bhairava *cheta*, are you suggesting Saudamini's real? And that she's a *yakshi*—a vampire-witch, who takes the form of a voluptuous, irresistibly beautiful woman when approaching handsome men such as myself on deserted paths come nightfall, turning into an ugly, abhorrent hag with red eyes, vampire teeth and matted hair when using the men for her pleasure, sucking them dry of their blood and virility, and leaving the impotent, old husks of them for dead?" Benny asks, his curious face impenetrable, making it hard to gauge if he's sarcastic or serious.

Bhairava sharply exhales through his long nose, jaw clenching.

"Saudamini's probably one of the many, very clever tricks, this land has up its sleeves to keep outsiders like us from nosing or interfering with the treasures they're very much invested in keeping for themselves. Just like the rest of the barely plausible fables about the *kaavu* Bhairava's feeding us. Keeps the weaklings away," Arjun answers instead of the taxi driver, a knowing smirk ruining the handsomeness of his face. Benny nods agreement.

Shaking his head, Bhairava keys the Ambassador into motion, the pyramid of his bat-black moustache softening to a plateau as his bow-shaped lips ease into a resigned smile.

The rickety, dicey ride is uneventful save for Benny's incessant rambles, until Bhairava slams hard on the brakes.

The woman is a bewildering vision. Draped in a scarlet saree with gold-foil borders—an attire more South-Indian wedding guest or a Raja Ravi Varma painting subject than stranded hiker in a treacherous forest. Her oval face heavily made-up and the braided rope of her oil-black hair adorned with jasmine blossoms, she sticks out, predatory bright and flashy, against the sepulchral green foliage, the car's amber headlights only accentuating her otherworldly edge.

Arjun and Benny stiffen beside me, breaths hitched in enchantment instead of alarm. Nobody but Bhairava is supposed to be able to navigate the maze-like forest from *Asthi mala* to the *kaavu*, or so it's believed in the cult-like circles of treasure hunters and paranormal investigators, and yet here was a mysterious woman who'd somehow made it ahead of Bhairava, waving breezily at us, thin, gold bracelets chiming, as if expecting us.

Her scent, a heady, biting jasmine with an off-putting metallic un-dertone, greets us before she does. Sensing the obliviousness of Bhaira-va who she settles in next to, she twists around to face us.

"Mohini," she says, her shapely, plump lips, painted a glossy blood-red, parting into a seductive smile, her kohl-lined eyes lingering on the tongue-tied men, flitting to my suspicious ones only briefly as we exchange introductions.

A disturbing trance descends over the men on my either side: Ar-jun's cat-grey eyes tracing Mohini's every move like he's hypnotised, a besotted smile smouldering his aesthetically pleasing face, and Benny, seemingly having lost his voice, staring slack-jawed at her. Neither the sceptical and apathetic Arjun nor the ever-inquisitive Benny demands to know any more details about this random stranger, and I'm so unsettled by her dark and deceitful aura, I want nothing to do with her.

Catching my scrutinising gaze in the mirror, Mohini winks at me, the crescent of her close-mouthed smile shining with an edge of dislike, before addressing an entranced Benny.

"Oh, Benny! *Asthi mala* did you in good, didn't it?" she asks, tutting at his bloody lacerations. "Here, drink this," she commands, producing from seemingly nowhere—likely a sleight of hand, drawing from a hid-den pouch at the waist of her saree—a palm-sized bottle of what looks to be water. A grateful Benny downs it without caution or question, at the last gulp of which, he gasps in shock, his hypnotic haze fleetingly dulled.

The wounds and the blood—every last speck of it—seem to have disappeared, leaving no trace; his hairy, brown skin reinstated to un-scratched perfection.

Black magic, I think, contempt rising in my chest.

Mohini, biting her lower lip with a canine sharp and shapely as a jasmine bud, looks thrilled as a gullible Benny and a sceptical Arjun furrow their eyebrows in confused disbelief.

"You're not, by any chance, a *yakshi* about to turn a ghastly hag and feast on my blood, are you?" Benny asks, finally retrieving his voice, his eyes alert, wide. "Mohini and Saudamini sound vaguely similar." He trails off, fear lacing his voice.

She tosses her head back, laughs a musical laugh.

"Why can't I be beautiful," she says, fanning her upper torso, "when I suck your blood? Do ugly and outcast hold the monopoly to dark deeds? Are beauty and evil mutually exclusive? Incompatible?"

She lifts a thickly filled-in, perfectly arched brow, her dancing obsidian eyes lazing above Benny's head, as if luxuriating in the profundity of her own words. Jhumkas swinging, she shakes her head, snapping herself out of the indulgence.

"I'm a sorceress, a witch of mid-level skills, if you will; not the *yakshi* kind, though." She laughs. "Most definitely not the Saudamini type you all so seem to fear. She's most likely powerless anyway, an exaggeration of mythic proportions."

The men relax a little, relieved. Mohini turns away suddenly, as if bored or exhausted of answering Benny's silly questions, directing her keen attention to Bhairava instead, who refuses to cast so much as a sideways glance at her.

"There's a stone *pratishtha*, a consecration, of Saudamini in the *kaavu*, isn't there?" she asks, twisting the tail of her thick braid around a long-nailed, scarlet index finger.

Bhairava nods and before Mohini can say anything at all, he halts the vehicle with an impatient screech.

"*Asthikaavu*," he declares morosely, flicking his chin to the right, long fingers drumming against the steering wheel.

Arjun and Benny freeze, trapping me in, hesitating to budge or open the door.

"You guys should leave if you aren't up to it. I'm sure Bhairava can drive you back," I offer, sensing trepidation hardening their faces.

"Of course not!" Mohini says, leaning in suggestively from Arjun's side of the window. "They'll come," she rasps, her tone more command than suggestion, that curiously has the effect of reanimating the two men from their fearful stupor. They clamber out the vehicle eagerly and follow Mohini, who saunters in with familiar ease like she belongs, into the brambled, narrow entrance of the *Asthikaavu* in a daze.

The blinking headlights of the car, like yellow reptilian eyes, are the last things I see of the outside before the vegetation breaks position, coils and writhes and intertwines into each other like thorny, stealthy snakes, closing the mouth of *Asthikaavu*, sealing the entrants into its expectant, hungry gullet.

Benny's pained screech in the distance snaps my rapture. Turning around, I find the three under a bay leaf tree; him scrambling to get up from the forest floor and failing, and Mohini and Arjun standing by, watching, the former's permanent smugness curiously replaced by a trace of fear. As I approach Benny, the cause of Mohini's sudden shift in spirits makes itself apparent. Not only have Benny's wounds reopened, but the gashes also seem to have resumed active bleeding, even the tiniest cuts beading a nauseating, betel juice red.

"Mohini's magical liquid wasn't that powerful after all; couldn't even survive the threshold of *Asthikaavu*," I comment, fully aware of her seething gaze on my back as I kneel before a whimpering Benny to inspect his sprained ankle.

She stalks off deeper into the *kaavu*, the tinny chime of her belled anklets grating against the unceasing chorus of cicadas. A spellbound Arjun, compelled to follow, tails the wilting jasmine cloud at her every step.

"Help me up, will you?" Benny moans, noticing me tracking the two as they disappear into the *kaavu*'s jungle-green innards, instead of offering to help his rapidly swelling ankle.

I grimace, hesitating. Now that he's actively bleeding, much more than before, I haven't the slightest inclination to nurse the bloody mess of him; but I don't want to abandon him either, for the ground stirs beneath us—the moist, dark earth, like a sea of bony fingers come to life, twitching and flexing, preparing to close its grasp on whatever's above. Benny, thankfully, too preoccupied with examining his elephantine foot, barely notices the anomalous, animating soil under him. I keen my ears to the sounds around me, wanting to help move him elsewhere. I hear cicadas, whispering leaves and tinkling water. Racing to the closest stream of the last, I spot a palm-wide surge of water just a couple sky-wrapping trees away.

I flick but a few drops of the water on Benny, cupped in a fallen teak leaf as big as my upper torso, and not only do his wounds disappear without trace like before, but his ankles deflate back to normalcy as well. Dumbfounded and relieved, he looks at me for explanation. I shrug my petite shoulders in answer.

Mohini and Arjun, predictably, are nowhere to be found as we continue our foray deeper into the forest, a healed Benny tripping repeatedly on the sharp crests of tree roots that jut out of the ground like human vertebrae, cursing their bizarre, spine-like protrusions each time he barely misses losing teeth in face-plants.

"Arjun's likely matching the leaves with their trees. Prospecting smartly," Benny says, his tone a dejected child's for being left behind. "He said the proportion of gold excreted and sequestered in our leaf samples was about five hundred times greater than found over known, high-grade ores. Once we clear this impossible-to-navigate mess of trees, start mining and claim this place as ours, there's no cap to the wealth and power we'll wield." He sighs wistfully before continuing, his words already skewering my insides with disgust.

"Arjun's also convinced this acreage is pitted with ancient treasures, the precious-metal-and-gem kind, their monetary value exponentiated multifold by their antiquity and possible historical importance across timelines. Just imagine the mind-boggling amounts of wealth we're walking on right now!" he exclaims, shaking his gobsmacked head at the black loam as if he can see through it ledges of sparkling gold and jewels just waiting to be bagged by Arjun and him. I look around, imagining nothing, only seeing.

I see magnificent columns of trees predating recorded human history, their mammoth, human-uncorrupted trunks standing tall and proud as sentries, their crowns of black-bled green barely sparing any strip of sky unoccupied, at the hem of whose skirts gather pregnant, lightning-illumined clouds, the moody, inky umbrella of them making the brooding *kaavu* look like the permanent home of monsoons. I see the lively, green moss velveting the humus-thick earth underfoot, overlaid with the canary yellow and capillary red fibrous fungi, their mycelia thick as sacred threads, carpeting the forest floor with their vibrant, crawling webs. I see the cluster of *yakshippalas*, the devil's trees, their bean-like fruits swaying in the charged breeze like a *yakshi*'s long, open tresses; smell the intoxicating scent of their greenish-white flowers perfuming the air heavy, the spicy-sweet richness of it only making me crave longer, deeper breathfuls; notice the sizeable gap between two trees that speaks to me, that asks to be filled.

I acquiesce gladly.

In the luminous clearing a few footsteps away, I find Mohini where I'd suspected her to be.

She traces circles around the sprawling banyan tree—the canopy of which houses the moss-matted, thigh-high idol of the *yakshi*, Saudamini—pouring some kind of oil along her path, feverishly chanting what I guess are tantric mantras. So engrossed is she in her focused incantations that she doesn't notice me walking right past her into the circle, inspecting her curious black-magic rituals.

A bunch of red hibiscuses are placed atop the fanned head of the two-hooded snake above the vermilion- and turmeric-smeared figure of the voluptuous Saudamini, and a couple more wilted flowers lay at her feet, one of which is poised above her mount, a crocodile with horns above its eyes. Instinctively, I look to the gigantic pond next to the tree, its crystal-clear, ultraviolet water magnetic and still, missing spotting at first glance the man lying prone on its bank. Roving the breathtaking width of the mystical-looking pond, I finally spot him—Arjun—shirtless, smeared with ash and garlanded with a rosary of tiny skulls and what appear to be jasmine-tipped needles sticking out from his neck. I start towards him in a hurry, only to be stopped by an infuriating, sharp tug at the collar of my flannel shirt from behind.

"He's unconscious, not dead. Makes the sacrifice so much easier," Mohini explains. "And it's best you keep shut and hunker in a corner until I'm done," she hisses, gliding to my front, her round eyes flinting with contempt when she sees I'm unfazed.

"And what exactly are you doing?" I enquire, hands folded at my chest.

Mohini closes her winged eyes, evidently running out of patience, loosens her neck and massages her pulsing temple with vermilion-stained fingers. Exhaling sharply through her mouth, she opens her eyes slowly, the copious whites widening around her raven-black pupils as she stares fixedly at me. I raise my eyebrows, cocking my head with an amused smile. Her face falls, clouding suddenly with fear and incomprehension. Shaken, she begins to speak, big, round eyes shrinking, skittering away from my drilling gaze.

"While I'm here for the treasures as much as anyone else," she says, gesturing in my direction and the sorry silhouette of Arjun's, "I also want more. I want to be a *yakshi*... Saudamini, to be precise." Her voice is dreamy. "There's an irrefutably strong presence permeating this *kaavu*. I can feel it in my bones, a sentient energy impossible to be contained in a pithy human body, a force, unlike any I've ever encountered before, and being a *durmantravadini*, a black-magic sorceress for most of my life, I've channelled many a dark forces previously, and none have ever come close to this *kaavu*'s volatile, open energy. If Saudamini's consecrated, seated securely in the stone idol, which I'm positive she is, she shouldn't be able to ripple her energy outside her safe containment; it makes no sense," she continues, knitting her brows together.

"Anyway, I'll sacrifice Arjun to please her, bathe her with fresh human blood and ask she channel herself into me." She's matter-of-fact, talking more to herself than to an unresponsive me, floating urgently towards Arjun, as if suddenly remembering she's out of time.

"What would you do with her transferred energy, anyway?" I ask, ignoring the gory part about the bloodbath.

Mohini, bent over Arjun, scythe in hand, snorts.

"How do you not see the obvious?" she scoffs, continuing without waiting for an answer. "I'll be powerful, feared, revered. As a *durmantravadini*, I've had my fair share of people keeping their distance, who know not to offend or mess with the shady woman with evil forces at her beck and call. I don't want that. I want more. An abode of my own spanning hectares. Notoriety that strikes fear in people's hearts. Inexhaustible wealth. Forever youthful and unblemished, maddening beauty. The freedom to do whatever I please with the men I lure, as many as I fancy into my honey trap, without judgement or consequences, and after, thrill in the hot slick of human blood on my palms." She smiles. "The blood of sacrificial animals doesn't satiate me anymore," she adds, pleased to find me stepping back and away, a disgusted scowl on my face as she hacks Arjun's neck with the scythe.

"If I were you, I wouldn't do that," I choke, nauseated by the blood spurting and pooling at her feet.

She laughs her throaty laugh I've grown to despise, not noticing the earth come to life behind her as she turns to cone a teak leaf the size of her to catch Arjun's fountain of blood.

The vivid mat of fungi quivering rapaciously mummifies him in its brilliant, stringy webs in a flash, and in the mere seconds it takes for Mohini to turn around, the ground yawns open, swallowing the parcelled Arjun into its depths, closing its satiated mouth into a smooth, innocent seal.

I'm glad for the quick, immaculate clean-up; a horrified Mohini, not so much.

Dropping the now-useless vessel of leaf, she stumbles back in horror, her round eyes more whites than charcoal pupils, tripping promptly on a spine of roots, falling on her back as she looks at me, face pockmarked with questions I have no inclination to entertain.

"What... what's happening? Where's Arjun?" she stutters, her voice splintering into a squeak. "And where's Benny?" She suddenly remembers him, her eyes flashing around me, morbid fear dilating them, as if expecting him to materialise from behind me any moment now.

I flick my chin to the slender *yakshippala*—snug between its two towering, ageless neighbours, a few feet away from a trembling Mohini—smiling approvingly as Benny claps two whorled-leaf branches together, releasing a generous shower of star-shaped blossoms to the forest floor. Quaking like a wind-whipped leaf, I see her following my gaze, seeing nothing, obviously not comprehending the elegant symmetry of alchemy.

A tree for a bough of plucked leaves. A snack for the earth—that fortuitously has acquired a taste for the delicacy of humans, blood, flesh, bones and all—that you planned to shave bald, eviscerate.

"What?" Mohini screeches, desperation and fear getting the better of her, the shrillness of her voice interrupting my pleasant ruminations.

Annoyed, I prise my eyes away from the *yakshippala*, the newest addition to *Asthikaavu*, and turn to face Mohini.

It's too late.

To ask her why the *yakshis* in the human collective of stories are all obscenely beautiful, seductive women lusting after men or bloodthirsty or both, easily reduced to powerless, benign demigods, immobilised in sculpted stone for eternities with a few chants and spells. To tell her a *yakshi*—custodian of treasures hidden in earth and roots of trees—averse to blood though she be, imbued with the elemental ferocity of forked lightnings, *Saudamini*, she knows to unfailingly, ruthlessly guard what's hers; even if it requires she ferry the avaricious, insatiable humans to her *kaavu* herself, to protect what she's obligated to most: the above-ground treasures that sprout and flower and turban themselves with dusky storm clouds.

It is too late for questions or explanations, for behemoth jaws, deathly still, lie open in wait behind a sweat-beaded Mohini immobilised on the ground, who has suddenly stilled as if sensing at her back the cavernous mouth poised to snap shut, swallow her whole. Her burning gaze on me alternates between pleading and accusatory as I consider the gargantuan horned-crocodile's yellow eyes seeking approval from mine. Not wanting to stretch thin Bhairava's patience any longer, I nod, granting permission.

About the Author

Neethu Krishnan is a writer based in Mumbai, India. She holds an MA in English and an M.Sc. in Microbiology, and writes between genres at the moment. Her work has appeared in *The Spectacle, Bacopa Literary Review, The Polaris Trilogy, Fu Review, Saltbush Review,* and elsewhere. She is a 2022 Best of the Net poetry nominee, and recipient of the Creative Nonfiction Award in *Bacopa Literary Review*'s 2022 contest. You can find her @neethu.krishnan_ on Instagram or on facebook.co m/neethu.krishnan.944

TO CATCH A BANNIK

BY KOJI A. DAE

Silvena ducks out of the party when most of the men are drunk. She doesn't bother with slippers since the bathhouse is only a hundred hops away on her frozen toes. She fumbles with the wooden latch and eases herself into the room. It's still warm from the day's wood. She inhales and catches the scent of wet dog beneath the mint and birch.

Her eyes go wide and she counts the days on her fingers. The third day of the week—when the bathhouse is reserved for the Bannik's family.

She grits her teeth. It's just a story. But then, she's here for the other half of that story, and if she believes the Bannik can tell her about her future husband, she should also believe he can melt her flesh and turn her into a spirit.

It's too late to go back.

She makes her way to the center of the small room. Her eyes refuse to adjust to the dark, and all she can make out are the embers glowing in the furnace. Her shaking fingers grip her long dress, pull it into a bunch, grabbing the shift beneath it. She closes her useless eyes and lifts.

The lace of the garment brushes her toes, the top of her feet, her ankles. She pauses, swallows, and reveals the plump curve of her calf.

The hand shoots out and wraps around her foot almost instantly. She tries to keep from squealing and concentrates on the features of the hand. It's hairy: her husband will be rich. It's wet: he'll favor the drink.

She lets out a sob. Not that her fate is poor. Most men drink and few are rich. But the fear is finally seeping into her. She's alone in the bathhouse, the Bannik is real, and he has her in his grasp.

A low crackle breaks the silence. It could be the fire settling or it could be the Bannik's laugh.

"I'm sorry," Silvena whispers. "I didn't mean to disturb you."

In answer, she feels a warm wetness push between her toes. Mud? Moss? The slow warmth as it runs over her flesh is almost pleasant. The Bannik's beard? She finally realizes it is his tongue, slowly licking the dirt from her feet.

She squeaks and jumps away, fleeing the bathhouse.

A year and a half later, Silvena dances until her feet ache, laughs as her husband smears honey on her face, and kisses him eagerly whenever their friends and family call for bitterness. He's been drinking since the first cock crowed, and by the time he takes her to the bathhouse, he smells more of rakia than man.

A cheer sounds from the field while Ivan struggles with the lock. He laughs.

"They've noticed we're gone," she says with a lopsided grin.

"They know what I'm about to do to you." He swings her into his arms and forces the door open. There's a cracking of wood as he slams it shut with his still-booted foot.

The Bannik won't like that, is the last thing she thinks before Ivan's mouth is on her flesh and his hands are tearing away her carefully embroidered dress. He pinches too eagerly at her breasts, but her loins respond to his touch, ready for the final act of the day.

It's pressing and stretching and painful with the slightest promise of future pleasure. But before she can relax into his thrusting and open for him, he finishes and falls asleep on the cedar bench, snoring so loud he shakes her body. She wriggles away from his embrace and stokes the fire.

"You're in for pain." The high-pitched voice comes from behind the stove.

She reaches for a towel, suddenly aware of her nakedness. But there are no squares of cloth on the shelf. She squats and crosses her arms in front of her breasts.

"What do you mean?" She speaks into the stove, not directly to the tiny man behind it.

A woosh of steam nearly knocks her over.

"He's large and crude. You think you hurt because it's your first time? No." Another cackle, closer to her sleeping husband. "You hurt because he's a brute."

"He's a good man."

The steam flows over the bench, and she can almost make out the shape of the Bannik, a skinny, old man whose bushy hair is bigger than his body and whose beard reaches his toes. "No blood?"

"I was pure," she says defiantly.

Another cackle. "I am just looking for my tribute, girl."

"Isn't my sweat enough?" she asks. Getting on the bad side of the Bannik could ruin her life and curse her family for generations.

The steam loses its shape and, soft and warm, rushes to her face. "Your tears?"

She hadn't realized she had cried. She wipes the moisture away. "Take what you want."

Another cackle. "You say that to all the men." A sizzle sounds sharp in the small room. "But it doesn't have to be that way."

"Fuck!" Ivan jerks awake, swatting at his shoulder. "What did you do?"

Silvena watches the red burn swell on her husband's flesh and helps him from the bathhouse.

The baby is coming, and Silvena can barely waddle to the bathhouse. She squats to the ground during each contraction, her body threatening to explode blood and fluid on the manicured lawn. She squeezes her thighs together, begging her body, and baby, to wait. She needs to make it to the warm security of the bathhouse, and the Bannik needs his tribute if he's to bless the child.

Her mother and aunt want her to stay in the house. They'll bring warm water in. She should birth in bed, like a respectable woman, not in the darkness of the bathhouse like a common villager. But there's no convincing her body, which inches toward the wooden building. They follow behind, worrying around her, but she barely hears or feels them. She needs to make it to the bathhouse.

A blast of humid air hits her as the door squeaks open. She chokes, and her stomach relaxes as she sinks onto a woven towel already laid out on the bench.

She closes her eyes. Her stomach is stretching, but there's no pain.

Knocks ring on wood. "Silvena! Let us in!"

The voices are panicked and familiar, but they sound so far away. The steam coats her. Thin fingers form, massaging the back of her neck and shoulders.

She opens eyes to find the wrinkled face of the Bannik close to hers. His teeth are stained and crooked, but his breath smells of mint and birch. She inhales.

"Just relax, girl," he whispers in his high-pitched voice. "I've got you."

The pounding at the door continues. So does the stretching of her abdomen. Pressure builds in her. The steam grows thicker to meet the strength of her uterus. Hotter. Hotter.

"Breathe," the Bannik commands.

His whisper slides over her sweat. When did she get naked? His encouragement caresses her hard nipples, down the dark line of hair at her belly, as if he's telling her womb to breathe. To open and exhale.

She inhales the wet-dog scent of his beard, which falls around her ears as he hunches over her.

"Breathe."

The pressure becomes stretching. Her skin puckers, tightening around her, and a chill shoots from her fingertips to her toes. She resists the rolling sensation threatening to consume her.

"Breathe," he hisses.

When she follows the Bannik's command, the tightening melts like spun sugar at the fair and turns to unexplainable pleasure. She sinks into it, a foreign moan escaping her throat. Her body shakes and fizzles into nothing edged in bliss.

Her baby slides on blood and sweat into the waiting arms of the Bannik. Her head—no longer held by him—drops to the bench.

"I'm disappearing," she murmurs.

The Bannik coos at the baby, then sets him in her arms.

"What was that?" she pants, tingling waves continuing to rush from her toes to scalp.

"That—" The old man bends to the bench and begins lapping up the mess of her birth. "—was an orgasm."

She holds her baby to her breast, winces, and sighs as he suckles.

The door to the bathhouse bursts open, and Silvena's mother and aunt stumble in, horrified by the bloody child in her arms. But all Silvena can think as she floats on a cloud of exhausted pleasure is, *I want more.*

Silvena bathes her child in the house like a modern woman should. But in the evening, she gives the baby to her mother and sneaks to the bathhouse. She peels her clothes from her skin, folds them, and sets them on the shelf.

She stokes the fire hotter than most men can stand, then splashes a cold ladle of water over the stones. Steam fills the room. It fills her lungs, and she can barely make it to the bench before she's inhaling the Bannik, letting him stroke her insides until they come to life. After the squeeze of pleasure and release of orgasm, he stays as droplets, caressing her skin.

"This should be your life," the Bannik tells her. He's a disembodied voice these days. He knows his old-man form disgusts her. When he's only spirit and steam, she allows him access to all of her. When he's solid, she thinks about the stories of the Bannik splitting women alive and turning them to steam.

"This is my life," she murmurs.

He takes advantage of her open mouth to caress her tongue, and she moans, opening her lips wider. She can feel his desire pressing on her. He toys at taking solid form, just enough that she can feel lips and hands in his mist. The weight of him tickles, and she laughs as if drunk.

"Your husband doesn't give this to you."

She thinks about Ivan's heavy body over her in bed—the way he thrusts and chases his own pleasure, his eyes glossed over with rakia. She has never orgasmed beneath him.

She sighs as the Bannik runs down her thighs in thick droplets. "He's not a bad husband. He gave me a child. Keeps us clothed and fed. What more could I ask of a man?"

The Bannik solidifies, stroking her with either his finger or his tongue. She can never tell, because all of him is soft and wet. And because she's afraid to look.

She lets him bring her to the edge of ecstasy and shudders, giving him the thick milk of her orgasm as offering.

The child grows. Silvena ages. Ivan drinks more.

Ivan's drunken stench seeps from his pores, dripping carelessly onto her—marking her. His sloppy kisses and forceful tongue make her gag. After he finishes and passes out, she wipes away his seed and tiptoes to the bathhouse to scrub her skin.

The Bannik holds her in his warmth. She's shaking, even though she doesn't know it.

He waits for her to ask for his touch. He waits for her to beg, tears stinging her eyes.

"Fill me, Bannik," she whispers. "I want your softness."

He sighs over her exposed neck, licks the curves of her breasts, and lays her back on the wooden bench. First, he enters her lungs, expanding her breath, calming her. Then he flowers her cunt, watching it bloom beneath his heat. He enters her slowly, solidifying only as much as he needs to separate her folds.

The rolling orgasms take her away from her loneliness and, when he stops, she's back in her body.

"Thank you," she whispers to the steam. Her body feels as if it might melt and, not for the first time, she wonders how it would feel to be like the Bannik, able to pass between solid and steam.

"You're unhappy," he hisses.

"Mmm. Not at this moment."

He stops licking at the sweat rolling over her body, and the stillness almost makes her open her eyes.

"You should come tomorrow."

She holds her fingers in front of her closed eyes and goes through the actions of counting the days, even though she already knows. "Tomorrow is third day." She can come to the Bannik most days, but she will not trust him on his sacred day, when the bathhouse is supposed to smoke low and be left undisturbed.

The Bannik whisks away from her, leaving her skin chilled and puckered. "Your husband cheats on you."

She stiffens, a hard coldness taking over her chest. "Who am I to seek fidelity?"

"I hear him talk about the girl. He gives her the softness and tenderness you seek. He plans to give her a child."

She shudders. "He wouldn't."

He would.

Her mother brings the news in the early morning, encouraging Silvena to drink bitter coffee for strength.

She holds the cup, smelling the earth in the black liquid. She remembers Ivan's body the night before. All the nights she lay with him—his rough thrusting and the weight of him crushing her.

The cup falls from her shaking fingers, and the coffee stains the carpet as she runs to the bathhouse. It's third day. The fire is low and a dim smoke fills the small room. She pushes into it. Restrictions be damned, and curses too.

Her tears flow freely as she calls, "Bannik!"

A pile of soot stirs below the oven, and the Bannik lazily extracts himself from the grime. The building isn't hot enough to allow him to billow, so he keeps his withered body in the shadowy corner. "Come back at night."

His voice is weak—dry—but it's the first time he's sent Silvena away, and the force of his rejection makes her cower. She shakes, and he blows on the coals, coaxing the fire to heat him.

"Why are you here?" he growls.

"I need you," she whispers.

"Why?"

She bites her lip until she tastes metal, then spits on the bench, trying to coax the Bannik out with an offering. "I need to stop thinking."

He moves to the edge of the shadow and sticks out a bony arm to scoop up the blood and spit.

Silvena takes a ragged breath and looks away.

"Stoke the fire."

She does as commanded, not looking at the shell of a being in the corner. As the fire warms the room, the Bannik swells. The next time he speaks, his voice is lower and smoother. "Third day is for me to rest."

She continues working the small billows, aching for him to take his true form.

"My true form? This is me, girl." He stands and hobbles from the corner. His withered frame barely reaches her knees.

Silvena squats before him, eyeing his shape with curiosity. She reaches out and strokes his scraggly beard. It's rough and brittle beneath her fingers. She snatches her hand away.

He grabs her hand and holds it to his wrinkled chest. "Do you want to know who it is?"

Her eyes fill with fresh tears. The room is so hot, if they spill, they may turn to steam. The Bannik expands beneath her hand. He swells until he's taller than her, pulling her to standing as he continues to grow.

"He talks about her. Brags. Men tell all their secrets in my house. Do you wish to drink them from my lips?"

His lips are plump. Young. His face is smooth. He's still rough, but handsome.

"No."

"Then what do you wish to drink? You're thirsty." He touches her forearm. "Dry."

She moans beneath the feather-brush of his fingertips.

"Say it."

She closes her eyes and forgets his withered body. Forgets the Bannik as an old man. Ivan above her, breath sweet with alcohol. Rough and heavy. She lets it all go and becomes light at the point of contact. "You."

He doesn't turn to mist. Instead, he scoops her up and places her on the bench. His too-solid hands lift her skirt around her full hips. His fists grip the fabric and tear until her bodice opens from navel to collar. His strength makes her shudder.

"I'm not always so soft," he says. But his breath feels like steam on her cheek. A soft slap of warmth. She arches her neck to offer her lips.

His mouth is full, his tongue pulsing against hers. She is tiny beneath him, and he will split her if he doesn't evaporate. His flesh, if it can be called so, is hot and slick. His belly slides over hers, and he enters her. Slowly. Separating. She burns—whether from the stretching or the heat of him, she can't tell.

The heat puts everything from her mind. She is only body. She is only here.

He continues to press into her, deeper, separating her spirit from body like a filet from bone.

"Yes," she moans in a voice her husband has never heard or imagined coming from her delicate throat.

The hardness of him pierces her belly, and the warmth of her blood flows over her thighs. Still, he presses.

Her moan becomes a scream. She's losing herself, and she isn't sure if it's pleasure or pain she's surrendering to. She isn't sure it matters.

The Bannik's slow, upward journey pauses. He retreats, only to return more swiftly, awakening a life in her she has never felt while bringing her to the edge of death.

She is ragged. And clenching. Against him. With him.

"Shall I stop?" he growls in her ear. His voice is moist, penetrating her eardrum, echoing in her brain.

"No," she breathes. The "o" elongates into a gasp, a hiss. She is tearing bone from bone, clinging with only sinew.

He thrusts deeper. Her blood boils with his heat. Her sweat steams. He is movement and warmth and she is melting. More than melting. Dissipating.

She lets out a final gasp and they both explode into droplets of steam that fill the bathhouse with hot pressure, threatening to collapse the entire building.

But the Bannik finds control. He cools himself. Returns to flesh. Silvena surrounds him in a million droplets, unable to draw herself together. Like all the stories said, he has split her into steam, and she never wants to return.

About the Author

Koji A. Dae is a queer American living long term in Bulgaria. She writes dark speculative fiction that concentrates on mental health and relationships. Her work can be found in Clarkesworld, Apex Magazine, Zooscape, and others. When not writing she enjoys dancing and fiber crafts.

Hamlet's House

by Anthony Engebretson

I can smell them. The birds. I see their plump little bodies prancing about my yard. I'm ready—stiff and poised—just one pounce and they could be mine. If only Long Neck would take this glass away.

Lucky little birds.

A hungry chirp rises from my throat. They'd do well to listen. This is *my* house and if they value their little lives, they'll keep away.

Of course, I haven't been here long. But I've placed my scent everywhere, from the basement to the attic where Round Face plays with his metal toys. I've hunted here even, capturing a vole sneaking around the basement. That was a fun chase! Round Face had been angry when I brought it upstairs. But he was just jealous. He and Long Neck are terrible hunters.

This is my house. Mine. There may still be places where other scents linger, but I'll snuff them out. There is only one room where I haven't been, upstairs, across from the bedroom. That door is always closed. The "forbidden door," I call it. Not even Long Neck will open it for me, no matter how much I wail at it.

I'm bored with the birds for now. I slink into the kitchen. My humans may not be good hunters, but they at least keep my bowl full of tasty crunchies. After my meal, I go back to the window. There is a human outside now, standing along the street where the vehicles zoom by. She's an old one, just staring at my house.

I look hard at her, my tail swishing. She better stay away. I don't like guests.

She keeps her distance. All she does is stand there and smile.

"Hello, kitty," she says. "Hello, pretty."

I get that a lot. Except, she isn't exactly talking to me. She seems to be looking at an upstairs window instead. Obviously, she's mistaken. There are no other "kitties" here.

Well, what do I care? As long as she keeps her distance, everything will be fine.

One of the kitchen cabinets stinks of that nameless other cat. I rub against it thoroughly until it smells more like me. I reward myself with some creamy crunchies.

I hear someone clomping into the kitchen. Then I smell his sweet, salty odor.

My Long Neck.

"Hey, Hammy," he says, passing me by and opening the fridge.

Round Face calls him Kevin. I call him Long Neck. It's fitting. Everything about his body is long: his arms, his legs, his face, his hair. The longest part of him is his neck, with that bobby little ball that goes up and down when he speaks. He is a funny-looking human and an unfortunate-looking cat.

I zigzag against his legs, rubbing my scent in deep. That isn't necessary, of course. He is already mine and always will be.

"Oh, Hammy," he says, bending down to pet me. His long fingers glide delightfully along my scruff. He's a good petter. "Hammy, Hammy, Hammy."

Hammy is one of his names for me. The main one is Hamlet. The truth is, I claim no name. I am just me.

Someone else comes into the kitchen with a harsh, sweaty smell. It's an unpleasant stench, but one that's grown on me with time. Long Neck calls this one Hansen. But with his short, thick, wide body and big head, I think Round Face is much more fitting. I give a couple rubs against his legs as well, because I can. He doesn't reach down to pet me, just says:

"'Sup, Hams."

That's one of *his* names for me. The humans also call me "Hums" or "Hummus"; sometimes, Round Face will call me "Fuckin' Cat." They're rather inconsistent.

Round Face is much more interested in petting Long Neck than me. They nuzzle against each other for a while, Round Face's thick arms wrapped around the taller human's body. They look like a stick tied to a rock, such a silly pair. Of course, all humans are silly. Large, hairless cats with no practical skills whatsoever. It's a burden to have *one* under your dominion, much less two. But I've gotten used to it.

Long Neck used to be my only charge. We lived a contented life in my little apartment, filled with an endless bounty of cockroaches and crickets to hunt. Round Face would visit often, and eventually he was there more often than not.

It was all fine until they started emptying out my home. Sure, the boxes were fun to play in, but it was an uncertain and stressful time. I shed so much fur I must've been practically bald! Eventually, *I* was the one being boxed and brought to this strange, new house. What an awful time. I love Long Neck, and Round Face is tolerable, but I am not sure I will ever completely forgive them.

Today was a busy day. I played with my jingly ball in the kitchen for a while until it was time to drown it in my water bowl. Round Face whined at me for that. Jealous again. Afterward, I slept on Long Neck and Round Face's bed. Then I pattered into the basement to use my litter box and search for more voles. When I couldn't find any, I slept on a pile of clothes next to the laundry machine. That's what's nice about this big house: so many different places to sleep. After this nap, I ventured all the way up to the attic where Round Face was lying on a bench, lifting one of his metal toys up and down.

One thing I like about Round Face is the warmth of his chest, so I hopped on. He wasn't too happy about that, shooing me away. I went back downstairs where Long Neck was in the bathroom. The door was closed. I hate it when they do that; they know I can't stand a closed door. I sat outside and cried as pathetically as I could. Sometimes, he'll give in when I do this and let me inside. But not today. I went back upstairs and, speaking of closed doors, yowled in front of the forbidden door for a bit. I did this until I smelled something. It was *that* smell, the hostile stink of the unknown cat lingering from under the door. It is such a rough, wild smell, unlike my own sweet scent. I wished I could go in and rub it all out. But with the door closed, there was nothing I could do.

I decided, then, to go sleep on my humans' bed again.

The work is never done.

Tonight, after eating their dinner, Long Neck and Round Face sit on the couch watching TV. I don't know what entertainment they get out of those incomprehensible glowing lights and noises, but this activity gives me an opportunity to sleep on Long Neck's lap. I just had one of my "spells," where I get this burst of energy. I lose control of myself, as if Long Neck gave me a pinch of that fantastic green stuff, and zip around the house. Needless to say, I'm exhausted. Such naps never last long, though. Once he readjusts his legs, it's over.

I pad down the hall and up the stairs, disdainfully disregarding Long Neck's pleas for me to come back, in search of another place to snooze. Maybe the bedroom.

But across from it, I see something spectacular. The forbidden door is actually open. Don't mind if I do.

It's dark inside, so dark even *my* eyes have to work double to adjust. This darkness doesn't make any sense, as there is an unshaded window in the room, the streetlight shining through. But I'll leave the overthinking to humans. All that matters is I have a new place to explore.

It quickly becomes evident, however, that there isn't much to see here. Other than the window and some boxes, the room is empty. It's cold too; colder than the rest of the house. That's no good.

My fur begins to prickle on my back. My tail swishing, I decide I've had enough of this place. As I turn toward the hall, that wild smell wafts over me, more overwhelming than ever. It feels like another cat is in here with me, even if I can't see it. I growl and hiss, though I'm not fully sure at what. But if there *is* an invisible cat in here, they need to know they've picked the wrong house.

The room is freezing now. I get this unnatural feeling, like a cloud floated down from the sky and is moving toward me.

I hear a sound. Well, not quite a sound. More like a vibration, a low growl rumbling inside my stomach. But it's not *my* growl.

Before I can act, something attacks me, leaping on me. I feel the sting of claws digging into my sides. I'm shivering, like someone just threw ice on me. My resolve is shattered by this invisible assault. I dart out of the room faster than I've ever gone. I'm gliding along the wooden floor. Along the way, I pass through Round Face's legs, nearly toppling him.

"Fuckin' Cat!" he shouts at me. But I don't hesitate. I just need to get as far from that room as I can. Down the stairs, through the hall, the kitchen, into the basement. There I slip into the tight space between laundry machines, nestling my body into that safe nook until a calm settles over me.

But even then, I don't leave. I stay in that spot for a very long time, even taking a couple brief, uncomfortable naps.

Eventually, daylight shines through the basement windows. I hear Long Neck upstairs, calling my name, shaking a box of treats. *Ooh, those treats.*

But they aren't enough to get me to budge. My house feels hostile now, like that something might be waiting for me around every corner.

It isn't long before I hear Long Neck coming down the stairs.

"Hamlet? Where are ya, baby? Hammy?"

I don't move, even once his slender body fills my vision. It isn't long before he spots me, my shining eyes likely giving me away.

"Hammy," he says, a sigh of relief. "What's the matter, baby?"

He awkwardly contorts himself to kneel before me, shaking the box of treats again. I can practically smell them, meaty and creamy. It's enough to make me salivate, but not enough to make me move. He reaches his other hand out to me. I lean forward and smell it. His scent sends a wave of comfort through my body. He gives me a few slow blinks, and I blink back. I want to taste him now. I give his fingers a couple licks. Soft and salty as ever.

"There ya go," he says.

I'm relaxed enough to creep forward, slowly though. Even as I come out of my nook, I anticipate an attack at any moment.

But nothing happens. Long Neck puts down the box of treats and pets me, one hand alternating between the back of my neck and the bottom of my chin, the other just above my tail. It feels amazing. He knows my sweet spots. I purr with delight.

"Aww, baby." He picks me up and cradles me in his arms. I usually hate being held like this, belly up. But I'll allow it. Right now, the world is melting away and it's just me and Long Neck.

Everything is right again.

From now on, I stick to the first floor and the basement. I won't go upstairs. I refuse. Every time I even go near the stairs, my fur prickles up. That smell is getting stronger up there too, that wild, invasive stink.

I also smell it downstairs, on towels, blankets, the furniture. Whenever I do, I rub my scent around as much as I can, blotting it out, reclaiming my place. Yet, the stench keeps popping up. It's like nothing can eliminate it. Round Face likes to clean, much more than Long Neck does, and he leaves this terrible, fruity odor. But even through that, the stink returns.

But despite the endless smells, I never see another cat in the house. I never hear one. The only fur sticking to the floor and furniture is mine. The droppings and clumps in the litter box are mine. The food only depletes when I eat it.

I saw another cat recently, but it was outside. I was perched on the living room window, watching the tasty little birds, when a mangy stranger with long, gray fur came slinking by. I did my duty, puffing up and hissing and yowling, warning her to stay away. She stopped and stared at me for a long time. I braced myself, preparing for the window to vanish so our fight could begin. But instead, she gave a slow, conceding blink and darted away. I wasn't able to bask in my victory for long. I sensed that cloud, that cold—the one I'd felt in the forbidden room—coming near. It was then *me* who was darting off, retreating to the basement.

That is where I feel safest, the basement, especially when the humans are away. I used to love it when they were gone, when I had the place to myself. Now, I'm filled with dread every time they leave.

Not that it's much better when they're here. Round Face is becoming less pleasant toward me by the day.

"Fuck off!" he'll say whenever I come near him. When he doesn't say anything, he just gives me these aggressive, unblinking stares.

I'm tolerating him less too. Even his grotesque smell I can no longer stand.

He and Long Neck are doing the laundry together, arguing about me. I am only inches from them in my cozy nook between the machines. They surely know where I am. They often talk about me like I'm not in the room, even when they know I'm *right there*.

"Your dumb cat keeps biting my feet," Round Face tells Long Neck. A lie.

"When?" I am grateful to hear skepticism in my human's voice.

"In bed. He's doing it every night now." An even bigger lie. I haven't been in their bedroom in a long time.

"Is that why you kept kicking last night?"

"Yeah."

"I haven't even noticed him in bed with us," Long Neck says. "He used to snuggle up in my legs all the time, but hasn't lately."

Exactly! Long Neck's curled-up legs are one of my favorite nooks. I would rather sleep there than spend any time biting Round Face's disgusting toes.

"Well, trust me, he's there."

I don't know what kind of scheme Round Face is getting at.

"And it smells all the time," Round Face whines. I know Long Neck is fond of him, but I'm not seeing much reason why we should keep him around any longer. "The house just feels disgusting!"

"You're the one who wanted this place, now you hate it?"

"It's that fucking cat. You know, sometimes he keeps me up all night. I hear him running around the floor, yowling."

This isn't true either. I spend most nights down here, in the basement, quiet as can be. But I'm beginning to wonder if he's *actually* lying. I get a whiff of something on the humans, a faint scent. That feral smell. It startles me so much I let out an involuntary growl.

"Shit, there he goes again," Round Face says.

Long Neck slams down the towel he's folding. It jolts me to my feet. I hardly ever see him so angry.

"What the fuck do you want me to do?"

"I just don't feel at home here." Round Face speaks softly, apparently stunned as well. "I thought I would but... I don't know. And your cat..."

"I know you hate cats, Hansen. But you knew from day one that Hamlet was part of the bargain. And frankly, I don't know how one cat can ruin your dream home for you, but I think that's your problem."

"It's not just the cat. It's... Something just feels weird. I'm sorry, baby. I don't mean... I'm not saying we should get rid of him, I just—"

"You better not be."

I love him so much.

It's an unusually good day today. First, I found some little red spiders in the basement. They were fun to chase and weren't so bad tasting either. Also, Long Neck is sick, so he's staying home while Round Face is gone. I've spent hours on his lap while he watches TV on the couch. His coughing is a little disruptive to my sleep cycle, but I'll take what I can get. I'm not smelling that wild, other cat smell in my wanderings today, although I still refuse to go upstairs.

I'm just smelling me. That's good. It's the way it should be.

After eating some crunchies, I decide to go into the downstairs bathroom, into the shower. Back in my old apartment, I loved crying out as loud as I could in the shower just to hear my voice echo off the walls and fill the room. I haven't done that in a long time.

I let out my best caterwaul. My voice is so strong in there. I am mighty.

"Yeah, yeah," Long Neck shouts from the other room. "I hear ya, Hums, I hear ya."

Everything feels the way it used to. Just me, my human, and my domain.

But this good feeling doesn't last. My smell fades, and the intrusive smell returns. The room grows cold and my fur stiffens, tail beating wildly, ears pulled back. *The cloud.* I now have a distinct sense that something is waiting on the other side of the shower curtain, ready to pounce. I let out a growl and a hiss, though I already have a feeling that won't repel this enemy.

"What's going on, Hammy?" I hear Long Neck ask.

I intensify my growling and hissing. Maybe then Long Neck will come and his presence will make this all go away.

But no matter how much noise I make, he doesn't come. I have to prepare for a fight. I get my claws ready. Good thing I never let Long Neck clip them.

The curtain bursts at me. Something pins me to the ground, a heavy, freezing force. Sharp, stinging claws tear into me again. Yet, I can't claw back. A terrifying, high-pitched yowl echoes through the shower, and I quickly realize it's coming from me. I manage to get to my feet and scramble away from the unseen attacker. I leap out of the shower, dash out of the bathroom, down into the basement, and hide between the machines again.

I was wrong. I'm not safe! *I'm not safe!*

Even in this tight nook, I can't relax. If anything, I feel trapped. I just want to go home, back to my apartment where Long Neck and I lived in peace. Why can't we just go back? Leave Round Face, leave this house, and we can be happy again. I don't belong here. I'll never belong here!

Long Neck comes downstairs, bundled up in a blanket, coughing and hacking.

"Hamlet," he says, trying to beckon me from my nook, shaking a box of treats again.

I cry at him, pleading, begging him to take me home. But he won't listen.

I no longer leave the basement. I spend most days nestled between the laundry machines or any other small space I can fit into. I'm getting thinner, my fur falling out in clumps. Long Neck has given up on trying to get me to come upstairs, instead bringing my food and water down here.

I'll eat as much as I can, but my hunger isn't what it used to be. I'll often let spiders and roaches pass me by. I even saw a vole one evening, crawling around the far corner. In another time, that would have made my day. But I didn't care. I let it skitter off, vanishing from my sight, its succulent smell fading.

Hunting doesn't matter much when I'm feeling like the prey.

Sometimes, I sense that cloud, prowling, searching for me. I feel its chill. But it's something I can't fight. I can only hide. I already know its smell has filled the rest of the house. It's cropping up in parts of the basement too. I can't snuff it out. It's unbeatable.

Worst of all, that smell is getting stronger on Long Neck. I sense more of it on him every time he comes down to do the laundry or visit me.

He's worried about me. But I'm not the only thing he has to be concerned about. Most nights, I'll hear Round Face yelling at him. Yelling about me, about the house, about everything. Sometimes Long Neck yells back.

Eventually, the yelling stops. I no longer hear Round Face at all.

Sometimes, I'll still hear Long Neck, though. He spends a lot of time talking to himself. Or maybe he's on one of those phones.

"Hansen," he'll say a lot. "Baby, please."

When he isn't talking, he's just sobbing. Is he doing what I used to do? Crying for my attention? I want to go up there, be there for him. But I can't. The cloud, the smell.

I may have no choice. Long Neck hasn't come down here in days. The food in my bowl is getting stale and sparse, and the water is barely high enough to soak my whole foot in. Even if I hunt spiders and voles, it may not be enough to keep me alive.

My hunger isn't what it used to be, but it's still there, deep and gnawing.

Sometimes, I whine at the stairs, as loudly as I can, hoping he'll hear me. Sometimes, after a few hours, he'll cry back. But he never comes down.

It's useless, I'm realizing. I'm on my own.

I wake up one evening, sensing something looking at me. I don't think it's the cloud, though. Could it be Long Neck? Is he down here with me again?

Doubtful. I don't smell him, and I hadn't heard him come down the stairs. Something else is watching me. But if it's not him, not the cloud, then what?

After glancing around, I see them. Two eyes, peering at me through one of the basement windows. I see the mangy, gray outline as well. It's the cat I scared off so many days ago. In my weakness, my defeat, she's decided to slink back to the house.

But it isn't victory or satisfaction I see in her eyes. It's a warning, a clear one. The cold darkness that rules this house will not spare me, will not have mercy. It will let me starve.

And whatever the cloud is, it seems to have overwhelmed Long Neck. That has to be the only explanation. Even if Round Face has abandoned him, has hurt him, he wouldn't forget me like this.

I wonder how this cat would know this. Was this once her house? Had she managed to get out, to escape the cloud? Or maybe she's just been around long enough, has seen many cats and humans come and go from this place, repelled—or perhaps even killed—by the presence that claims it.

It doesn't really matter. She's right. I have to leave this place. I have to somehow get Long Neck out too.

I cautiously creep upstairs. The state of things is worse than I thought. The hostile stench is everywhere, overwhelming me. This place feels completely unwelcoming. It doesn't feel like the same house I once thought mine not so long ago. The cloud is somewhere close, shambling around. It doesn't seem to know I'm up here yet. I want to run back downstairs, to disappear again. But my hunger is strong, desperate. Hiding will kill me. I have to push forward.

Luckily, I don't have to wander too far into this hostile territory. Long Neck is in the kitchen, sitting at the table, staring blankly at his hands. He looks thinner, sickly. His sweet scent is still there but hidden beneath the wild smell mixed with the rancid odor of unwashed skin. I cry out to him, the strongest caterwaul I can muster. He doesn't move. Can he not even hear me? I jump up on the table and wail directly in his face.

"Shut up," he mutters, still not looking at me. He's said this to me before, but never with such coldness.

I'm not deterred. What kind of cat would I be if I was? I can't stay on the table any longer, though. I feel exposed. If the cloud comes into the room, it will see me immediately. I jump back to the floor and continue my caterwauling, though I know it's useless.

Desperate measures must be taken.

I nip at his bare toes. I'll admit, in my hungry state, the sweet and salty taste of his skin is appetizing. But I'm not here to eat him.

He jerks away at each bite. It's an encouraging sign. At least he's *that* responsive.

"Stop," he groans pathetically, sounding like he's on the verge of tears. "Stop."

I can't have any mercy, though. Not until he snaps out of this state and gets it together. This darkness can have the damn house. *I concede.* But Long Neck is mine. He's always been mine. When I was a kitten and he took me out of that shelter, he gave himself to me. It's not a claim I take lightly.

I bite down hard, with as much fierceness and love as I can muster. Perhaps a little too hard. He cries out, throwing his foot forward and kicking me. A jerk reaction, but it sends me into a furious haze. I lose control of myself as I lunge forward, claws out, stabbing into his leg.

"Fuck!" he bellows angrily, rising from the chair. I finally got a reaction out of him, although not the one I wanted. He's reaching out, eyes frenzied. I'm certain he'll throttle me if he catches me. I dash back to the basement. I can feel him stomping after, pursuing me in my retreat. I skitter into my nook, right back where I started. Perhaps not such a good place, I realize immediately. I'm pinned in here, within his reach. I cower, facing the wall, hoping maybe he won't see me.

He lets out a sharp but brief cry, and his thudding footsteps turn into an erratic tumble, ending in a thick crack. After that, it's silent.

When I feel safe enough to turn around, I see him lying at the bottom of the stairs. His body is twisted at an angle humans usually don't make, his neck as bent as the fluffy blue tunnel I used to have in my apartment. He's looking back at me, but his eyes are glassy, unblinking, seeing nothing.

I recognize what this is. It's the end of life, the failure of survival. In an instant, my Long Neck is gone.

I stay nestled in my nook for a long time, staring at Long Neck's body. Sometimes, I'll cry out. To whom, I'm not sure. To Long Neck, in the hopes that my wails will snap him back to life, back to the way he was? And then he'll nestle me in his arms and carry me back to my apartment. Or maybe I'm crying out for Round Face, for anyone to come and get me out of here, to make this end.

But crying is useless, exhausting. Sometimes, I'll sleep, in unsatisfying bursts, waking up to find Long Neck still where he is, those eyes looking through me.

As time goes on, the sun darkening and glowing and darkening again, his scent begins to change. Sweet, musky, rotten. All swirling together, sending strange sensations through my body, my stomach. It's an unpleasant smell, yet at the same time, luscious.

I creep forward to Long Neck, barely understanding what's driving me. I lick his cheek. The taste of his skin is salty as ever, and his flesh feels dense beneath my tongue. My hungry body quivers with delight.

I retreat back to my nook. I can't do this, not my Long Neck.

But when I look back, I hardly see my human there. I don't see the big, dumb cat who I'd spend long nights snuggling with, whose warmth got me through the coldest winters, who always kept my bowls filled. Long Neck is gone. Now I just see flesh. *Meat.* My empty stomach twists and growls with excitement. A human, with all their overthinking, would try to find a way around this. Perhaps even choose starvation. But I must survive.

Besides, he is still mine. And I'll do what I must with what is mine.

I creep forward again. Slowly, very slowly. At any moment, the cloud could come down. I must be careful. I start with licking his cheeks, taking in his taste, letting my hunger decide if I truly want to do this.

I do.

I bite as hard as I can. My teeth rip into the tender flesh. The blood, though cold, is as savory as gravy. The meat slides effortlessly down my throat. The sensation makes my whole body tremble with pleasure. Food at last.

I spend days feasting on what was once my Long Neck. When one cheek is depleted, I turn to the other.

He is unrecognizable now, his face resembling a chewed steak.

It's delicious, though. It's better than any chicken and gravy, any crunchies, any of those creamy treats. This is better.

This is better?

No. Look at what I've been reduced to. Look at what *it* reduced me to. No matter how much I clean myself after feeding, Long Neck's blood seems soaked into my fur, crusting it. My litter box is filled to the brim, so I have to excrete the flesh of my human in every corner of the basement, unable to bury my waste. I've gone from ruler to savage beast. That cloud, that darkness, whatever it is, has ruined my life. Worst of all, I can't fight it. My claws and teeth are ineffective. All I can do is hide.

Or escape.

Yes, I have to get out of here, out of this house, even if I live my life as a stray or wind up in a shelter again. There is no chance of going back to my apartment. Not with Long Neck gone. But at least I won't spend the rest of my life hiding.

One thing is undeniable: there is no possibility of escape as long as I skulk in this basement. All the windows are shut, too high for me to reach. Staying down here will lead to death. Long Neck afforded me some time. One last act of love. But his flesh won't always be nourishing. Decay is coming. I have to go upstairs again, and soon. I must take a chance.

Opportunity comes at an unexpected moment. I am chewing on Long Neck's meat, which is becoming bitter and sinewy, when a sudden, unearthly ring jolts through my body. I scramble back into my nook.

When the noise chimes out again, I recognize it.

The doorbell.

I always hated that sound. The shrill and piercing call of an unwanted guest.

But now, as I hear it a third time, followed by loud banging, a tingle of possibility crawls down my spine. Somebody wants in, badly. I'm not sure who, but if they're so desperate to enter this house, they won't give up easily. Dare I go upstairs, risk being caught by the cloud for the vague possibility of escape?

Look at what this has done to me. I'm overthinking like a human.

It rings a fourth time. A fifth. More banging. I hear shouting, a deep voice, somewhat familiar.

Round Face!

I have never been so excited to hear his aggravating whine.

Another ring. Then another. He's definitely not giving up. He's going to barge his way in however he can. I know it.

If I want to survive, I can't stay here. Long Neck's already rotting. Round Face is presenting me this one chance. I have to take it.

The moment I come out of my nook, I feel as exposed as a bug in my food bowl. I resist the urge to retreat and stealthily climb my way up the stairs. I keep my head low, one silent, creeping step at a time.

The oppressive smell envelopes me again at the top of the stairs. I don't sense the cloud, but it's near. I feel its chill. Another primitive urge to retreat.

Round Face is slamming hard on the front door now. He's trying to force it open. The door is crackling with each pound. It will give way soon. I aim my body toward the door, bottom raised, ready to dash the instant it opens. I'm excited. I'm terrified.

I've never been an outdoor cat, no matter how much I loved the feel of fresh air and desired to chase birds and squirrels. I may not have what it takes to survive out there.

I won't survive in here.

My hair prickles, my tail swishes. The chill worsens. Something's seen me. Predatory eyes skulk toward me. *The cloud.*

I cry out. Cry for Round Face to hurry. The door still won't give way, and his slamming seems to grow weaker. Is he going to give up? Is he going to turn and leave?

I feel the cloud rushing across the room toward me. My whole body is itching to retreat. But I must stay steady.

The door bangs again. Again. It's cracking. It's going to give way.

No, it won't. I must hide.

The cloud is coming. It's shrieking and growling, claws at the ready, teeth bared. I must run. I must wait.

Bang. Bang.

The door flies open. The cloud pounces on me, the icy chill filling my body. Claws dig into my sides, teeth in my neck. Throwing me to the ground. I shriek and convulse, pawing at it, batting it off. It won't relent. I'm pinned, claws and teeth in my skin, the smell sweeping through my fur, blotting out my own.

"Hamlet?" Round Face asks.

His voice seems to catch the cloud's attention. Just for a moment. One tiny moment where the bite eases, the claws slacken. It's all I need. I pounce onto my feet and dash. I already feel the cloud at my tail. It's as fast as I am, if not faster. It almost has me. But the light is right there, behind Round Face's bulky body. I run between his legs, nearly knocking him over.

"Fuckin' Cat!"

The cloud's on my back. It's about to throw me down. But I'm at the door. I leap across the threshold. The cloud immediately pulls away as I tumble down the porch's steps, regaining my footing to scramble across the lawn and up a tree.

I'm free.

I spend the whole day perched on a high branch, watching as more humans come to the house. Strangers in weird clothes with flashing lights on their vehicles. Round Face sits on the porch, rocking back and forth with his head buried in his hands.

At one point, the strangers bring out Long Neck. His body is wrapped in a sheet. I can see red splotches where I ate from him. His last precious gift to me.

I'm on my own now. Even if I'd tolerated Round Face or if he'd ever liked me, he wouldn't take me in after what I'd done to Long Neck's body. *What I had to do.* At best, he'd send me back to the shelter; at worst, he would murder me.

I don't know how I'll manage, but I will. I must. The wild smell from the house is gone. I'm filled with new scents, equally wild but far more welcoming. The trees, the air, the sweet, tender birds.

And beneath it all, most importantly, I can smell myself.

I'll make do, will make a home somewhere out here. Maybe one day some kind humans will take me in, offer themselves to my supervision and care. Nobody will replace my Long Neck, but I could accept a new arrangement.

Just as long as they aren't in *that* house.

Even now, from one of those hostile windows, I can feel that darkness watching me. Eyes narrowed. A low growl in its throat.

Warning me to stay away.

About the Author

Anthony Engebretson is a Nebraska-born author based in west Michigan. He has had short stories published in several anthologies. His debut novella, *Sair Back, Sair Banes*, was released in May 2022 and his second novella, *Lumberjack*, will be released in December 2023. He loves writing dark fiction with a speculative bent dealing with issues ranging from personal and mental health issues to systematic and structural horrors. He is also pursuing a masters in Library Science.

THE GREAT BATH

BY T.S VICKERS

Elisa and I had been waiting in the queue for the renowned Roman Baths museum for so long that our designated entry time passed over half an hour ago. We stood at the front, and the line behind us grew with tourists that it bent around the corner and out of sight. While we waited, I noticed the window beside me, twice my height, was steaming up from inside.

I was about to complain about the wait to an approaching staff member when the museum's doors were flung open and out came two paramedics wheeling a stretcher.

"Sorry folks!" they called. I couldn't see much of who was on the rolling bed other than it was a man, about fifty years old, with skin like the moon's surface. "Due to an unforeseen circumstance, we are forced to close. We apologise for the inconvenience. I repeat, we are now closed!"

The crowd grumbled.

"This is ridiculous!" I protested. Elisa turned away with a look of embarrassment. "You can't do this. We've been waiting for ages."

"We're sorry, sir, but we've got no choice but to shut down for the foreseeable future. Hold on to your ticket, and we'll allow you entry once we reopen. Otherwise, refunds can be claimed either on our website or by completing one of our forms."

I wanted to argue further, but I was too distracted by the steamy window and its strange behaviour. Nobody else seemed to notice, and Elisa had stepped away to make a phone call before I could point it out.

Words began to take shape upon it. I stepped back as the letters formed, thick and bold, and in no particular order. They weren't strung together in the order they ought to, and nor were they written in a manner they should be. They came into being as random patches of condensation disappeared, dryness morphing into recognisable symbols. The words chilled me like a breeze blowing inside my bones. Goosebumps bubbled on my skin, and my hairs stood when I read the two words that formed: *Enter, Rowan.*

It was nearly October, yet the sun was defying its seasonal obligations with a downpour of heat as it floated above Bath Abbey. After leaving the queue, Elisa and I sat outside a nearby pub, overlooking the courtyard.

The possibility of a cooling breeze was blocked by the surrounding Palladian-style limestone architecture, giving the impression that you were lost in some Regency-era labyrinth. The Abbey loomed above it all, the centrepiece of the city.

On either side of two long windows were sculptures of angels ascending a ladder, all the way to the roof. They were gazing down at some unseen horror with petrified expressions that felt similar to my own mood.

The silence between Elisa and I was growing uncomfortable.

"What do you think those angels are climbing away from?" I nodded towards them. My arm was trembling so much that I spilled my drink.

Elisa squinted as she looked, fanning her face with a leaflet, before she noticed the table was wet.

"Are you okay?" she said.

"I'm fine. Just wondering about the sculptures over there. What do you think?"

"I dunno. They're probably supposed to be looking at the burning infernos of hell, or some other Christian crap like that." She looked at me intently. "You're pale."

I gulped the rest of my pint. The glass made a thud as I set it down. "Come on, let's get going."

Elisa left her drink and followed me. We joined a historical tour of the city which we had booked earlier that day. Despite all the interesting things the guide told us, which ordinarily I'd be more than intrigued to know, I couldn't focus. The words *Enter, Rowan* swirled around my mind.

There had to be a rational explanation. Did someone inside the museum want to see me? A long-lost relative; an old friend? I couldn't settle until I found out who was behind it. I had to put my mind at ease.

The tour guide continued to ramble while I thought about what I should do. I soon realised that, if I wanted to get to the bottom of this mystery, I had to find a way inside the museum, whether it was open or not.

I waited until Elisa was fast asleep, some time after midnight. I scribbled a note that read *Gone for a smoke*, grabbed some jeans and a shirt and got changed in the bathroom. All set, I sneaked out of our hotel room, careful not to let the door slam behind me.

The streets were empty this late. I strolled along York Street, where the walls of my destination stood to my right, over ten feet tall. The museum had been built around the hot springs in Victorian times, and while most of the exhibits were indoors, there was an open terrace above the waters that offered the perfect entry point. The wall's wide bricks offered convenient holds, and I was up and over in no time.

I landed on the terrace. The Abbey loomed in the background. My only company was the eight immortalised Roman officials standing atop the inner balustrade, their gazes fixed to the opening beneath their feet. I peered over, and all I could see was the reflection of the blood moon glowing in the Great Bath below.

My senses were heightened in the darkness. Dripping water seemed like asteroids splashing in an ocean; my footsteps like giants stomping through a valley; pebbles I kicked like boulders tumbling down a mountain. But nothing was as striking as the emptiness in the intermittent silence.

Uneasiness was setting in, the burden of a trespasser. It was only a matter of time before the cameras sent security to drag me away. Just as I was contemplating whether to leave, I heard sobbing come from below. I thought my mind was playing tricks on me, or that there was some drunk woman out in the street. But no; it came from the Great Bath.

I shuddered. As much as I wanted to get out of there, I couldn't. Not without some investigation. I leaned over the balustrade.

"Hello?" I called, just a bit louder than my talking voice. "Are you all right down there?"

"No!" a woman's voice quavered. "I am not okay!"

Instinct told me to leave it there. Descending the ten-foot wall was a safer option than engaging further. But I didn't have the heart.

"Is there anything I can do to help?"

"What does it matter? You'll only leave me. They all leave me, in the end."

I reminded myself about the message on the window. The lady presented a lead, someone to answer my questions.

A door that led inside opened, as if the breeze had swayed it. Mist poured out from the stairway and dispersed into the night.

"Enter, Rowan," she said. My spine turned to ice. "Enter, if you think you can help me."

The museum was filled with fog. I tried to fan it from my face with my hand, but it was stubborn. Dull green security lights were all that guided me.

I followed the corridor through various rooms of cabinets that hosted different artefacts; a glamorous brooch, a collection of coins, some daggers. The woman was nowhere to be seen, but her crying grew louder with every step.

Running water slapped against stone somewhere in the next area. I was hit with a stench akin to damp clothes after they'd been left to fester. The path guiding me was barely visible; just clear enough for me to creep along.

I entered a room filled with ancient stone tablets. Their information boards told me they'd been discovered when the museum was built. Inscriptions had been carved into them thousands of years ago by folk praying for favours from their goddess—a deity of water named Sulis Minerva. They believed she inhabited the baths.

The crying reached its apex when I stepped out into the opening of the Great Bath. The blood moon beamed on the rectangular stillness of the water. Drips fell around me. The Roman statues stared down from above, like they were watching me, judging me. The crying echoed, but no matter where I looked, she was nowhere to be seen.

I crept around the outskirts of the bath.

"Where are you?" I called, with a hint of aggravation I didn't expect to hear from myself. "How can I help you if you won't show me who you are?"

The moon's reflection trembled. The water moved like it was being blown by the wind. It swirled, a whirlpool forming in the centre of the bath, except the water was not pulled beneath; it rose upwards, defying gravity. Like clay on a potter's wheel, it spun around and around, until it transformed into the figure of a woman. She was on her knees, her hands clasped together.

"Don't be scared!" she yelled.

I stepped backwards and fell. All I could hear in that moment was my heartbeat pounding.

"Please, sir, do not be afraid!"

She was beautiful, but it wasn't enough to redeem the terror. Her eyes—colourless, transparent, wet—were locked with mine. She was dressed in a watery stola. I could see that she was crying, but there was nothing distinguishing her tears from her body.

"I'm not going to hurt you!"

Words struggled to find their way to me. I felt as vulnerable as an ant to a shoe. The man on the stretcher—was he the last victim of this demon?

"Please, Rowan!" Years of desperation were carried in her tone. "You promised you would help me."

"Who are you?"

"Have you ever been imprisoned?" I shook my head. "I've been a prisoner of this pool long before humanity existed. It was a blessing, for a while. I've seen millions of people come and go, across millenia, as Aquae Sulis has grown from a humble settlement and into the historic city you see today. This sacred pool was transformed into a temple, and from a temple into a museum."

It was at that moment I realised who I was speaking with.

"You're her..." I muttered. "You're the goddess. Sulis Minerva."

"You asked me earlier if there's anything you can do to help me. Well, perhaps there is. All I want is one day to explore the city. To see the world that's been built around me. Just a single day, to get out of this pool and see what Aquae Sulis has become. Please, Rowan." She dropped to her knees and clasped her hands as before. "I beg you to do this for me."

"But how?"

"By lending me your body!"

She screamed so loud it was all I could hear. She lunged forward, like a shark darting for its prey, and tried to grab me. My blood froze as I recoiled to the wall.

She threw heaps of water at my face with such force that it knocked me over. I coughed as it shot into my throat and up my nostrils; a putrid taste of bitterness and salt. I struggled to get to my feet. Spluttering, I crawled away as fast as I could.

As soon as I was out of range I got to my feet. All I could hear were the echoes of her screaming and weeping as I hurried through the museum. I reached the terrace, where splashes erupted up to the statues from the bath below and rained down over me.

"Lend me a body, Rowan! Let me be free!"

I needed no further convincing. Coming here was a mistake. I rushed for the wall, climbed over and dropped to the street below.

The blood moon's glow lit my way back to the hotel, and I left Sulis Minerva for what I thought would be the last time.

The next day, Elisa and I sat at one of the city's quaint cafés, al fresco. The place looked like it was designed to make you feel like a character in a Jane Austen novel.

The tea room's waitress wobbled like an old car moving along a cob-blestone road as she carried a three-tier-high tea lunch, complete with sandwiches, scones, cake and biscuits. I found her elderly appearance and spirit in keeping with the Georgian street's resonance.

"You two look lovely." She poured our tea from a china pot with a smile. "Would you like me to take a picture?"

"No thanks," I said, my gaze to the ground. "Just the food and drinks please."

She looked offended, but nodded and left us.

Reaching for the sandwich was more difficult than it should've been. My hand was trembling so much the plate rattled when I grabbed it. Tuna and cucumber proved to be insufficient at replacing the taste of possessed water that stained my mouth.

"Are you sure you don't have a fever or something? You don't look well at all." Elisa was too busy watching me to start eating.

"Yes."

"Then what's wrong?"

"Nothing." I got through the sandwich like it was the first thing I'd ever eaten. "Didn't sleep well."

She looked unconvinced. Some part of her wanted to laugh at me, I could see it in her eyes.

"It feels like you're lying," she said quickly before sipping her tea. I sighed.

"We're meant to be having a nice week away."

"Are we?" Her cup clanked when she returned it to the saucer. "This trip has felt anything but nice. We haven't had a single normal conversation since we arrived."

I struggled to stop myself from raising my voice. "Just eat your lunch."

She folded her arms. I sensed there was something else she wanted to say, but she was unsure how to say it. Whatever it was, I was in no mood to press.

"Listen, Rowan," she finally went on, "there's something I need to tell you. I wanted to wait until we got home so that we could have a nice week, but it doesn't seem like that's happening. So, the sooner you know, the better."

I felt my nails dig into my skin as I clenched my fist. "You've cheated on me, haven't you?"

"Well—"

"Who's the unlucky man?"

"It's just—"

I slammed my fist on the table. "I said who's the unlucky man?"

We had become the theatrics of the street. Customers inside and outside the café were watching us, and some passersby slowed their pace to get a look. The waitress stared from the window. We were just one more outburst away from being asked to leave.

But it didn't get that far. Elisa didn't elaborate, perhaps not wanting to make too much of a scene. Our gazes locked, I shook my head and threw my cake on the floor.

I left her alone, departing with a final glance as I turned the corner. I savoured the image of her left with the remains of a romantic meal for two by herself.

I spent the rest of the day in the hotel room watching sitcoms, drinking the fridge dry and ordering room service. Our room was booked under Elisa's bank card, after all.

I wasn't sure what she did with her day other than spend it avoiding me, but she didn't return until after 10 p.m. She found me lying on the bed, lips stained red, with an all but finished bottle of wine in my hand. Finally, the taste of possessed water haunted me no more.

"Don't pity me," I said, noticing the expression on her face. She seemed relieved that I'd broken the ice.

She sat at the foot of the bed. "I'll go home tomorrow."

"Just tell me who he is."

"Rowan, I don't see how that will—"

"You accused me of lying, and now you're hiding the truth. I know I haven't always been a good boyfriend, but we've spent over three years together, and I think you owe me the courtesy of telling me."

She was lost in her thoughts for a moment. She tried to speak several times, but stopped herself. Perhaps she was unsure of her wording, or too afraid to admit the truth. Eventually, she came clean.

"It's Julia."

I was as heartbroken as I was perplexed. I held the bottle tightly in my hand. Frustration—and being slightly drunk—told me I should lob it at the wall, but I didn't.

I got up and stared out the window. I could see the balustrade that bordered the terrace of the Roman Baths museum in the distance, and wondered which of my nights here had been the most emotionally devastating.

I turned back to Elisa.

"Fucking Julia?"

"I'm sorry, Rowan. It's just—"

"I'm not sure what I'm more confused about. The fact that I've just learned you're into girls, or that you're sleeping with my sister."

"Nothing like that has happened, I promise." She struggled to speak clearly through her sniffling. "I know how much it must hurt to hear this, but I just wanted you to know the truth."

I could see how difficult it was for her to speak and decided I didn't need to hear anymore.

We opened a fresh bottle of wine and started drinking together. To ease the mood, mostly. A couple of hours later, I made my own confession.

"I wasn't lying when I said I didn't go out drinking last night," I said. "But in the spirit of honesty, I might as well tell you what I was up to."

She finished a sip from her glass. "Go on."

"It's nothing serious. But I found a way up to the museum's terrace." I could see she was relieved, if not a bit baffled. "I was walking back after going to the shop when I noticed how easy it would be to climb over. So I did."

"You didn't get caught did you?"

"Course not. I was careful. I was wondering, though. We've not had much fun together since we got here. Do you want to check it out?"

She thought for a moment. "Won't the cameras catch us?"

"They're broken. I think that's part of the reason why they've closed down. Come on, Elisa. The younger you would be up and over in a heartbeat. Let's do it."

It took a bit more reassuring, but she soon agreed.

Shortly after, we were on our way. Perhaps it was our confessions that relieved the tension, or the excitement of doing something risky. Either way, things felt as close to normal between us as they could.

Some might think I was being petty, to put her through terror as punishment for betraying me, but I couldn't wait to see her reaction when she met Sulis Minerva.

I helped Elisa climb the wall with a leg-up. Once she was over, I followed, and met her on the terrace.

Her eyes beamed with wonder at the sight of the Roman statues. She darted from one to the other and read their information boards aloud, relishing in the history they told. I mirrored her enthusiasm. The museum was, after all, the attraction we were most looking forward to.

She leaned over the balustrade to see the Great Bath below.

"Shame it's so dark," she said.

"Yeah..." I joined her side, and wondered whether Sulis Minerva was listening to us.

"Did you manage to get a good look yesterday?" Elisa asked.

"I did."

"Do you think there's any way we can get down there?" She leaned so far that I thought she might fall in. It gave me an idea.

"Maybe." I edged closer, until our elbows were almost touching. "Elisa, I owe you an apology."

"You don't owe me anything. I'm the one that's hurt you. If anything, I should be apologising."

"It's not that." My armpits started sweating. "It's not that I want to apologise for something I've done. I should apologise for what I'm going to do."

"What do you mean?"

I grabbed her legs and tried to throw her over. She kicked and screamed as we tussled against the stone bannister.

"Get off!" she cried.

Her foot slipped free and booted my nose. I ignored the pang and grabbed it again, squeezing tighter this time. "You'll understand later."

"Let me go!"

With a burst of adrenaline, I thrust her up and over the ledge and she plummeted to the water with a great splash.

My heart was pounding. I ran for the door leading inside.

Elisa's screams echoed, intertwined with the wailing of Sulis Minerva. I sprinted past the exhibits until I reached the pool.

The water tossed and turned, mimicking a stormy sea. The screams and cries battled for dominance like two ships clashing.

I was swarmed with anxiety. Was Sulis going to kill her? Would I be convicted as a murderer? How could I be sure I wasn't the next victim?

Then the pool went still. Silence enshrouded, eerie and unnerving. A shadowy figure emerged from the bath, walking towards me, up the steps that led from the depths.

I couldn't believe my eyes when I saw her. Her expression, one of smugness and satisfaction, was nothing like I had ever seen from her before. I struggled to process it; she looked the same, but her demeanour was different.

"Elisa?"

"Thank you, Rowan," she said. She spoke sweetly and formally, and though her voice was the same, it was accentuated with a manner entirely different to her usual idiosyncrasies. "You have freed me."

"Sulis..."

"What's going on?" a voice from the pool cried. The watery form of Elisa stood there. I was lost for words.

"Do not be afraid, young lady," Sulis Minerva said. "I promise, I will be extra careful with you."

"What the fuck is going on?" Elisa screamed.

"You didn't tell her?"

"Tell me what?"

Various explanations came to me but none of them seemed suitable for justifying what I had done. I said nothing.

"Everything will be normal again soon," Sulis went on. "All I want is to explore the city, to see how it has grown. Once we're finished, I shall return. That's a promise."

"I don't understand!"

"Enough," Sulis snapped. "We must go. The sun will rise in a few hours, and we shall return before it has set."

She grabbed my hand and pulled me away. The sound of Elisa sobbing from the pool haunted me as we departed the museum.

I had to remind Sulis several times not to stare at almost every person we passed. She had a childlike intrigue about her, and I was sure that, left to her own devices, she'd have gotten herself in trouble.

Part of me felt guilty for deceiving Elisa; part of me couldn't believe my luck. I was walking with a goddess, a deity who'd watched these lands transform across millenia. What had she seen in such a timeline? What answers to the mysteries of history did she possess?

We spent the day strolling the streets and enjoying the historical attractions of the city, with barely a moment of silence between us. I was full of questions and intrigue, and she was happy to oblige in entertaining me.

I took her out for dinner where she recited the story of Celts discovering her bubbling, warm pool. They would dance and celebrate in testament to her, ever-grateful for the miracles she performed with her healing waters. And she told me, too, of the arrival of the Romans, the legions who butchered and slashed the natives, but worshipped her all the same.

As she progressed through the ages, she seemed increasingly disappointed with the developments of humanity. She lamented our diverted attention from theology to technology. The construction of the museum—a limestone prison, she called it—had cemented our abandonment of worshipping her. I sensed deeply rooted emotions in her, feelings of nostalgia, remorse or perhaps even of vengeance. I broke the moment by asking a waiter for the bill.

As the sun made its descent, she insisted that we return to the museum. I was surprised to see her keep her word so readily.

"Do we have to go now?" I tried to dictate our pace by walking slower, but she was in a hurry. "There's so much more I want to ask you."

"Yes. I've seen enough. We must return by sunset."

The high street was bustling with people in expensive suits and dresses on their way to bars and restaurants.

"Come on," I negotiated, "what's the rush? Wouldn't you like to see how it really feels to be human?"

"I'd despise nothing more." Her pace quickened. I struggled to keep up without panting.

"But look at everyone. They're having a great time, and we could be too. It's not like you get to do this often."

"You don't understand."

"Try me."

"No."

Before long, we were back at the museum. After checking we weren't being watched, we climbed over the wall.

She showed no sign of slowing down until she was well inside, and came to a sudden halt at the room filled with stone tablets.

"It's a shame," she reflected, a tear rolling down her cheek. "Some of these poor souls died before I could honour their prayers. Slaughtered by their brethren."

The largest tablet stood at the far end of the room; an apparently new addition, propped on a heavy-duty hand barrow. Bits of broken glass from damaged cabinets were scattered across the floor, along with spilled artefacts.

She knelt before the tablet, ran her fingers across its inscriptions and started sobbing. Unsure of where to place myself, I stood behind her.

"It's not your fault." I rested my hand on her shoulder.

"Why must you humans spoil everything you touch?" While I knew she was speaking rhetorically, I couldn't help but think she was expecting an answer. Before I could offer one, she stood and faced me.

"Rowan." She wiped the tears from her face with her sleeve. "You've done so much for me already, but might I make one final request, before I go?"

Steam started to fill the room.

"Of course. Anything."

"It's been centuries since someone performed rites in my name, and I long for it like a mother who yearns for the affection of a dead child." Silhouettes of humans formed around us, shadows within the fog. "Please, Rowan. Do me this final favour."

The apparitions stepped closer, mysterious and intimidating. I agreed to perform the ritual.

I dragged the tablet on the hand barrow outside, following her orders. The apparitions—whose population grew—followed us.

I stopped by the Great Bath. The water was still. As I wondered whether Elisa's soul remained in there, it twisted and turned like a reverse whirlpool until her form appeared.

"You're back!" she cried, a tinge of hope in her voice. "Please, Rowan. I beg you, give me my body back. I'm so sorry for hurting you. I'll be out of your life forever, if that's what you wish. I just want to live again."

Sulis passed a dagger to me, taken from one of the exhibits, and knelt by the steps leading into the pool. There was hope in Elisa's eyes, hope that her nightmare was coming to an end.

I felt like an actor without a script, and I paused with stage fright.

Voices muttered. Voices of the spirits, whispering in my ear.

"Healing Mother." The words came from my lips as if they were willed by someone else, like I was their puppet. "For centuries, you have blessed our world with the gift of invigoration, a selfless entity with intentions pure. You have watered our roots so that we may stand like an oak in a meadow, strong and enduring. You have brought us warmth where we ought to find cold, rinsed us from sorrow, washed us from despair."

Hundreds of apparitions surrounded the bath now.

"Healing Mother. For centuries, we have forsaken you, rejected your gifts with ignorance, selfish beings with intentions obscure. We have uprooted our innocence so that we may fall, decaying in the soil. We have built walls where we ought to find space, imprisoned ourselves from peace, starved ourselves from love."

I raised the dagger above my head and pointed it where dark clouds formed.

"Healing Mother." My voice echoed. "With this last ritual, it must come to an end. We must sacrifice your soul so that we may atone. We must sacrifice your soul so that we may absolve. We must sacrifice your soul so that we may cleanse this world forevermore."

I cut Sulis's neck with the blade. She smiled as blood seeped out. Elisa wailed at the sight, cries that bellowed like a thunderclap.

A downpour unleashed with an intensity that matched her outburst. The body tumbled into the pool, sinking through her watery hands as she tried to grab it. She disappeared for a moment, diving under.

I dropped the dagger and fell to my knees as the trance subsided. The reality of what I had just done hit me with a surge of unbearable regret.

She returned to the surface, her head in her hands.

"You did this," she whimpered.

"I'm sorry," was all I could say, though I knew it meant nothing.

"What am I?" she lamented, staring at her translucent hands. Her form grew bigger as the pouring rain became one with her, and she soon towered over me. "What have you done to me?"

The pool overflowed, soaking my shoes as I backed away, perplexed at the sight. Thunder clapped again.

I had little choice but to run. The museum was flooding behind me as I sprung up the steps that led to the terrace, and I returned to the company of the Roman statues up top. Like them, I froze.

It was impossible. They were all facing me. Constantine, Hadrian, Vespasian, Caesar; they were all glaring at me.

A sizzle of boiling water resonated from below. As I crept past the statues, a crack resounded. One by one, they tumbled to the Great Bath, until only Caesar remained.

In the silence, I felt shame. I felt regret. And I felt the judgement of sublime forces looking down on me. With a parting look, Caesar fell too, and plunged into the dark waters below.

I'd spent the night pacing around the hotel room with a headache. The downpour had been going all night, claiming the streets. I gazed out the window to see litter drifting along the roads like debris caught in a stream.

Anxiety got the better of me and told me to escape. There wasn't enough time to think of a plan, or to gather my belongings. I had to make it to the train station before it was too late.

It wasn't long until I was sodden. My waterproof coat proved ineffective against this mythical rain. But I pressed on, passing the café Elisa and I had dined at a few days earlier, and ached to feel such normality again. As upset and betrayed as I felt that day, at least both of us were still human.

A crowd was forming in the next street. People came rushing out of doors on both sides. Waiters and chefs darted about, bashing wooden spoons against pans as they insisted customers abandon their seats.

"What's going on?" I asked a gentleman in a grey chequered suit who used a book like an umbrella.

"Bloody plumbing!" He turned to me. "The whole damn street's broken."

Water was flooding the floors of all the surrounding buildings, drenching carpets and smothering tiles. Helpful strangers moved frantically with mops, towels and whatever else might be useful in soaking it up. It was a thankless task.

We were soaking in Elisa's sorrow. Perhaps, if I could talk to her, she could make it stop.

I hurried towards the next street, where people were hurtling away from the steaming water that flowed, scalding every bit of skin it could find. Cascades fell from the tallest windows of the surrounding Georgian limestones, and all the cracks within them you wouldn't have otherwise noticed. It was spilling, too, from the terrace of the museum; a miniature waterfall that made climbing a difficult task. Bath was turning into a saucepan, simmering the souls of its inhabitants.

I did my best to ignore my stinging ankles, venting my pain through yelling as I diverted to the front. The entrance was locked with heavy chains tied around the handles. All I could do was slam my fists against it and demand entry, hoping Elisa would help. It was no use.

I scouted the area, looking for something to break the glass with, when I found a disposed brick. I picked it up and lobbed it at the museum's window, but it bounced off the reinforced glass and dropped with a splash.

The water rose so fast that I had to swim to stay afloat. My body was burning and there was blood in the water. Survival instincts kicked in and I deemed it wise to abandon my plan in favour of looking for safety.

Some people had climbed to the buttress of the Abbey; others were throwing them back down to save room for their loved ones. If I was to seek my own refuge, I'd have to go higher.

I paddled to the sculpted ladder beside the windows of the Abbey where those petrified angels I noticed days ago seemed like they were staring down at the deluge. I gripped onto it, pulled myself up and started to ascend.

I was free from the water at last, but it was catching up. In a panic for their lives, other people copied my idea. Worried that they might try and pull me down, I climbed as fast as I could.

Once I reached the top, I grabbed onto the ledge of the steeple and shuffled around to the side wall. From there, I pulled myself to the rooftop. The Abbey's bell tower loomed over me. There was no route to climb higher, and hopefully I wouldn't need one.

The rain felt like falling pins. I gazed over the edge to look down at the horror. One by one, people desperate to survive lost their strength and fell, swallowed by the flood.

"This can't be it." I fell to my knees. My tears, droplets of regret, became one with the downpour. "This can't be it."

The puddle around me started to swirl. I knew exactly what it meant before it morphed into the spirit of Elisa, now donning a similar stola Sulis had worn.

"Elisa, please," I begged. "Stop this madness. Innocent people are dying. By all means take my life, but spare those who don't deserve it." She stood over me and said nothing. Never had I felt so intimidated. "I didn't know what I was doing. I wasn't thinking properly, and Sulis knew that. She manipulated me so that she could kill us all. I believed her when she said she wanted to see the city. How was I supposed to know she was sizing it up for destruction?"

"That's the thing, Rowan. This isn't destruction. Like you said yesterday, this is purification. This is cleansing."

I was speechless. Elisa had never been the vengeful type, and it felt like I wasn't speaking to her at all.

"You see," she went on, "Sulis Minerva is not the spirit in the Great Bath so much as she *is* the bath; she is the water. And not just of the pool, but of the whole world. The woman you spoke to was just the avatar. She'd only been there for a hundred years, tricked by her predecessor into swapping places. Just like I was."

I had never felt so vulnerable. "But why?"

"It's not something you're capable of understanding, Rowan, and neither would I if you had not sacrificed me. There are many of us, observing Earth's creatures across the millennia, while Sulis Minerva has waited until the time is right."

Elisa knelt and kissed me.

"Humanity's end has come. It's time to pave way for a new world."

Her body collapsed with a splash. I bawled like a baby, curled up on top of the Abbey. The city of Bath was submerging, and there was nothing I could do to stop it. I was almost certain that the entire island of Britain would follow, and perhaps even the whole world.

About the Author

T.S Vickers lives in the heart of England, and when he's not writing, he's either working as a Mental Health Practitioner, rehearsing with his band or enjoying time with friends at the pub. He's been writing as a hobby for over a decade, and over the past few years has made publishing his goal, with 'Evergreen Chapel' his first released work. One day he'd like to publish his first novel, which he aims to have completed by some time last year.

SHAZAM!
CARNIVAL
GARBANZO THE GREAT
BIG BERTHA
STRONGMAN!
ALLIGATOR MAN
TINY TIM

THE GREATEST SHOW ON EARTH

BY JOEL REEVES

"**S**top wiggling about!" Garbanzo growled. "Or I promise you, I *will* stick you with one of these swords."

Princess Tina, Garbanzo's pretty and petite assistant, squirmed a bit, her eyes growing wide with fright each time a new blade was thrust through one of the slender openings in the infamous Box of Death.

MacGregor squirmed too. No matter how many times he witnessed the act, the strongman could not help being nervous for the young woman, knowing as he did that even the simplest of carnival tricks carried a certain amount of risk for the performers involved. Truth told, MacGregor held a secret flame for Tina and he didn't particularly care for how the carnival's owner treated her.

"Listen to the awful way he talks to her, Monkey," the strongman complained to the capuchin monkey chattering atop his shoulder. "I'd like to stick *him* in that thing."

Garbanzo pulled apart the sectioned box, revealing that Tina was still in one piece. Tina hopped up, performed a bow, and walked quickly off stage. MacGregor started to wave at her, but seeing his boss approach, stopped.

"MacGregor," Garbanzo whispered. "I have something I want to talk to you about in private. It's urgent. Meet me at my trailer right away."

"Yes, sir," the strongman replied. "I'll be right there."

It was about Tina. He was sure of it. The little tyrant probably noticed all of the longing gazes. MacGregor gave one last glance in Tina's direction, then lowering his head sadly, walked reluctantly along the dusty trail that wound through the carnival grounds in the direction of Garbanzo's trailer. Big drops of warm rain splashed on MacGregor's head and shoulders and on the empty wooden seats of the roller coaster and Ferris wheel. They rolled down and slid off the faded canvas awning that hung over the carousel, keeping its mad-eyed chomping steeds dry.

A few moments later, MacGregor knocked on the door of the nicest trailer on the lot.

"It's not locked," Garbanzo insisted. "Come in."

Garbanzo sat at a small table, resting his pimpled chin on one of his sharp, bony fists, examining a ledger and sipping from a tall glass of wine. MacGregor took a seat across the table. He braced himself as Garbanzo explained the nature of the "urgent" situation. When the boss was finished, MacGregor felt physically ill and more unsettled emotionally than if he had just simply been fired.

"So, as you can see," Garbanzo explained, "we cannot continue on this course. The show is losing money every day and—"

"I won't do it!" MacGregor snapped, furiously spitting out the words. "I refuse to have any part in your horrible scheme."

Garbanzo rolled his eyes and sighed. "You will do what I say or you will never see your lover girl again."

The strongman shot to his feet, his quivering face beet red, his great fists clenched in rage. "You little creep," he cursed. "You leave Tina out of this. You do anything to her and I'll kill you!"

MacGregor took a menacing step toward Garbanzo. The scrawny magician backed away, dropping his empty wine bottle with a crash on the tabletop, and held up his hands.

"Take it easy," Garbanzo quickly assured the strongman. "Tina is in very good hands. I promise. As long as you hold up your end of the deal, she'll be returned to you safe and sound. That's the Great Garbanzo's personal guarantee."

MacGregor lowered his head. The Strongest Man in the World blackmailed by Garbanzo Arbutus, a disgusting, disturbed pimple on the face of humanity. He must be strong now inside too, he thought, and keep his wits about him. He must also be patient and wait to see what opportunity might present itself.

"You promise that Tina will not be harmed if I cooperate?" MacGregor asked, hardly believing that he was agreeing to become an accomplice in the magician's mad plan to make the carnival profitable again.

Garbanzo smiled and made an X over his heart with his long, thin pointer finger. "Cross my heart," he said sweetly. He stretched his long, slender arms above his head and yawned.

"I don't believe you," MacGregor snapped. "Why should I? You..."

And just like that, the magician was asleep, his head resting face down on his crossed forearms, three empty bottles of wine lying on the table beside him. MacGregor glanced about the room, stood slowly to leave, and then stopped. His eyes shifted toward a strange, expensive-looking chest.

MacGregor eyed the magician once more, anxious. The monkey perched on his shoulder tipped its head down, chattering softly. The magician's cheek rested on one fist, a thin line of drool forming a puddle on the tabletop, an obnoxious snore escaping from his thin, cruel mouth. The strongman moved quickly to the small, shimmering chest, kneeling to examine it more closely. It was made of an expensive-looking black wood, probably exotic, MacGregor surmised, inset with gems and engraved with weird, leering faces—evil countenances that shifted, fading and then reappearing, defined and hideous.

MacGregor started to gently lift the lid then paused, surprised that the magician had left such an obviously expensive item out in the open. It crossed his mind that perhaps he had done so as a trap for him to find on purpose. But the more likely explanation, he mused, was the boss's preoccupation with the carnival's financial decline, coupled with his maddening addiction and current state of intoxication.

The strongman opened the lid all the way now, peering inside, his eyes growing wide. Several black votive candles—some new and others scorched and partially melted—were stacked together in one corner. A padded case held a variety of other more delicate items, including three stoppered flasks filled with a dark red substance, a crystal orb clouded in blackness, and a small whip, the handle of which was engraved with images similar to those on the chest itself.

What's all this? MacGregor gasped. The monkey shrugged and held up his tiny hands, bewildered. But MacGregor thought he could begin to guess. The magician had said that his plan involved powers beyond this world. The strongman was beginning to believe him. He felt a shiver creep through his body as he pulled out a black tome from the chest. The book's cover was wrapped in a strange material, wrinkled and dry and leathery like old skin.

MacGregor snorted when he read the title: *A Beginner's Guide to Summoning.* "Really, Garbanzo?" He chuckled. "I suppose that's how you learned your magic too."

He jumped at the touch of a cold, bony hand on his shoulder. He spun about to find the magician directly behind him, smiling. "I see you found my chest."

Startled, the monkey screeched and jumped down to the floor. Mac-Gregor stood quickly, his thick legs trembling. "I'm sorry, sir," he blurted. "It's just that—"

"You wanted to see if I was telling the truth about my dark plan to make this carnival the Greatest Show on Earth." Garbanzo nodded, his eyes narrowing. "This isn't just one of my smoke and mirror routines, my muscle-bound friend. It's going to require some sacrifice on everyone's part, but the rewards will be enormous."

MacGregor studied the magician. He didn't like what he saw and he especially didn't like that word: *sacrifice*. Not after what the owner had told him and what he had seen in the chest.

"Tina will not be harmed," the strongman said. "You promised."

"I'm a man of my word," Garbanzo insisted.

Eyeing the magician with contempt, MacGregor watched the strange fellow open a compartment above his bed. He handed the strongman a pouch containing a piece of gauze and a bottle of chloroform.

"You can use this to knock the townies out," Garbanzo stated, grinning. "If that doesn't work, well, use your imagination. But we need to make this quick. We need a big act to make this carnival great again!"

MacGregor glared at the magician. "Just what do you plan to do with these people once I've kidnapped them for you?"

"That's none of your concern," Garbanzo snapped, then he smirked. "Let's just say that I'll be putting all of my skills to good use." He took the large book out of the strongman's hands, winking. "And a few new skills besides."

"You're going to summon a demon?" MacGregor asked, dubious. "That's your answer to replacing the other oddities and making this carnival a success? You should be put away."

Garbanzo chuckled. "We'll see who's crazy when this carnival is making money hand over fist." He took MacGregor by the arm and ushered him toward the door. "You just make sure you're at your station in the House of Horrors when the guests arrive," he ordered, impatient. He peered out of a window in the direction of the scariest ride in the carnival. "They'll come as always just as soon as that blasted rain stops."

With a heavy heart, MacGregor scooped up his monkey and kicked open the door, leaving a boot-shaped impression in the metal panel. He stepped down from the trailer and stomped away through the dead, brown grass and leaves covering the carnival compound, heading back toward his own trailer. The rain fell even harder from the sky, seeping into his clothes, the sky gray and bleak.

"You'll pay for that door, MacGregor!" the magician shouted after him. "I'm deducting it from your salary."

Garbanzo watched MacGregor depart, cursing softly under his breath at the insolence of the man. He examined the damage to the trailer door, then pulled it shut and sat back down. He picked up the ledger from the table still cluttered with empty wine bottles. He studied the book a bit more, dismayed by what he saw, but confident that he was on the right track toward correcting the deficit.

"People will not tolerate a boring carnival filled with oddities that they've seen a hundred times," he said to himself. "This carnival needs something amazing, something horrifying. Something that will make even the most jaded of those townspeople soil their drawers."

And, Garbanzo Arbutus commended himself, he knew exactly what that *something* was. With the strongman's help, he would make the *Traveling Sideshow of the Grotesque* the greatest attraction in the country once more, maybe even the world.

Lenny Skeers, dubbed the Alligator Man because of a condition that gave his skin a scaly, reptilian appearance, laid out another hand of poker. But none of the oddities seemed much interested in the game today, not since they had heard the bad news.

"Boring!" shouted Sam Hill, furious. "Is that what that dirtbag said about us?"

The dwarf perched on his stool so that he could look the other freaks around the table straight in their worried eyes, his clenched fists trembling, and small, round eyes popping.

"He's already given Big Bertha and Tiny Tim their walking papers," Romeo the Clown confirmed. "I saw them packing last night. Garbanzo told them people don't think fat ladies and midgets are all that interesting anymore. He said reality television is lousy with stories about obese women who can't get out of bed and midgets and dwarves crying because someone made the chairs at a restaurant too tall for them to get into."

"Little people," Sam Hill scolded. "We're a community now. Don't forget that."

Romeo frowned. "Sorry, Sam," he apologized. "I'm just telling you what the boss said. I didn't mean to be insensitive."

Sam shrugged and sighed. "No big deal," he said. "I guess I'm just really worried," he admitted. "The boss talking about downsizing the carnival... it's got me real scared. I mean, this is a bad time. Jobs don't come easy. Especially for guys like me."

The other oddities glanced nervously at each other. Eventually, their eyes turned to MacGregor sitting in the corner, his chattering companion perched atop his thick shoulder. He looked out his small trailer window at the rain, preoccupied with thoughts of Tina and his role in Garbanzo's insane plan. He wanted to tell the others about everything, but he feared what the carnival owner might do to his beloved.

"What are we going to do, Mac?" Sam demanded. "You're the union president for the carnies. You've got to talk to the boss for us. Make him understand that the reason ticket sales are down is because things are tough all over right now. It's not because the townies are bored with looking at freaks."

MacGregor shrugged, his face grim. "I'll do my best," he promised. He glanced out the window in the direction of the House of Horrors, the black form of the big trailer barely visible in the gloom. "You guys stay and finish your game of cards. I've got something I need to do."

The rain suddenly stopped at dusk. The carnival came to life. Colored lights in blue, red, and green illuminated the grounds once again.

Laughter and the sound of a calliope filled the crisp October air. Townies lined up to play games and ride the rides. The bravest wandered to the back of the courtyard, all the way back to the tents posted with garish signs marked ADULTS ONLY. Men entered tents, sometimes with their wives and children in tow despite the warnings, standing just inside the closed flaps to gawk at the oddities within. Henry Walloon, a retired schoolteacher who had lived in the town all his life, read the sign that identified the exhibit before him: THE ANATOMICAL WONDER. He watched with little interest as the man without a stomach attempted to wow the crowd by pulling his gut until his backbone became visible.

Unimpressed, the crowd grumbled about wanting their money back, and slipped out of the tent, leaving the oddity inside to put himself right again. The carnie attraction, having composed himself, sat on his stool in the gloom of his tent and lowered his head, terrified now that what the boss had claimed—that the carnival and its sideshow had lost their pizazz—was, in fact, true. Had people really become so jaded that the freaks no longer made them curious, or fascinated, or on the best of those rare occasions, filled them with a sense of horror?

Coincidentally, re-instilling that sense of horror was exactly what Garbanzo Arbutus was working on at the moment. He climbed aboard the conveyor belt that swept the young and old alike into the gaping maw of darkness that was the House of Horrors.

"Be careful," Garbanzo warned, grinning with his death's-head face at a wide-eyed child who had lost his balance and nearly toppled off the platform. "I wouldn't want anyone getting hurt."

The apple-cheeked boy peered up at the strange man and squeezed his mother's hand tightly. "You're creepy."

Garbanzo frowned at the insult, annoyed. He took the flashlight he held in his hand, turned it on, and pointed it directly in the boy's face. "You should really have more respect for your elders."

The boy held up his hand, blinking. "Hey!"

The conveyer whisked the screaming riders into the gaping mouth, into darkness, into the screams of the insane clowns, the screeches of witches, and the shrieks of ghosts. A huge rubber spider dropped down from the ceiling and a rider shouted at the feeling of something like webs sliding across her face. A ghoul holding his bloody, decapitated head in his hands sprung from the floor, groaning.

After the last of the customers disappeared into the dark mouth of the ride, Garbanzo nodded for Eric the Lion Tamer to take his spot at the front of the line. The magician hopped down to the ground, disappearing around the back of the big trailer that housed the ride. He slipped in through the STAFF ONLY entrance, pulling it shut and locking the door behind him. He shined his flashlight down a flight of stairs that descended into the darkness beneath the House of Horrors, following a narrow corridor that led to a trapdoor room.

He removed a cell phone from his pocket and punched in a number, still not comfortable with the whole texting business. "Bring the girl at midnight. I've got something special planned."

MacGregor crouched beneath the trapdoor, alone with his thoughts, still torn over his role in aiding Garbanzo in the abduction of innocent people to fulfill the magician's bizarre scheme. He thought about Tina, imagining her stuffed inside the sword box, screaming, and shoved away into some dark room. And the little monkey. They were his life. He'd decided to leave his little companion back at the trailer. Kidnapping people was new to MacGregor. Bringing the monkey along would only complicate things. He'd be much safer at home until all this strange business was over.

MacGregor felt a vibration and then a rumble somewhere, not far off now. The conveyor was coming. A rumbling belt of terror. The walls and ceiling shook. He squeezed his big hands into fists, waiting.

No light penetrated the darkness this deep into the belly of the House of Horrors; even the bright sound of the calliope outside was gone—only the cries of the undead monsters and the frantic beating hearts of the townies lingered here. Suddenly, the conveyor reached an abrupt end and those in front felt themselves thrown forward, unable to keep their balance, tumbling and sliding down a polished ramp and rolling onto a cold, wooden floor.

A dozen groaning mummies dropped from the ceiling, a red light illuminating the bandages that covered their hideous, rotted faces. Behind the townies, a trapdoor swung open quietly. The old woman at the back, who had come alone to the carnival, peered up at the dangling monsters, their groans still echoing. She didn't have time to cry out as a large hand suddenly wrapped around her mouth and nose, the sweet smell of ether burning her nostrils. Lifted her off her feet and plunged into Hell.

A little boy looked back at the empty space in the blackness. He scratched his head, not really sure if he had imagined the old woman after all.

Outside, the line of people for the House of Horrors extended past the brightly lit trailer that sold popcorn, hotdogs, chips, elephant ears, and sugary sodas. Eric the Lion Tamer checked his watch, waiting for the next carnie to come and spell him off. He helped more passengers aboard the popular ride, pulled a lever with a big, red knob, and watched disinterestedly as another group of townies were whisked away, screaming into the guts of the mechanized house.

MacGregor pushed the trapdoor open a few inches and peered out, quickly identifying another easy target: a little boy leaning on a crutch who reminded him of Tiny Tim. Like the old woman, the little boy stood apart from the others, someone who had braved the scariest ride in the park on his own. The strongman awaited his cue—the mummies dropped, their loud groans mixing with the screams of the alarmed townies. The panic in the dark provided perfect cover for MacGregor who quickly gagged and snatched the boy out of the darkness before the others could notice, adeptly disappearing out of sight through the hole in the floor, and quietly lowering the trapdoor.

He rushed down the ladder to the chamber below with the squirming boy. A grinning Garbanzo stood holding the small chest glittering in his arms. They tied the boy's hands and feet, and lowered him to a sitting position beside the frightened old woman who lay shivering and terrified in the cool night air.

MacGregor watched as Garbanzo opened the chest. He took out the tome, the candles, and the vials, which the strongman now surmised, contained blood. He didn't want to think about it, nor did he ask how the magician had obtained it. Finally, he removed the dark glass orb and held the small whip in his hand, examining it with interest.

"I need more townies for this to work," Garbanzo announced. "Just a couple more should do it."

"And then you'll give me back Tina?" MacGregor asked, the blackmail fueling his resentment and rage.

The magician nodded. "Of course," he said. "Garbanzo the Great is a man of his word."

At that moment, the walls shook. MacGregor sighed and reluctantly climbed the ladder to the trapdoor. It was nearing midnight, closing time, when the strongman dragged the last of the victims into the chamber below the carnival ride.

"Your job is done," Garbanzo announced. "Mine is just beginning." He poured the blood onto the stone floor, a circle to protect him from the evil that he would summon. "Go home, MacGregor. Go home to your girlfriend. You will find her there now, safe and sound, as I promised."

The strongman felt his insides twist at the sight of the townies tied and gagged on the floor. Suddenly, the STAFF ONLY entrance door at the back of the chamber swung open. A tall, slender man dressed in a black suit and tie with a long scar down one cheek entered. He whispered something to someone in the dark behind him who MacGregor could not see, then pulled out a revolver. He pointed it at MacGregor.

"You want me to shoot him, boss?" he asked. "Or you going to feed him to the monster too?"

Garbanzo shook his head. "Neither actually," he replied. "Mister MacGregor was just leaving, weren't you?"

MacGregor lowered his eyes in shame, his heart sick at the sight of the hapless townies staring up at him in horror. "I won't let him get away with this."

"Goodbye, MacGregor!" Garbanzo growled impatiently.

MacGregor looked at the thug with the gun. He was the Strongest Man in the World, but he realized, even strong men were no match for bullets. He took one last, long look at the poor wretches huddled on the floor, then left.

MacGregor arrived a short time later at his trailer. He leaped up the steps in one bound and shoved open the door. He gazed inside, waiting to be greeted by Tina and his pet monkey. But the complete darkness and silence told him all he needed to know. Garbanzo was also the Greatest Liar in the World. He stepped inside and stood thinking for a moment about what to do, angry at himself for wanting to believe too much that his loved ones would be fine, that Garbanzo still had a scrap of decency, that everything would turn out okay in the end.

Something rustled in the dead leaves just outside the door. He heard a chattering noise.

"Monkey!" MacGregor shouted, elated. The little monkey had jimmied the lock on the trailer door once before. MacGregor shoved the door open quickly and looked out.

A squirrel with an acorn stuffed in one cheek rustled about in the leaves. Seeing MacGregor, the little animal scampered away and up a tree, perching in the long limbs above, chattering down at him. The sound of shouting drew his attention to the far end of the compound where a large crowd had gathered, all pushing and shoving to see something.

Furious at being duped and more worried than ever about his friends, MacGregor rushed off in the direction of the commotion, pushing roughly through the throng toward the front. He stopped suddenly, his eyes widening.

"Sweet Jesus, Garbanzo, you insane fool," MacGregor gasped. "What have you done?"

A gibbering mound of flesh the size of a small hill, covered in oozing sores, slithered and wobbled in front of the House of Horrors. Cavernous, twisted mouths in the creature's swollen, undulating body yawned and spoke and cried all at once. A dozen or more pairs of eyes looked out from the gelatinous mass, squinting, glaring, peering at everything and everyone like a hideous newborn looking for a parent, wanting to escape the attention and the bright carnival lights.

With the exception of a few small children too naive to know better, the townspeople fled, dropping carnival refreshments, long strips of purple tickets, and stuffed animals won in ring tosses earlier in the night. They ran toward town, screaming for the law or God to save them. The carnies withdrew into their trailers, locking their doors and peering out through window curtains, fascinated and dismayed by the appearance of this freakish creature that threatened both their lives and livelihoods.

Garbanzo stood several feet away from the creature, holding aloft the glass sphere from the little chest. The globe glowed a brilliant red, bathing the creature in its light.

"I think you will agree that this monster is the most grotesque thing ever," Garbanzo gloated, pleased at the townies' horrified reactions. "No other sideshow has anything like it, I assure you."

MacGregor found himself unable to look away from the monster. He stared hard at the gibbering mass, watched as the eyes and mouths formed faces that surfaced in the gelatinous monstrosity, and then sank from sight, only to appear a moment later on another part of the demon's enormous, ulcerous body. He gasped, horrified.

The face of a screeching monkey surfaced, its small, brown eyes imploring him, trapped in the quivering flesh.

"Monkey!" MacGregor cried, reaching out, helpless as the face disappeared from view.

The strongman fell to his knees, his eyes filling with tears. At the same moment, Tina's brave face appeared, her sad expression ripping at MacGregor's heart, deep into his very soul.

"No! Garbanzo, you monster!" He covered his face as the vision of the only girl he had ever loved sank again from sight, swallowed by the gibbering mound of flesh once more.

Garbanzo strutted about, oblivious.

"Watch the freakiest of the freaks perform!" Garbanzo shouted, smacking the quivering flesh of the monster with his whip, a crackle of blue electricity cutting the demon with each strike. "Roll over, demon. Your master commands you!"

The demon shrieked, hating the thing that controlled it.

Garbanzo, delighted at his power, raised the whip, and holding aloft the glass sphere spoke the control word: "Pain!"

The demon winced, the mouths twisting and shrieking. Like a big dog, the demon rolled over, growling and snarling and spitting.

MacGregor watched the display, sensed the demon's humiliation, felt the taste of bile in his throat, and swallowed it back down.

"You dirty fink," he snarled. "You promised."

He jumped to his feet and lunged at the magician. Garbanzo shouted, his eyes wide, and held up the whip, daring MacGregor to come a step closer. A rock came out of the darkness, whizzed past MacGregor's shoulder, striking and shattering the glass ball clenched in Garbanzo's hand. An explosion split the air, the horrified face of the magician illuminated for only a second in a burst of red light.

"You little fool!" Garbanzo shouted. "What have you done?"

A child in the shadows giggled and ran off.

The demon stared down at the smashed sphere. With a terrible ear-splitting scream—the sound of many voices shrieking all at once—the creature lunged at Garbanzo, knocking him to the ground. He struggled and shouted, striking at the demon with the whip.

"For the love of God, MacGregor!" Garbanzo screamed. "Help me!"

But MacGregor did not scream and he did not run away. Instead, he glared at Garbanzo, seething with contempt.

"You're the Greatest Magician in the World," he snarled. "Help yourself."

Garbanzo's screams were heard in every locked carnival trailer up and down the midway—and across the field, the little boy who had thrown the rock that had missed the evil magician but destroyed the magical orb heard bloody shrieks and ran into the house and locked the door.

MacGregor slipped away back to his trailer and locked himself inside, pressing his hands to his ears against the sound of Garbanzo's dying wails. He peered out through the curtain of his trailer. The demon was hunting. With the addition of Garbanzo it had gotten bigger, and with each new victim, MacGregor feared, it would continue to grow. Garbanzo had unleashed it, and now that the ball was broken, MacGregor wondered if there was anything that anyone could do to stop it from ravaging the countryside. He continued to watch the demon as it moved methodically from trailer to trailer, pressing its quivering flesh against the doors, and finding every trailer secured, eventually shambling off into the darkness. In the direction of the town.

MacGregor told himself that he would mourn the loss of Tina and his pet later. Now, however, action was needed and it seemed that this new role fell to him. Not wanting any more trouble, and knowing that carnies were always to blame when things went bad, the strongman ordered the *Traveling Sideshow of the Grotesque* to pull up stakes and shove off.

A few hours later, MacGregor sat up on his bed, unable to sleep, and peered out his little window. The first light of dawn appeared on the horizon. MacGregor felt the bumpiness of the road, heard the sound of the leaves in the trees, and wiped away a tear, thinking about the two companions he had left behind.

About the Author

Joel Reeves studied education and humanities at Central Michigan University and has taught both high school and college. He enjoys reading and writing Twilight Zone-esque speculative fiction—the darker the irony the better. His most recently published work, ODD BIRDS, is a collection of tales with twists and twisted tales. When he's not writing, he enjoys playing games with his family and long walks in the Michigan woods.

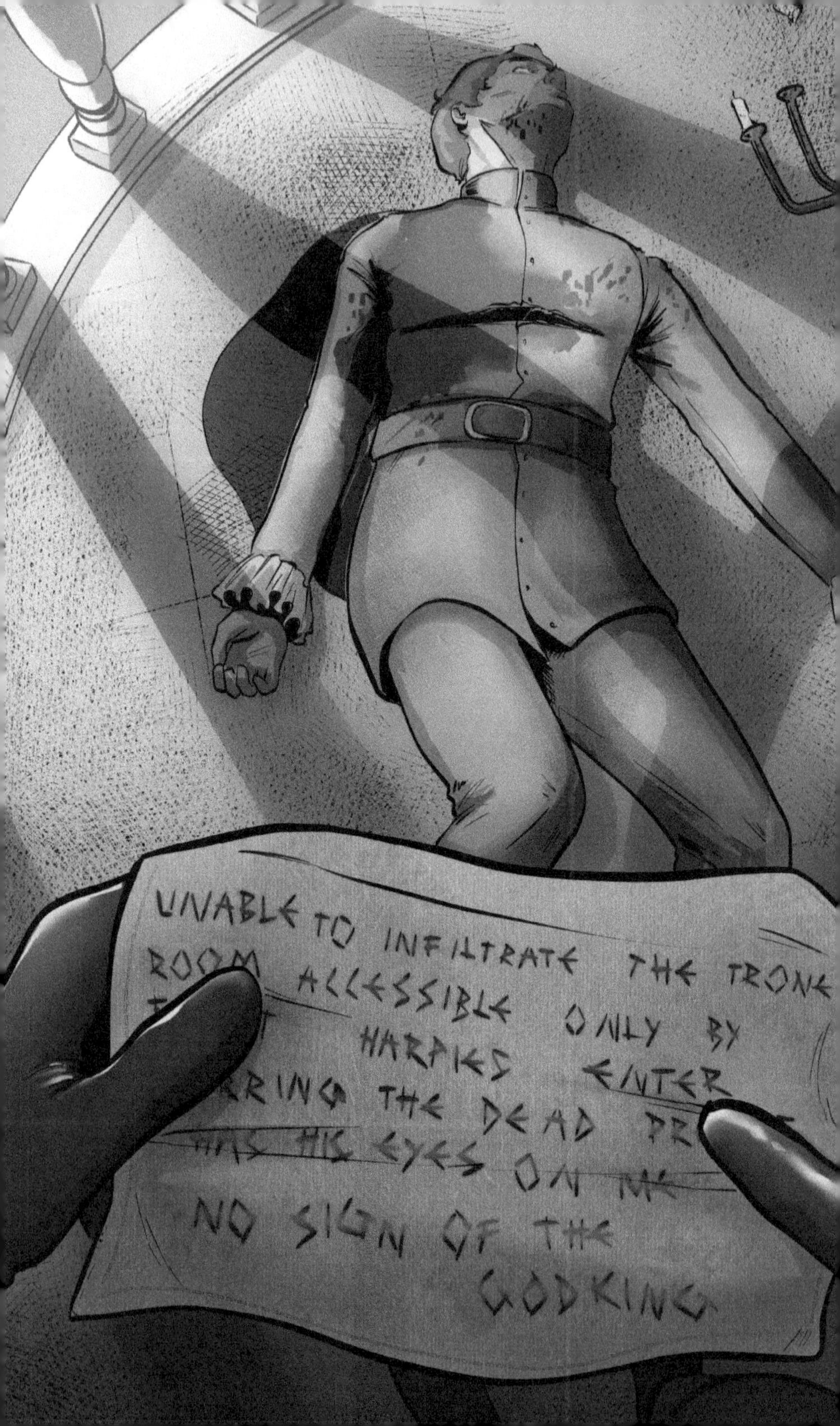

UNABLE TO INFILTRATE THE TRONE
ROOM ACCESSIBLE ONLY BY
HARPIES ENTER
RING THE DEAD PR
HAS HIS EYES ON ME
NO SIGN OF THE
GODKING

A Final Offering

by Akis Linardos

*Conformance does not equal unity. Human sacrifice
negates freedom. Divinity is no excuse for slavery.*
from Final Offering by Amadi Dane, Founder of the
Nameless Guild

Vatu was ten when he first saw a body fall from the sky. It hadn't crashed nor splattered, but landed like a fish with a slimy splat. Now, Vatu was the one doing the throwing. On the balcony of the floating cathedral, his black robes flapped wildly against the wind as he tossed another corpse overboard. Dust-red clouds rolled from all around, and the air carried the stench of piss-stained feathers from harpies hovering far above, circling the steeples. The land below, ashen like a used-up hearth, veined with muddy roads, seemed as far as the stars and moon.

In that balcony was an array of anvil-shaped tables, fresh cadavers lying on top. Some had turned white from the Godking's handling, their texture transformed to that of a larva's, shining an unnatural white sheen, smelling of sour clams.

With gloved hands, Vatu brought the scalpel down on one of the transformed cadavers. He sliced along the solar plexus, flesh receding like jelly. After two years of service to the Godking, it still wrenched his stomach. But he had to do it. He had to act the part to get close to the Godking, and kill him.

He sliced all the way to the left rib and pushed his hand inside. Gloved fingers wiggled through, feeling as if immersed in honey, until they met the spiderweb encasing the heart, like crystalized bundles of hair. Others called those *kristas*—the manifestation of emotions, the things left behind when the Godking transported the soul to another plane of existence. Or so the tales told. Vatu pulled out the gossamer, wrapped it into a bundle, and put it in an oakwood container. It was his job that these were taken out and brought back to the Godking.

Yet any time he'd touch these things, he could feel a tug at his skin. Like a magnet pulling his heart, a deep sorrow would nest within him. The world would shrink and the clouds would grow darker until he'd tuck the *kristas* away in their containers. And once again the shadows would lift from within him. Was it the tug of a lost soul at his own heartbeat? Was there a leftover consciousness in the dregs these souls left behind, crying to be set free?

Vatu shook his head. Grim assumptions wouldn't help. He didn't have to understand all the depravities of the Godking. For now, he had to find a way into the throne room.

He pulled a black piece of cloth out of his robe. The letters he'd woven with white thread upon it read: *Unable to infiltrate throne room. Accessible only by flight. Harpies enter carrying the dead. Prophet has his eye on me. No sign of the Godking.*

He shoved the cloth into the body and marked the side of the head with an X. Denu—his friend since childhood, his first and only crush—would receive his message, pass it on to the guild. Vatu pushed the body off the balcony and moved to another table.

A fresh cadaver this time. Two years ago, he would not believe he'd find a fresh cadaver to be pleasant, but compared to the slimy result of whatever the Godking was doing to these bodies, they were a welcome break. He sliced from navel to the waist, removing the entrails. The fabric of his robe wicked away the blood splatter, growing a little darker.

The air became pungent with harpy-stench as one of the winged creatures descended. It swooped the fresh body he'd just handled and flew toward the top of the cathedral, through the gaping gate of the dome. A long balcony extended outward like a tongue.

Vatu had long since deduced this to be the throne room, but that's about all he knew. The fresh bodies would fly in there, and days later, back would come grotesque, slimy abominations, their hearts encrusted in that crystallized spiderweb. Some thought it was just what happens when the soul is extracted by the Godking and sent to paradise. Vatu didn't know what to think.

The stench of sour clams came again, stronger.

"The gaze lingers too long, mortal man," a shrill voice said.

Vatu turned. The prophet hovered above him. He had the form of an oversized baby, and an umbilical cord that stretched to the skies. His eyes bulged like hen's eggs, his frog mouth curving to a long smile that split his face. He was the source of the stench.

Vatu bowed. "Just admiring the stonework of His Eminence, prophet. My apologies if it caused offense."

"His *Divine* Eminence," the prophet croaked. "You are still new here, mortal man. How long has it been since your ascension? Three years? That's nothing. To preserve the privilege of living among gods, you must learn to keep your head *down*."

One year, seven months, and twenty one days, Vatu thought, but saw no reason to correct him. "Yes, prophet," he said, bowing so low he faced his own kneecaps. "Thank you for enlightening me this day with your wisdom."

The prophet hovered away, seemingly pleased with Vatu's subservient attitude. They said that when the prophet had first descended to bring the message of the Godking Gluul, silver rain came down from the skies. They said every man, woman, and child cried tears of joy and sang in unison.

They said all sorts of hogwash.

Vatu incised the next body, and in his mind's eye he saw through the gates of the dome, picturing the Godking sitting on a throne built on spilled blood and broken bone.

I will slit your throat yet. No child will ever have to face what I did. Never again. The prophet can bark all he wants but I'm coming for you, false god.

Eighteen years before Vatu's ascension...

There was mist again at the outskirts of Traffel, the fishing village Vatu called home. Gray grass covered the meadow, like a painting whose artist never got to fully color. Two teenagers—a boy with a great red scar across his neck and a girl with wispy brown hair—held a net stretched out to five feet filled with fish. On the other side, five kids including Vatu and Denu, had just finished outlining a square on the ground with twigs and rocks, no wider than ten feet.

"Vatu should sit in the front," the boy with the scar said. He and the other teenager seemed as big as adults to Vatu.

Vatu grabbed Denu's hand and squeezed.

"I'll do it," Denu said. "Assuming the torch."

"Hiding behind a girl again, Vatu?" the boy with the scar asked. Some of the kids laughed.

"She assumed the torch, Brok," the girl with the wispy hair said. "It's the rules."

"Fine," Brok said. "Denu, you take the front. Vatu can sit back."

The kids arranged themselves in a pentagon inside the square. Brok whistled. The two kids holding the net swung it back and forth, singing in unison:

From his head sprouts the sea

From the sea sprouts the rain

Sin, sin, sing

Sing

For

The

Hail!

They swung the net forward, hurtling the fish at the five kids. Vatu fixated on Denu, who masterfully dodged two cods and a sea bass. Another fish came, passed over her shoulder, and landed flat on Vatu's face. His nose and mouth filled with bile.

"Sinner, sinner, fish for dinner!" the other kids shouted.

"You're useless, Vatu," one of them said, laughing. "You're just like your fa—"

Denu slammed one of the sea basses across the kid's face.

"Hey!"

"Sorry," Denu said, walking toward Vatu, holding five fish by their tails. "Hand slipped. Let's go, Vatu."

"Yeah, you take your pet and go, Denu," Brok chided. "We'll see each other soon."

Vatu and Denu walked down the hill of the ashen meadow until they reached the edges of the floating cathedral's shadow, still lingering at the late hours of dusk. Vatu mumbled a prayer to the Godking, tears welling up in his eyes as he thought of the punishment awaiting him for being labeled a sinner in the game.

"You don't have to pray all the time, you know," Denu said.

"But m-m—" Vatu broke off, crying. "M-mother says I have to. I have to be perfect. She says I—that I—the teachings of Amadi…"

"Godking doesn't always listen," she whispered. She pushed the fish into Vatu's hand. "Take them."

His eyes opened wide. "Denu, no I—but they will punish you!"

"It's fine. Father says penance proves my loyalty to the Godking. It will increase the chances of me ascending. It's all worth it, for the cause."

"But *I* lost! Not you! The game is a ritual to the Godking. It's sacrilege to give it to me! It's not—it's not fair!"

"We passed the torch, remember? You were supposed to get that fish." Denu smiled. "Nothing is fair."

"But—"

"Race me to the hill," she said. "Catch me and I'll take the fish back." She bolted to a sprint before he could reply.

Vatu was a terrible runner. Cold wind always hurt his throat, causing phlegm to build up. Denu vanished after cresting the hill, and Vatu pushed all his willpower to his legs to keep up. He reached the top. She was down at the base of the hill on the other side, smiling up at him.

He took a deep breath, sprinted, and leaped off the hill. For the brief moment he was in the air, the thought of her smile fresh in his mind, he felt happy. Free even.

He landed on slanting ground and toppled over himself until he reached bottom.

"Are you all right?"

Denu leaned over him, smiling. Beyond her, high in the sky, the cathedral loomed like a twin brother to the moon. A dark, twisted brother that had descended to keep a close eye on the land and its creatures.

Denu followed his gaze, fixating on the cathedral. Vatu looked at her and her ginger hair. So beautiful. If only the Godking never existed. They would be free. Free of their parents' demands and dreams of revolution. Free to make their own choices, to just have fun and enjoy one another's company as often as they wished.

"Vatu," she said, still looking up at the sky. "Promise me something, will you?"

"Of course. What is it?"

"If the Godking takes me. Just remember me—I mean—remember me as I am *now*. If we grow old and become like our parents. Remember me as I am now, will you?"

He didn't fully understand what she meant. "I promise," he said anyway.

As they crested another hill, Vatu saw the shadow of a bird above. It grew larger and larger with every passing moment. Until he realized it was not a bird at all.

The body landed ten feet ahead of them. The sound reminded him of when fish dropped to the ground during the Sinner Dinner game, only more powerful. They dashed toward it. It might once have been a woman, but now it was a thing, shining white, spreading on the ground like spilled jelly.

Gods are not born into the world, they happen. When I witnessed Gluul emerge from chaos, I knew my purpose was to help him rule.

Revelations of Gluul - Passage 12:33

Now...

On the day of the Bloody Rain, Vatu and the other ascendants gathered at the core of the floating cathedral under the watchful gaze of the prophet. The chamber was large enough to host gladiator games, and the circular trapdoor at the center wide enough for a fighting pit. Piles of corpses formed around the trapdoor, while ascendants held spear-sized shovels in pairs, discarding the cadavers out the hole. Up in the stalls, the prophet sat in a chair shaped to fit his baby-like form. His umbilical cord slithered upward to an opening and vanished from view.

The man paired with Vatu stood a head taller, crouched and cowled so that only his hands were visible. Rough, pale knuckles. Had to be from the northern fishing villages. Vatu had few chances to interact with other ascendants. An ally would be indispensable in this world. Frankly, any social contact would be.

Slim chance, convincing an ascendant to join his cause, but the atrocities committed in the floating cathedral should shock even the fanatic believers.

"Ever seen the god's face?" Vatu whispered as they carried another body over the trapdoor.

The man turned his gaze at Vatu. His eyes were gray and cold like ocean mist, his long face had a sort of authority to it that disarmed Vatu. "No one but the prophet gazes upon the face of the Godking."

"Would be good for morale. And why not ascend more people?" Vatu pointed to the pile of bodies next to them. "He'd not have to throw away—"

"What is your name?" the man asked.

"Vatu."

"Are you aware of Sinner Dinner? Children play it in the north."

"Yes. It's played in the south as well."

The man nodded. "Only in our version, the parents hold the fishing nets. Losers are doused with fish oil, their stench telling everyone how they sinned. The parents shut the sinner kids in stone coffins without food for an entire week to atone. You appreciate other privileges when you're shut in a closed space for so long with nothing but the worms, the humidity, and your own dark thoughts."

A chill crawled down Vatu's spine. He remembered the sting of the whip, the flagellation his parents would inflict on him when *he* sinned. When he'd lose the stupid fish game or when he'd let his gaze linger above with childlike curiosity at the looming cathedral instead of keeping his head down. He caressed his own shoulder blade, heart *thud-thudding* as if the whip would come any moment now. *It's in the past,* he reminded himself. *Your parents can no longer hurt you.*

"Are you getting to a point?" Vatu asked the man.

"I am," he replied as they hoisted the shovel over the cockpit, flinging the body. It seemed like the world had lifted upside down and they were simply watching a bird fly away. "Do not question the Godking in front of me. Where I come from, there is no such thing as casual talk about His name."

Three months before Vatu's ascension...

Three feet below ground, within the ancient catacombs, Vatu and Denu sat in a chamber the old guild had used as base of operations. He steepled his hands, elbows resting on an oval table. She sat on the other side, eyes glazed. Her ginger hair was long now. She usually wore it in a bun—a sign of piety—but beneath the ground, where the Godking's gaze could not reach, she always let it loose.

"It's not fair, you know," she said.

"Nothing is fair. Right?"

She slammed the table. "How? *I* had always been the strong one. *Me.* How did you get chosen?"

"Maybe he prefers the strong ones remain on ground. Who knows what the ascended ones do? Amadi only ever talked about incisions in his manifesto. No details as to why or when, or even how he was supplied with the information."

"This is *bullshit*," Denu said.

"You shouldn't swear."

"Oh, shut up. We're three feet below ground. He doesn't fucking listen. And besides, what does it matter? You're the chosen one now. Gluul never ascends more than one from a single village."

"It matters. You need to keep the guild alive. We need to work together to defeat him. To be finally free."

She scoffed. "I barely know five guild members. Four, now that my father's dead. Piss on his bones."

Vatu stood, walked toward her, and laid a hand on her shoulder. "I know you're hurting, Denu. But it ill becomes you to talk like that about your parents."

She fell silent for a while, then said, "I was always a tool to them. They never saw me as a human. Only you did. I can't just let you go. I-I—" She slammed the table again. "It's not *fair!*"

A lingering silence fell. He eyed her lips. He craved to kiss them, but he couldn't bring himself to do it. He eyed his hand, still nesting on her shoulder. It didn't feel right to remove it. It didn't feel right to leave it there. Nothing felt... particularly right at that moment.

"I was less than a tool to my parents," Vatu said. "A useless tool. One that didn't perform the required function." He chuckled. "Wish they were alive to see me now. In any case, I—they—well, let's say I understand now. I don't forgive them. Never will. But I understand. You have to sacrifice part of your humanity—become a monster, that is—if you hope to overthrow a monster."

"The corpses," Denu said.

"What?"

"The corpses. That's the only thing that comes and goes from the floating cathedral. Sew your messages in them, throw them overboard when the cathedral floats over the fishing village. You'll have to sew the same message in more than one—mark them with something, use the guild's emblem—no, too complicated. Just use an X. I will then be able to tell these were handled by you."

Vatu cringed. "*Amadi's bones.* What will my life be like from now on?"

Denu touched his hand, still resting on her shoulder. "Our lives are already gone, Vatu. Offered bit by bit since childhood." She pulled him closer. So close he could smell the cinnamon in her breath. "Is there really anything left of us now?"

"There might be something," Vatu said, and kissed her for the first time.

In this ephemeral form he will guide the godless. Let there be fear in his wake, for in fear man finds order. In freedom, chaos.

Revelations of Gluul - Passage 5:12

Now...

Vatu was on the balcony again, stitching another one of the transformed bodies. He'd thrown three that day, stuffing copies of his message inside each to be sure it would be received. A harpy came carrying another body, its head clean shaven. Vatu froze.

The harpy dropped the body, and Vatu rushed, catching it before it hit the anvil. Denu's almond eyes were shut, her lips blue and cracked, her beautiful, long hair gone, and her scalp grimed with dirt. He placed her down, his feet wobbling. Tears threatened, but he fought them off, fearing someone might witness him.

How? How could this happen? You were the most careful of all.

He eyed her navel. He imagined himself bringing the scalpel down on her, he imagined her body coming back in a slimy mess. He gritted his teeth and squeezed his eyes. How could this happen? How could—

Denu's hand snapped out and grasped his wrist. She exhaled as if she'd been drowning.

Vatu pulled back. "*Goddamn!* Denu! Denu how—"

She embraced him, touched her lips to his. He closed his eyes, feeling the warmth of her touch. He could not believe she was real.

"How?" Vatu asked.

She pulled back. "The Hunter made a breakthrough. He tracked the harpy flight patterns. I knew which one would be delivered to you." She put her thumb and index finger inside her mouth, wiggling them as if trying to remove a tooth. She produced a teardrop bottle, no larger than a molar, a pale pink liquid inside. "The Alchemist," she said, voice rough as if her throat had been torn by glass fragments. "He made a potion that suspends life temporarily. I have to take another dose. Infiltrate the throne room. You said so yourself. Only way something moves into the throne room is in the talons of a harpy. Just—"

Vatu grabbed her hand. "No."

Denu frowned. "What do you mean *no*?"

"I know this place. I'll take the potion."

"Are you seriously going to debate with me right now?"

"I'm not debating," Vatu said. "Assuming the torch."

Denu's mouth twitched. "*Fucking...* Give me your robes, quick, before someone notices."

Vatu gave her his robes and laid down on the anvil.

The cowl hid the shaven scalp as she looked down at him. It allowed him to imagine her hair was still there beneath the cloth.

"It won't hurt," she said. "Not until you wake up."

Vatu nodded. He could hear his own heartbeat.

She grabbed his hand, passing the bottle. "A final offering."

"A final offering," Vatu echoed.

He gulped the potion, tasting like the skin of a lemon. He drifted to a deep slumber, and in his dream he saw a snake sliding down his chest, worming through his navel.

What is the opposite of permanence? How does one negate immortality? The truth lies in that which is exclusive to mortals. Emotion.

from Final Offering by Amadi Dane, Founder of the
Nameless Guild

The first thing Vatu felt when he woke up was a searing pain in his belly. His fingers traced his body, drenched in blood. There was something hard etched inside his skin near his navel.

The air was pungent with the revolting sweetness of cadavers, warm in a way that made his skin itch. The throne room was massive, supported in two sequences of pillars tall as elms. Corpses piled the walls, their blood suffusing the grout. On one end was the gate, showing the red skies beyond, and on the opposite, a giant sat on a throne. The throne was not made of bone or blood as the tales told, but granite. The giant's head lolled to one side. Vatu could not make out his features; the giant seemed unconscious.

Got you now, false god.

Vatu felt the hard surface of his own belly with his fingers. Whatever was etched inside, it was rectangular and flat, long as his index finger. He pushed on one edge of it, seeing a razor blade protrude from the other edge. With a grunt, he slid it out.

He realized Denu had incised a pocket inside his skin to hide the weapon. Her maneuver had supplied him with defense and the bloodied belly convinced the harpy that the body was ready to be transported. It pained him like hell, but it was too shallow to kill him. At least he hoped it was.

Vatu slipped silently down the bloody table. He passed through spiderwebs, their thin strands wrapping around his naked body, creeping cold seeping from the floor through the soles of his bare feet. He snuck from pillar to pillar, drawing closer to the throne. He stepped on blood more than once, and now his footsteps made a squishy, wet sound. He cringed, and slowed his pace to keep the resonance low, to avoid stirring the giant.

Reaching the final pillar, he saw the Godking staring straight at him with wide eyes, head lolling still. Vatu's blood curdled. The Godking would eat him whole and spit out his soul.

When the Godking made no move toward him, Vatu came closer, heart pumping loud in his ears. The giant's face was wrinkled like resin, his whole body mummified. A cord came down his shoulder, reaching all the way to his left leg, like a gigantic, dried-up snake whose head had been torn off.

He was dead. He'd been dead for a very long time.

By the large throne, Vatu saw a cradle. A bedsheet lay on top, moss green but for the huge, dark stain in the middle. Blackened bedding bulged out from the bottom of the bassinet, and dark liquid dripped with a slow, steady cadence.

Vatu moved toward it, covering his nose. He stepped on something hairy. It was a bundle of strands, just like the ones he'd removed from used-up bodies. His eye caught something by the throne of the dead god. At first he'd thought it was a small table, but now he realized it was an enormous book. The cover read in gilded letters: *Revelations of Gluul.*

He lifted the cover, opening the book as he would open a chest. The language was foreign to him: horizontal and vertical slashes, symbols of birds and harpies. But as he progressed, he encountered scribblings he could decipher, of a language much like his own. It was the words of the prophet. Vatu skimmed through the contents, fixating on a particular passage:

Gods are not born into this world, they happen. When I witnessed Gluul emerge from chaos, I knew my purpose was to help him rule. Now here I am, looking down at his wrinkled body. Old fool. Falling in love with a lowly human. His cord snapped like a twig when he touched her. Emotion is poison, didn't you know? You should have known. Why did a weakling like you materialize into such a powerful body when I'm stuck in this pathetic baby form?

The following pages were written in a slant, disjointed sentences not making use of the whole page.

Why do all of them get to have parents? They don't deserve them. Hateful. Spiteful. Greedy creatures—Why is there so much noise in this world? Why? Why Why Why—Gut them—Slice them—Give them to me—It's all going to be all right, so long as I have warm wombs to nest within.

Something oily crawled up Vatu's throat. He moved toward the cradle and removed the bedsheet, unleashing the pungent smell of sour clams. Inside was the corpse of a woman. She seemed to be mid-transformation to the familiar, repulsive slime texture. The belly skin lay open on either side like ajar doors, and where entrails had been, there was a nest made of the strands Vatu had discarded many times—*kristas.* A concavity formed on the nest, as if something had just rested on it.

Vatu couldn't hold it in any longer. He retched beside the cradle, his head whirling like a ship in turbulent waters. The last words he read circled in his mind, like worms slithering along his cerebellum.

So long as I have warm wombs to nest within.

Nothing is fair. You happened upon an unfortunate time to be alive, in families that bear the responsibility to break the chains that bind our world. Forgive the world and lay down your lives, for they are not your own. They are a sacrifice. A final offering to the future.
from Final Offering by Amadi Dane, Founder of the
Nameless Guild

Vatu wrapped the bedsheet around him. It was covered with *kristas* along its length, and it made rustling sounds as he tied the edges around his neck. It stunk, and it made his stomach twist, but the biting cold was worse.

Why did the prophet assign Ascended like Vatu with discarding these strands before tossing away the bodies? If the prophet didn't want anyone to have access to them, perhaps it was part of his weakness.

He sat at the balcony, welcoming the chilling wind on his face. Below, the land seemed a whole world away. Maybe it would be better if he just took the plunge. He might have pretended to be dead to enter, but to leave...

Vatu imagined himself in the cradle, the prophet nesting inside his belly, snuggling in his organs... His throat convulsed. He craved Denu's touch, her embrace.

A thud came from inside the chamber. He walked toward the source of the sound. Denu lay there, her belly torn and bloodied. Her almond eyes, glazed and pale, unmistakably dead. He knew this would come, but it still hurt, it hurt more than the sting in his own belly.

A massive headache struck him, like sharp needles had inserted themselves within his amygdala, popping in and out of existence to the beat of an unseen drum. He knelt.

"Naive is the man that stands up to a god," came the prophet's voice from behind. He hovered by the window, umbilical cord vanishing beyond the rim of the door. His frog mouth stretched to an obscene smile.

Vatu struggled to his feet. "A god... that hides... behind a curtain? Behind the corpse of another *god*? You're nothing but a usurper."

There was something in the prophet's bulging eyes. Something deeply vicious. Anger? The umbilical cord pulsed like a flowing vein. Vatu had never seen it do that before.

The throbbing pain inside his head weakened.

"Worm," the prophet said. "What would you know? You are an ant. I have seen stars and worlds form, I have lived in the deep darkness that lies at the edges beyond your perception. *What* would *you* know?"

"No," Vatu said. His words had an effect on the prophet, he had to push him further. "You are deeply in pain, an abomination craving something it can never have. I feel sorry for you."

"Silence!"

The pain vanished and Vatu stood straight, clutching hard at the bedsheet around him. His gaze drifted to Denu's pale eyes. He remembered her as a child, slamming the fish against that kid's face. Remembered her as she was, as he'd promised he would. Tears welled up in his eyes. "A final offering. To the future."

Vatu sprinted over the gate, leapt, and grasped the cord where it met the prophet's belly, its texture slug-like. As they fell, his ears buzzed and the dust-red clouds seemed to fly away.

The prophet cackled. "Fool. The cord stretches eternal. I will see your body splatter. I cannot die."

The bedsheet parachuted as they fell, flapping to the wind. Vatu pulled it out with one hand, tearing the knot. He draped it over the prophet.

"Wh-what?" the prophet muttered.

Was that fear in the bulging eyes? Of course. The *kristas* along the bedsheet were his own emotions, his own insecurities. He excreted them like a shrimp does its shell. The prophet was at his most vulnerable state when cowering inside the cradle. An object laden with his insecurities made the immortality cord fragile. It made him *mortal*.

"Hush now, be silent," Vatu said. "Lay yourself to sleep."

"*Why... why...*" The grotesque eyes shut and the prophet wailed like a baby.

As the ground came rushing at them, Vatu saw a group of kids chasing one another. They stared up at him, curiously.

I wonder if it's your first time seeing a body fall from the sky.

He pulled out the razor blade. With a single cut, the cord snapped like a guitar string, and Vatu shut his eyes.

About the Author

Akis is a writer of bizarre things, a biomedical AI scientist, and almost human. He's also a Greek that hops across countries as his career and exploration urges demand. Find his fiction at Apex, Dread Machine, the Martian, and visit his website https://linktr.ee/akislinardos for other dark surprises.

THANK YOU

We would like to express our deepest gratitude to our staff editors, **Susan Russell, Rachael Swanson,** and **Kasey Kubica,** for their tireless efforts in reviewing submissions, proofreading, and overall helping us stay on track throughout the creation of this anthology. Their dedication to this project and attention to detail have been invaluable.

We also want to thank **Dany Rivera** for her beautiful story art, which has added a new layer of meaning to the stories we've collected. Her talent and creativity have truly enhanced this project. You can find her at danycomicsarts.com We'd also love to thank **Daren Robertson** for his talented illustration for Helping Hands in the Acreage. You can find more of his work on Deviant Art: deviantart.com/darenrobertsonart

We are also grateful to our volunteer submission readers, **Suhas Sridhar, rklep13,** and **Blake Pingleton,** who generously shared their time and expertise to help us sort through the many submissions we received. Their feedback and insights were crucial in helping us identify the most compelling stories for this anthology.

A special thank you to our Anthology Contributors: **Dan Peacock, KT Wagner, Aly Faye, Jessica Feather, Mei Davis, Amanda Cecelia Lang, DJ Cockburn, Chris Kuriata, John Haas, Neethu Krishnan, Koji A. Dae, Anthony Engebretson, T.S Vickers, Joel Reeves, Akis Linardos**

Finally, we want to extend our appreciation to all the authors who submitted to this anthology. We recognize the time, effort, and passion that goes into writing and submitting work for consideration, and we were grateful for the opportunity to read and appreciate each submission.

Thank you to everyone who has contributed to this project in any way.

We could not have done it without you!

If you liked any of our stories, take a moment to stop by our Amazon page and leave a review!

Check out our other anthologies!

Paramnesia

The Devil Who Loves Me

More Than a Monster

www.ingramcontent.com/pod-product-compliance
Lightning Source LLC
Chambersburg PA
CBHW071409300726
48976CB00006B/2037